THE WHITE OWL

THE WHITE OWL

Edmund Snell

RAMBLE HOUSE

The White Owl
1930 by Edmund Snell

ISBN 13: 978-1-60543-510-7

ISBN 10: 1-60543-510-4

Cover Art: Gavin L. O'Keefe
Preparation: Fender Tucker

THE
WHITE
OWL

Prologue

"BY HEAVEN, DICK!" whispered Juan Mitzakis at my elbow. "It's here. I believe we've found it!"

I saw him throw down the pick and face me, a tall, olive-skinned giant of a man, dark-eyed, dark-haired, as handsome as Adonis, his strong white teeth as he smiled flashing in the light of a tremendous moon that threw dense shadows on the hilltop from the tangled thorn through which we had cut our way, from the crumbled ruins of a civilization that had flourished before Cortes and his legions had cast anchor at Vera Cruz. Let flat into the solid rock at our feet, laid bare by the efforts of a dusky labor party of eleven and our two selves, lay a heavy, iron door, rusted and pitted with age.

"The temple of Huitzilopochtli!" I muttered aloud.

Mitzakis smiled.

With sweeping movements of his long arms, he drove the bearers back along the narrow path through which they had come, snatching a crowbar from one of them as he went. Presently we were alone—two gaunt figures in sun-hats, singlets and shorts, oblivious of the host of greedy blood-suckers that whined around us in clouds, staring down at the door behind which, for all we knew, lay the dread secrets of ancient Mexico.

My companion shook his head at me. "Not Huitzilopochtli," he corrected softly. "He was the war-god of the Aztecs, Dick, before whose altars the priests hacked out the hearts of living victims. Unless I am badly at sea, we stand on the threshold of a grimmer deity, the worship of which involved practices before which those of the Inquisition paled into insignificance. The hieroglyphics I found in Guatemala show that this deity came to earth in fantastic shape in 1527, encountered some Spanish troops near this spot and was eventually driven into a cavern by the presence of mind of a Spanish priest and a crucifix."

I sat down on a boulder and filled my pipe.

"A legend, of course," I remarked.

Mitzakis dropped a hand on my shoulder.

"I wonder!" he said.

I stared up at him in astonishment.

"Juan!" I ejaculated. "Surely you don't believe—?"

For answer he removed the leather top from a quaint scabbard he carried at his belt and drew a slender object into the moonlight. I caught the flash of steel as he passed it me—six inches of tapering blade, flexible and incredibly keen, surmounted by a handle of some hard white substance I did not recognize, carved to represent an owl.

"I have never shown you this before," he murmured, staring towards the big stars that bejeweled the violet canopy of heaven. "It's a beast of a thing, Dick. I picked it up in the tomb of a priest of the cult and it was there that I saw the writings. I've tried to lose it, to destroy it, to throw it away—but I can't. It haunts me in my sleep and with it come pictures of a vast temple, of sacrificial stones weltering in blood and a woman of extraordinary beauty, whom ghostly voices call *Naia,* which apparently means 'The Nameless.' " His mood changed quite suddenly and he broke off with the boyish laugh that had sealed our bond of friendship when we first met at Cambridge. "Unutterable tosh, eh, Dick! Imaginative idiocy! Perhaps you're right. You know my origin. My father was a Greek merchant. That's where all the filthy lucre comes from! My mother was a Castilian who always claimed to have Toltec blood in her veins. Perhaps that accounts for my restless spirit of adventure!—What about prizing up this confounded door? We ought to manage it between us."

He had secured the crowbar as he spoke and, as he dropped it on to the metal plate, a deep booming noise reverberated over the entire hillside like the sounding of a great gong.

I rose somewhat wearily and reached for the pick.

"Stop a bit," I said, "the cement isn't all chipped away yet— What was the name of this deity, Juan?"

Mitzakis fixed me with his dark eyes.

"The White Owl," he answered in a low voice. For half an hour we worked in silence, struggling until our muscles ached, to undo the efforts of Spanish masons sweating on that same spot centuries before. Suddenly it gave an inch and dropped back again and my companion emitted a sigh of relief.

"It's coming, Dick! Shove the point in here. There! That's right. Put all your weight on the thing when I tell you . . . Now . . . !"

It came up, slowly at first, but gradually yielding. Six inches of dark aperture showed and Mitzakis wedged a stone under one end

with his foot. The next instant we had dropped our tools and retreated hastily into the bush, driven there by an odor indescribable
that came in hot waves from the bowels of the earth, a ghastly,
nauseating smell that hung on the hot air of night, bathing the
maze of cactus and thorn, wild olive and crumbling ruins, in a
faint yellow fog . . . Mitzakis clutched at his throat, and the silver
crucifix that he wore there snapped from its slender chain and fell
into the undergrowth. I picked it up, intending to give it him, but
he had fastened a handkerchief around his nose and mouth and
was back again to the site of his beloved exploration. I tucked the
thing in a pocket and joined him, securing the rope we had brought
to the iron trap. We pulled on it together and it tilted clear quite
suddenly, sending us both sitting heavily in a thorn-bush. Mitzakis
reached the aperture first—a gaping hole fully six feet square, still
throwing off fumes.

"By gad! it's deep!" he remarked, peering down through the
yellow mist.

He dropped a chunk of Spanish cement into the hole and we
both listened.

"Did you hear it fall?" he whispered at length.

I shook my head.

"Then it's still dropping!—My hat!"

At that moment a noise came from the inner depths like the
rushing of a tremendous wind, and a great white bird flew suddenly out and began circling in the darkness above, screeching
mournfully. I stepped back, staring up at it in mute astonishment.
It was stupendous . . . colossal . . .

"My God!" I heard Mitzakis shout. *"The White Owl!"*

It had perched on the branch of an olive tree not twenty paces
from us—a queer, stunted growth whose twisted bark hung like
the crumpled skin of some antediluvian reptile caught in the act of
sloughing. Watching it through that pallid mist, I caught its evil
eyes blinking at me. A sensation of utter loathing swept over me
and I drew my automatic from its holster.

"Don't be a fool!" Mitzakis shot at me. "You'll never hit it."

"What!" I retorted, "at twenty yards!"

The suddenness of its appearance had swept the legend of the
Toltec god clean from my mind. In my excitement I had not bothered to consider the significance of the fumes. At the back of my
head lurked the conviction that the cavern below had another entrance concealed by scrub through which this colossal specimen of
horned owl made its nocturnal forays in search of food. The brute

just sat there, its weird white lids closing and unclosing over those green lamps of eyes.

I fired at it—and nothing happened. The sound of my shot echoed and re-echoed over the moonlit range, rousing a snarling protest from some catlike monster that prowled the forests, and setting monkeys gibbering in the trees, but the white owl perched there motionless, unscathed.

I fired again—and still nothing happened.

"Dick!" Mitzakis called to me across the gap: "Better give it a miss. There's something here you and I don't understand. According to the writings, the temple of the White Owl held treasures of inestimable value, the vast hoardings of the priests that even Cortes' legions never dared search for. A century later two consecutive expeditions came here from Mexico City, and not a living soul got back to tell the tale. Possibly those bones we struck yesterday were some of them."

I folded my arms and stared at him.

"What are we going to do?" I asked.

He shrugged his shoulders.

"I don't know. Cover the place up and go back, I suppose."

His answer staggered me. Mitzakis had gone to prodigious lengths to persuade me to join him on this expedition. His private yacht *Felicidad* had cost him a small fortune in itself. Captain Lindsay and the crew were down at Tampico now, eating their heads off, while we—It was ludicrous!

"Go back!" I stammered. "Why, man alive, look what we've been through! Look at the privations, the weeks of forced marching, the publicity our adventure provoked at home! We can't just crawl back—with nothing!"

He was still looking at the white owl. His handsome features, as fine and clean-cut against the night as any sculptor could fashion, showed strangely white.

"I'm scared, Dick," he admitted quite frankly: "scared of the accursed brute on that branch and all that it stands for. You and I have been in tight corners together before this. You know I can hold my end up. You've never seen me show the white feather. But there's a cold hand on my stomach tonight and I haven't the courage of a louse left in me. It's these ruins and that hole—and my accursed Toltec blood. This thing has haunted me for months—ever since I found the knife and the writings. I had to come here. Renée begged me not to, but I wouldn't listen. You'll tell her, Dick, what happened—"

I skirted the hole and shook him.

"Tell her be hanged!" I shouted. "You'll tell her for yourself."

His head came slowly round and I saw in his eyes an expression I had never noticed there before.

"If I get back."

"If?—Of course you'll get back. What's to stop you?"

He pointed to the white owl, motionless where it had first rested, and the intense irritation this action aroused in me was immediately responsible for something I have bitterly regretted ever since.

I fired at it for a third time—and the brute came swooping straight for us, flapping clumsily. I remember stepping away from the gap instinctively, shielding my face with my left hand, giving it at close range a shot that should have told without question. Apparently I missed again, for it wheeled across to Mitzakis, now six feet from me, and knocked him clean from his stance. In a flash I saw the danger that threatened and leaped to save him, but a root caught my foot and I fell. I was up again in an instant, but it was too late. It was the most horrible yet most extraordinary spectacle I have ever witnessed: Mitzakis, clutching at a straw as the dark gap loomed beneath him, clung actually to the wing of the savage brute that had unbalanced him. For a second the two hung poised in space—and then the bird dived for the hidden cavern from which we had disturbed it, carrying my friend with it!

Loose earth and stones, brushed by the wings of the owl, scraped by Mitzakis' boots as he went, disappeared noiselessly into the depths. Mitzakis was gone! Trembling, bewildered, my teeth chattering like castanets in the dread stillness that wrapped this desert of scrub and rocks and moldering walls, I crawled to the edge of the gap and peered down . . . And then a fresh phenomenon drove me back—forked tongues of pallid flame that scorched my cheeks and flickered there undeniable, inexplicable . . .

"Juan!" I called aloud. "Mitzakis!—Are you there? Can you hear me?"

But only the echo of my own voice came back, distorted in my frenzied imagination until it sounded like the mocking laughter of demons . . . I fastened our rope to a tree and to my waist, intending to descend in search of him, only to be confronted again and again by an impassable barrier of fire. Stumbling along the rough road to camp, I aroused the men and took some of them back with me. *Leperos* and Indians they were, unreliable at most times, useless in an emergency. We replaced the door, hoping to direct the fire to another quarter, left it and lifted it off, but the flames persisted. An Indian touched the ground with his hand and pointed there significantly. It was growing uncomfortably hot: I could feel it through my shoes. He slunk off into the shadows and I never saw him again. Others followed suit. I caught one in the act and pulled him back. He threatened me with a knife and I knocked him down, but I knew that the situation was hopeless. A vague, superstitious dread had seized the lot of them—and in any case there was nothing to be done.

Sick at heart, I crawled back to my tent and tried to sleep, comforting myself with the hope that Mitzakis had reached a ledge beyond the radius of the flames, and that we should find him through some other entrance that we would look for with the dawn. I may have dozed off for a couple of seconds; I cannot say. However that may be, I remember sitting up with a start, conscious of the sound of movement outside. The tent-flap drew softly aside and my hand slipped beneath my pillow, seeking the pistol I kept there.

"Who is it?" I called.

There was no answer.

Suddenly a woman came through the aperture and stood in the entrance, the pale light from the hurricane-lamp by my side playing in the myriad jewels at her fingers, her throat and her hair. She was short and slight and very beautiful. I have but a dim recollection of the details of her barbaric attire, for my gaze was concentrated on her face that was dusky-white, and on her eyes that were as dark as the night itself.

"Who are you?" I demanded testily, "and what do you want?"

She placed a finger to her lips and spoke to me in fair Spanish.

"Go away from here," she whispered. "Go away while yet you are safe. He will come back to you—when he is ready!"

"When he is ready?" I echoed. "Who? Who do you mean?—Mitzakis?"

She inclined her head.

"Then—then you know all about him? You know where he is?"

"I know, white man," she responded.

A wild hope throbbed in me and I swung my feet to the ground, feeling for my shoes. This was wonderful—amazing. There was some unknown tribe living in the neighborhood, possibly in the caves themselves. This girl had found Mitzakis . . .

"I'll come with you," I said. "Is he all right?"

Her sudden agitation puzzled me.

"Oh, no! You do not understand. You cannot see him yet. Presently—in a little while—in twenty moons perhaps!"

"What!" I cried. "In twenty moons! I don't follow you. What on earth do you mean?"

She did not reply.

"Here! Come on!" I insisted. "Who sent you here?"

She crossed both hands over her breasts.

"The White Owl commands," she retorted simply, "and I obey!"

I had laced one shoe by this time and was stooping over the other.

"I see," I muttered. "Well, look here, young lady, I'm giving orders this morning and I fancy you're going to obey *me*. If it's reward your people are after, I can promise you anything you want, within reason—What's your name—to start with?"

A low ripple of laughter filled the tent, and the flame of the hurricane-lamp flared up suddenly and went out. I grabbed at my pistol again, suspecting some trick—and a mocking voice trailed to me from a distance.

"I am Naia,"—it said—and my wild pursuit to the tent-door showed me nothing but huddled forms slumbering in the open and the first bright rays of a Mexican dawn . . .

Chapter 1

AS I TURNED THE KEY OF MY FLAT in South Kensington, I heard the telephone in my study ringing.

For some reason the sound irritated me. It was a vile night outside and the entire metropolis was wrapped in that peculiar species of fog that comes immediately to a foreigner's mind when he speaks of London. I had had a busy day and I was tired, and the only combination of things that appealed to me at that moment was a quiet meal at home, a book, felt slippers and a fire.

My man Baines met me halfway along the hall.

"That's the telephone, sir," he informed me in a voice that suggested he was imparting a profound secret.

"I know, you idiot," I retorted. "I heard it."

He held open the door for me and switched on the light.

I picked up the receiver.

"Hullo?" I queried, perhaps a trifle more sharply than usual. "Coombes here. What is it?"

A ripple of laughter answered me.

"Good evening, Dick," said a woman's voice slightly distorted over the wire. "So glad to catch you in a good mood!—Guess who it is?"

"Sorry," I said. "I can't."

"Try again," suggested my fair tormentor.

I caught myself laughing in the glass opposite.

"Afraid I can't. I'm hopeless at guessing. Who are you?"

"Renée . . ."

"Not really?"

"Absolutely! Me—in the flesh!"

"Good lord!" I gasped. "What in the name of everything brings you to England?"

It was rather in the nature of a miracle. Renée de Salis was a sybarite—one of the most attractive sybarites I had ever met. I had never known her farther north than Biarritz from October to April. She had been comfortably off when I first met her, and now that poor Juan had bequeathed her his entire fortune she must have possessed a great deal more than she knew what to do with.

"You!" she replied briefly and with emphasis.

"I . . ."

"Why, yes. Aren't you flattered?"

"Tremendously."

"And curious? Confess now that you're curious."

I leaned on one elbow on the knee-hole desk and laughed again. When next she spoke I thought I detected a change in her manner.

"I can't explain now—over the phone. But I do want to see you badly, Dick, and tonight."

"Tonight?"

"Yes, tonight—now, if it's possible. Come and dine with me. Put off any other engagement you have and come. I must see you. It's most important."

I glanced at my fingers.

"Very well," I replied. "Where are you staying?"

"At the New Venice, Piccadilly. I can count on you?"

"Absolutely."

"It's ten to seven now. Shall we say in an hour's time?"

I consulted my watch.

"Provided I can find the station in the fog. I'll change now."

"Goodbye, Dick. You can't think how grateful I am."

"In an hour then," I said and hung up the receiver.

I glanced in at the sitting-room on my way to dress. The electric radiator on the red tiles threw out a pleasant, inviting glow. Susan, Baines's cat, sprawled at full length over my felt slippers. I pulled aside a curtain and looked out on to a world of jaundiced darkness, feeble street-lamps and flares. Somewhere in the yellow gloom an agitated driver was tooting his horn.

"It's a rotten night," confided Baines as I washed, "not fit for a dog to go out."

"I'm not a dog!" I retorted.

"No, sir," he responded without emotion. "Quite so."

A taxi all but ran me down as I crossed the road, and I passed the District station twice before I found it. By a stroke of luck, a train was waiting at the platform when I got down, and I found a seat, inwardly blessing the unknown genius who had first thought of subterranean travel. One change and a further bewildering ramble brought me to the steps of the New Venice shortly before eight. The fog accompanied me into the vestibule and the latest thing in elevators whirled me up to Renée's suite on the fourth floor.

She emerged from a doorway almost before her trim French maid had taken my coat.

"My dear!" she murmured. "Whatever must you think of me! I haven't been out since tea—and Marie tells me it's a perfect beast! Do come into the warm and let me look at you properly." She shuddered as she spoke. "Oh! how I hate London in winter!"

I followed her into a lounge of pink carpet and upholstery and an abundance of white enamel. Another electric radiator presented itself, and we sat down before it, while a waiter from the hotel staff concocted drinks.

"Why do you come here?" I asked.

She spread out a pair of the daintiest hands in creation.

"My dear man! You know I never do!"

"But," I objected, "you're here now!"

"I know, but that's an accident. We crossed by the night boat yesterday—and I've been recovering from it all day! Why don't they build that Channel tunnel, Dick? It'd be so much appreciated!"

"Rotten crossing?" I suggested sympathetically. "Rough luck!"

"Such rotten little boats, too, Dick. I can't think why they don't make them bigger."

"They would—if the harbors were large enough to take 'em."

"Then why not build bigger harbors. Isn't that logic?" She held up her glass to me. "Well, here's to seeing you, Dick. You haven't changed one little bit!"

"Haven't I?" I laughed. "After that I suppose I ought to tell you that you're looking prettier than ever! You are, you know."

She grimaced at me.

"I shouldn't believe it—even if you meant it—which, of course, you don't. In any case, I don't *feel* prettier. I feel a perfect sketch. If you could only have seen me, Dick, less than twenty-four hours ago, in that pokey little cabin! I'm glad you didn't anyway."

"I didn't," I answered, "so why worry!—You left Nice on Wednesday?"

Renée nodded.

"On Wednesday, Dick, by the *luxe*. Marie and I just packed up and ran away like a couple of frightened children—*to you.* "

I put down my glass.

"Yes, yes, I know," I protested. "But why to me?"

She looked at the waiter.

"You can go now," she told him. "Take those things into the next room—anywhere you like. Tell them to hurry along dinner."

The door closed and we were alone.

Renée de Salis bent towards me.

"Because you are the only man in the world who understands, Dick—the only man who *may* understand. And because I trust you more than any other I know. Do you know why we were frightened?—why we ran?—why I haven't slept a single wink until today?"

I shook my head.

"Because, Dick, we've seen a ghost!"

I stared at her.

"A *what?*" I gasped.

"A ghost, Dick. You won't believe me, but I'm not joking. I'm perfectly serious. Marie saw it too—at the Gallia Palace, in Nice, on Tuesday! I was in my room—just going to bed. Something tapped at my window and I told Marie to open it and find out what it was. There was a bird there, she told me, a strange white bird. And then *he* appeared there—Juan—Juan Mitzakis!"

I was conscious of a tingling sensation in my hair.

"Juan!" I cried incredulously. "Renée, what madness is this?"

"No madness at all, Dick. He came into my room, I tell you—and spoke to me."

I stared beyond her at heavy pink curtains, as new as the hotel itself, shutting out a fog-bound world. Between them and my questioning eyes there arose mind-pictures of a period more than eighteen months before . . . of moonlight and ruins and prickly cactus—and another fog, yellow and nauseous, streaming up through a square hole in the ground . . . of an evil bird perched on an olive tree, blinking at me . . . of Naia whispering to me in my tent . . . *"he will come back to you when he is ready!"* Up to that moment I had suppressed that portion of the story, believing that I had dreamed it. But now, in the lounge of Renée de Salis' luxurious suite, it sounded like a prophecy and the fulfillment of a prophecy. Mitzakis had come back! Perhaps, as Naia had foretold, *he was ready;* likelier still he had found that other entrance my men and I had sought for days in vain, and had fought his way alone to Tampico and the sea.

"But this is wonderful!" I blurted out.

"Yes," she agreed dully, "isn't it?"

"How did he come to you? By the window?"

"Oh, no, my dear; he just walked in at the door, as if he had a perfect right to do so. No knock, no warning, nothing. I turned and saw him standing there. I was glad, of course, frightfully glad. I fancy I said something to him; I don't remember. 'Hullo, Renée!' he cried, just like old times. I flew into his arms—and that queer tapping came on the window again. At the sound of it he seemed to stiffen. 'It's that confounded bird!' he muttered. 'Will it never leave me alone?' And then, Dick, he pushed me away from him and wrenched open the door. I caught his hand. It was as cold as death!"

I jumped from my chair and began pacing the room, my hands clasped behind me.

"Did Marie see him?" I queried.

"We both saw him. Marie was scared stiff! I left her counting her beads, pulled on a wrap and followed Juan. He didn't look at the elevator—just ran down the stairs like a madman, with his silk hat tilted to one side as he always used to wear it, and his coat over his arm. I called to him, but he didn't even glance at me. At the next landing I took the lift and almost caught him in the hall."

She paused and looked at me. "Dick! what do you think?"

"I don't know," I answered.

"There was a pretty, dark girl in a car outside. Just as I reached the steps I saw him jump in beside her and drive off into the night!"

I paused in front of her.

"Then that settles it," I declared. "It wasn't Juan. Some hotel thief more probably—come in after your jewels, hoping to find you out. Perhaps he resembled Mitzakis slightly, and in the excitement of the moment you were both deceived."

Renée stamped her foot.

"But it was Juan! What nonsense you talk, Dick! Do you think I shouldn't know him anywhere? He drove away with that girl."

"Did you take the number of the car?"

"My dear man, I ask you! Was I in a fit state to take the number of any car? I was speechless, heart-broken. To find him, alive and well, at one instant—and then in the clutches of some vile creature glittering like a jeweler's window!"

"He left no address?"

She rose swiftly and reached something from the mantelshelf.

"He left this. Marie found it on the carpet after we had gone."

I found myself staring at six inches of tapering blade, flexible and incredibly keen, surmounted by a hard white substance carved to represent a fantastic bird!

"By heaven!" I heard myself muttering. *"The White Owl!"*

Chapter 2

THE SAME WAITER, suave, foreign-looking and supremely self-satisfied, announced that dinner was ready. We drifted through a communicating door into the next room and sat down facing one another in surroundings more luxurious, if possible, than the last. Beauty and charm of personality is a combination that is unfortunately rare, but Renée de Salis possessed them both. In spite of everything, I was glad that I had risked my neck to cross a fog-bound metropolis at her bidding. In every sense I was an honored guest—honored to be opposite this small, very pampered little being, in her Paris frock of pale amber and just those few, discreetly-placed emeralds that accentuated the perfection of her fingers and failed to distract one's attention from a pale, wonderfully-molded face that did not entirely scorn the use of cosmetics. I sat there in my shabby dinner-jacket, marveling at the picture she made, watching the light from the alabaster bowl above playing in chest-nut curls that wreathed her head like a glorious, tight-fitting halo.

She caught me looking at her and smiled.

"Thank you, Dick!" she whispered. "I like it—from you!"

I wrinkled my forehead.

"Like what, Renée?—I didn't say anything."

"I know, but your silence is most eloquent, dear! And you know you are one of the few admirers I can tolerate.—It's a sweet frock, isn't it? Corinne's, Dick, in the Rue de la Paix. I get most things there now. And Corinne is a man, bigger than Carpentier — and he was gassed in the war! Isn't it ludicrous?"

I admitted that it was.

For almost an hour we chatted at random, raking up stupid reminiscences, cracking the feeblest of jokes, and laughing over them immoderately, until, I feel convinced, the young Italian in side-whiskers who administered to our needs imagined that either the cocktails or champagne—or quite possibly both—had gone to our heads. With the coffee and Curaçao he left us and, deprived as it were of our guardian angel, the daemon that had hovered some-where in the region of that elaborately-painted ceiling fluttered down. An eerie feeling gripped me—a sort of vague conviction that somewhere in the yellow pall outside the White Owl perched, watching us with its green eyes . . . But the phantom that was with us in the room was Mitzakis risen from the grave . . .

Hidden in the vast metropolis groups of otherwise sane people, societies existed with chairmen and committees and printed codes of procedure that frankly and openly believed in ghosts and supernatural phenomena. For my part, I boasted neither faith nor knowledge of these things, nor do I believe did Renée. And yet we sat there, refreshed with wine and a good meal, each grappling with a problem that had begun in the Toltec ruins of Mexico and continued a year and a half later in a fashionable hotel in Nice.

"He wanted to speak to me," said Renée quite suddenly. "He wanted to say something important—and the bird wouldn't let him!"

Her elbows were on the table, her chin in her cupped hands, and there was a tired look about her eyes that spoke of trouble and nights without sleep.

I pushed back my chair.

"When we first discussed this," I reminded her, "you told me you'd seen a ghost."

"I know. Marie thinks that still. You see, he appeared in the room so unexpectedly—just after she had seen that creature outside."

"And yet you slipped into his arms—perfectly solid arms, of course?"

"Oh, yes."

"And when you touched his hand, to detain him, it was very cold?"

I saw her shudder.

"Horribly cold! And Juan's hands were always like fire."

She closed her eyes, as if the mere recollection of the scene hurt her, and for minutes on end we remained there smoking, with the electric light playing on the silver, and the muffled noises of disorganized traffic drifting up from the street. Suddenly Renée rose.

"Let's go into the other room," she suggested. "It's cosier in there—and Luigi will be wanting to clear. We're being a frightful nuisance to you, aren't we, Dick?" she added, taking my arm. "But what else was there for us to do? I couldn't complain to the French police that my fiancé had turned up from the dead—and then run off with another woman! Even if they had believed me, what do you suppose they would have thought?"

I closed the door and watched her drop into her original place. Presently I passed her chair and picked up the knife again with the owl handle.

"I've another like this in my desk at home," I said. "Juan gave it to me, if you remember, on the night he disappeared. He found it in a tomb in Guatemala."

Renée looked up at me.

"Ghosts don't carry knives," she declared.

"No, I suppose not."

She reached over and touched my sleeve.

"Do sit down, there's a dear creature, and try to *look* comfortable, even if you don't feel it! Dick! It must have been Juan, mustn't it? Do you think he's in trouble? Do you think I should have stopped there, with Marie, and waited for him to come again? Dick!"

"What is it?"

"Supposing something ghastly has happened to him. Supposing his sufferings have driven him—mad! They might, you know. Living there in that underground place, this white owl legend might have preyed on his mind."

I bit my lip.

"But you saw the white owl yourself," I objected.

She shook her head.

"I saw something—something very vague. It was Marie who assured me it was a bird, and Marie's a bundle of nerves at the best of times. I heard the tapping, of course, but it might have been a bat or a large moth, or just anything. Don't you see what I mean, Dick? Poor Juan, half-starved, demented, escaping to the coast, working his passage perhaps to Europe—"

She paused, frowning heavily.

"Well," I commented. "Go on."

"Drifting somehow to the Riviera, drawn there possibly by some dim memory of myself, he caught sight of me in the street and followed me to my hotel. —Dick, I'll go back to Nice tomorrow!"

I put the knife back on the shelf.

"Make it Monday," I said, "and I'll come with you."

"Dick!"

I gave her a reassuring smile.

"I'm afraid I'll have to," I told her. "Juan was the best friend I ever had."

She curled herself up in the chair with a sigh of utter contentment. Quite obviously the arrangement suited her; quite possibly, and without the painful necessity of asking a favor, she had achieved precisely what she had come from the Riviera to do. \\liat of it? Apart from certain business arrangements which would have to be postponed, the arrangement was entirely agreeable to myself—and faced with the prospect of a journey south with so charming a personality as Renée de Salis, mere business faded into the background. Besides, I felt it was my duty to solve the mystery of this apparent reappearance of an old friend; and it is not so often that duty and pleasure combine!

"I think I shall call you 'Uncle Richard' in future," Renée was saying dreamily. "It's such a safe sort of relationship—and, after all, uncles can be any age they like! I knew a married woman once who had one of thirteen—and still at school. Wasn't it ridiculous? She used to call for him in term-time and take him out in an Eton suit to have ices! Would you like *me* to take you out and stand you ices, Uncle Richard?"

We both laughed.

"I should simply hate you to stand me ices," I retorted. "They invariably disagree with me!"

The phantom of Juan Mitzakis descended again, and the forehead of the spoiled child in the chair puckered into a delightful frown.

"I must show you Juan's papers," she decided. "His bankers sent them me in a black tin box. Marie and I spent a whole week going through them, deciding which we should keep. Did you know he was writing a book?"

I shook my head.

"Well, he was, Uncle Richard. There are pages and pages of it in the box, all bound together, and an envelope of photographs which apparently he intended to use as illustrations. I read it and it frightened me. Dick, do you honestly believe the people of ancient Mexico practiced those ghastly rites?"

I shrugged my shoulders.

"They have always enjoyed a somewhat sinister reputation," I said.

"Tying their victims up and cutting out their hearts, I mean; torturing them while they were still alive! According to Juan, women used to take part in these dreadful orgies. *Women*, Dick!"

"It was the fashion in those days," I assured her, "and fashion has always led women to incredible lengths. You know that yourself."

Renée sighed.

"I suppose that's true, but it's not a very pleasant thing to reflect upon. Juan's book was so real though, so terribly convincing. It would never strike one that he had pieced it together from things he had found on his travels, from hieroglyphics in musty Toltec tombs. One would imagine he had actually been present at these gatherings of white-robed priests, that he had rubbed shoulders with the crowds assembled there lusting for blood . . . that he had actually seen the White Owl flutter over the vast multitude—and perch on the shoulders of the man who was to use the knife."

I started to my feet.

"Renée!" I gasped. "How did you learn all this?"

"I read it in the book, Uncle Richard, and it kept me awake for weeks! There was a list of names at the end—thirty or forty prominent Spaniards who had incurred the wrath of the White Owl and who were doomed to perish at his altar—De Garcia, Lopez, Manzanarez, Figuera—You see, I remember some of them even now—*'He who sees the White Owl—dies!'* she chanted so suddenly and realistically that something cold trickled down my spine.

"You shouldn't have read that book," I declared sternly.

"I know, but I couldn't help it. It just led you on. 'A sudden hush fell on the temple,' " she quoted at random, " 'and every man present covered his face. There came the sound of a gong and a fluttering of giant wings, as the grim bird of sacrifice was released. Only one of all that vast multitude felt the creature pause, the touch of its talons on his flesh. Not daring to look, he called his own name aloud and the High Priest by the stone altar repeated it. Again the fluttering, fading off into the distance, an eerie shriek perhaps—and then the gong . . . In the tense silence that followed, a woman's voice, clear penetrating, chanted the single sentence of a creed: *'He who sees—'* "

I touched her arm.

"I don't think we'll have that again," I said. "I don't know that I like it. Remember, Marie saw the White Owl at Nice—and I shot at it three times in Mexico!"

She observed me curiously.

"It was a wonderful book, Uncle Richard!" she sighed.

"It must have been!"

She sat up suddenly, listening.

"What was that noise?" she demanded, and her gaze was directed towards the curtained window. "There! Don't you hear it?"

"Water dripping outside," I answered, but I wasn't by any means as certain as I sounded. It came again, a distinct rustling noise against the pane. "I'll go and look," I added.

I strode across. Pulling aside one curtain, I peered through misted glass into Piccadilly, as foul and uninviting as I have ever know it. Just blurred lights and gloom and ghostly traffic moving vaguely. I let it fall again and turned to Renée.

"There's nothing there," I said.

She flashed me a wan smile.

"Only nerves, eh, Dick? We're all nerves tonight! You'd like a drink, wouldn't you? I'll ring the bell." I had barely left the window when a movement at the far end of the room caught my eye. The door was slowly opening. I was wondering if it were Marie when a white hand appeared in the aperture, groping along the architrave. It found the switch—and paused. The next instant the room was plunged in darkness.

Renée called to me.

"Uncle Richard! Dick! What's happened? Has something fused?"

An ornament toppled from the mantelpiece and crashed to fragments on the tiles. I closed with a shadowy figure whose legs showed suddenly in the glow from the radiator. A knee, planted skillfully in the pit of my stomach, winded me completely, and the intruder tore himself away, making with stealthy footsteps for the exit. I heard the *snick* as the door closed softly. Crawling painfully in his wake, I turned on the light again. At that instant the outer door banged.

Renée was kneeling on her chair.

"My dear!" she exclaimed in an awed whisper. "How extraordinary! We must ring up the management. But you're hurt—"

"Just winded," I said. "The beggar was too quick for me. Where d'you keep your telephone?"

She was standing by the fender now, looking from the fragments of blue vase to the place from which it had fallen. I saw her beckon me.

"Dick! Come here a moment."

I obeyed.

"Can you see that knife anywhere? It was here just now."

I pushed back a chair, looking for it.

"No," I declared at length, "it's gone right enough."

She caught the lapels of my coat and looked up at me, her dark eyes as big as saucers.

"Of course it's gone. Don't you see what it means, Dick? It was Juan! He came back for his knife. He wanted it. The bird was there too—outside."

Chapter 3

IT WAS PAST ELEVEN when I left the New Venice and still the fog
had not lifted. I had interviewed the management on Renée's behalf, explaining that an unknown intruder had let himself into the
suite, apparently with the help of a spare key, had broken a vase
and removed a trifling souvenir. I thought it inadvisable to add
anything further. The management, represented by a portly, clean-
shaven gentleman in morning attire (to avoid, I supposed, the in-
dignity of being mistaken for a head waiter) expressed itself pro-
foundly shocked at the occurrence. It promised full investigation
and hoped that the matter would not be allowed to go further. As
an earnest of its good intentions, it placed an hotel detective on
duty outside.

Renée seemed satisfied with this arrangement, and I could see
that she was tired. There was nothing left for me to do but go
home.

I was hugging the right-hand pavement, making for Piccadilly
Circus and the tube station, when a fresh phase of this extraordinary adventure began. I became aware of footsteps following close
behind me in the fog. I looked back, but could see nothing; slowed
down only to hear the unknown stranger slacken speed, keeping as
it were a measured distance from me in the enveloping gloom;
hurried to hear him pattering after me in a manner that was distinctly unnerving. Nor was it hallucination, an eerie echo of my
own footfalls produced by the fog, because my tracker took
shorter paces.

A group of youths fresh from a theater gallery, shouting, laughing, whistling the tune that had taken their fancy, straggled out of
the yellow pall and were gone again, and still the footsteps continued with grim persistence. Smiling to myself, I turned completely
round, marking time like an infantryman on parade.

The ruse was surprisingly effective. It solved my mystery in an
instant, only to create another more perplexing than the first.

A figure walked right into me at a spot where a street-light fee-
bly penetrated the gloom—the figure of a woman, hatless, slim
and wrapped in an expensive fur coat! Before I could avoid the

collision, her warm body had come in contact with my chest. Frightened eyes from a pale, beautiful face looked up into my own.

"Oh!" she gasped, and her voice had a slightly foreign ring. "I—I'm so sorry! I did not see you!"

She swayed suddenly as if she were about to fall. I caught both her elbows. At that instant something in my brain *clicked*. The grip of my fingers tightened on sable sleeves damped with fog and I found myself staring in mute astonishment at dusky white features nestling in a voluminous, up-turned collar, framed in a wealth of dark hair to which tiny beads of moisture from the dank atmosphere clung.

"Naia!" I whispered hoarsely.

She strove to free herself.

"I don't understand you. Please let me go. I have an appointment."

A strange fragrance assailed my nostrils as I held her there, the mysterious mingling of exotic flowers that bridged a gap of months and carried me back to an eventful night in a tent on a Mexican hillside—and a woman in barbaric garb watching me in the light of a hurricane-lamp. The scene was different, the barbaric clothing exchanged for fashionable European attire, and yet I was convinced there was no mistake.

"You will deny, perhaps, that you were following me?" I insinuated.

She shook her head and tried to avoid my gaze.

"I do not know you," she moaned. "I have never seen you in my life. I am a stranger here . . . I only arrived from Paris this morning. Please let me go. You are hurting me."

I nodded grimly. Already I was beginning to see daylight. In encountering this wild creature from the Mexican hinterland in a fog-camouflaged Piccadilly I had hit upon a clue that gave Renée's story of the returned Mitzakis confirmation.

"I want to talk to you, Naia," I said. "I want to know what you have done with Juan Mitzakis—and why it was you left Nice together!"

She trembled violently. I could feel it through her coat. But her dark eyes, when next they were turned on me, carried not fear but fury unchained.

"You fool!" she shot at me in a tense whisper. "You damn' fool!"

She was struggling like a panther now. Stooping suddenly, she buried her teeth in my left wrist, tore herself bodily away from me and began running towards the Circus. Painfully conscious of the spot where she had bitten me, I followed, resolved to cling to her like grim death until I had discovered with whom it was she had this mysterious appointment. The feeling of tiredness that had crept over me on the New Venice had vanished completely. I was throbbing with subdued excitement, alert, buoyed-up with the conviction that I was on the verge of an astounding discovery. There were portions of this extraordinary jig-saw of events that would have to be fiddled into their proper places in the morning: Why Naia had been detailed to shadow me in Piccadilly was one of them. But, firmly impressed on my mind at that moment, was the fact that the woman of the car outside the Gallia Palace and the girl I had just met were one and the same. Nor did I harbor the slightest doubt as to her identity. She had wriggled and hedged— but she had never actually denied it. And, just at the time when I was patting myself on the back for my astuteness in recognizing her, she had culminated by labeling me a fool! Her parting epithet intrigued me. It appeared to suggest that the knowledge I possessed was dangerous to myself. In any case, it admitted I was right.

She was still hurrying on ahead, alternately vanishing and reappearing in the fog. The diffused lights of the Circus made freak effects ahead of us, while busses, hours behind their schedule, taxis and private cars lumbered along behind that yellow wall to our left, moving in a queer, uncanny way like a phantom mechanized army caught in a barrage of gas.

It was the worst fog in my memory. I felt that the papers in the morning, particularly those that delighted in records of any sort, would assuredly pronounce this as one.

We bore suddenly to the right and presently the alluring stranger who professed to have no knowledge of London inveigled me on a nightmare journey across a main thoroughfare! I tripped on the curbstone at the far side just as a police-whistle sounded in unpleasant proximity to my ear. I lunged into a tall constable in a cape who was bending over a dim form on the pavement. He straightened himself and grabbed my arm.

"Just a moment, sir," he said gruffly. "There's been a bit of trouble 'ere. Perhaps you'd be good enough to lend a hand."

I looked round me helplessly. Naia had disappeared. This slight delay had given her all the time she needed to elude me. Luck, that was of vast importance in such an affair and on such a night, had in one stroke robbed me of my chances of seeing Juan and pitch-forked me into one of those distressing responsibilities all quiet-living citizens instinctively avoid.

"All right," I answered without enthusiasm. "What is it? What do you want me to do?"

He had dropped on one knee and was fumbling beneath his cape for something.

"Just 'old up 'is 'ead—get one arm under 'is shoulders while I—"

He broke off suddenly, leaving the remainder to my imagina-tion. I endeavored to comply. I had a sort of blurred vision of a woman in dark clothes sobbing hysterically, of the policeman's trousered legs and boots, and of a little, olive-featured elderly man, with glassy eyes staring upwards and unbuttoned overcoat revealing an expanse of white shirt sodden with blood.

"What is it, constable?" I murmured. "Street accident?"

I was supporting the small man's back when the question an-swered itself. It was more than an accident—it was murder! The knife that had administered the fatal thrust was sticking there now, with the blood welling out over it and streaming down to a dark pool that showed on the flagstones like a grotesque map. My gaze clung to that knife—held there by an odd fascination that I was at a loss to understand. And, as I stared, its white handle stood out in sudden relief against a background of black overcoat that had fallen across the shirt. My senses reeled.

"My God!" I said aloud; but nobody seemed to notice. I cleared my throat. "You can't do anything for him, constable," I added. "He's dead! The poor chap's been stabbed to the heart. Did you notice the knife, by the way? It has a handle like an owl!"

The constable peered at it.

"Well, now!" he exclaimed, displaying intense professional in-terest, "so it 'as! Curious that—isn't it?"

A sallow youth, with an abundance of white scarf at his throat, plunged into the charmed circle and recognized the woman. Somewhere about that time it dawned on me that we were within a stone's-throw of the Haymarket Theatre.

"Margharita!" he exclaimed in Spanish, seeing nobody but her. "Where have you been all this time? We have been looking for you with the car. You promised to wait in the foyer. Is your uncle here?"

She uttered a little, choking sob and clung to him desperately. I saw her point to the pavement and the dark eyes of the man follow her finger.

"Dios!" came his horrified whisper, and again *"Dios!"*

His Southern temperament carried him beyond the point of tears.

"Manzanarez!" he sobbed, addressing the still form on the pavement. "Luiz! Speak to me. Who was it—struck you?"

The constable touched his arm and whispered something in his ear, and I caught the warning bell of the ambulance through the fog.

Chapter 4

Luiz Manzanarez!

The name haunted me as I jolted on the Underground towards Kensington. I paused on a cold threshold, fumbling for my latch-key, and the grim happenings of the night, vague, disjointed sections of a vast puzzle, jerked themselves suddenly into place to form a fantastic whole that set me shuddering.

I closed the door and hung up my hat and coat. Susan, Baines's cat, had sneaked in with me. Her purring, as she rubbed herself against everything within reach, sounded strangely like the ticking-over of a multi-cylindered automobile in the street below. It was a pleasant, companionable noise. It accompanied me from the hall to the sideboard where the decanter was, and presently to the fireside and a chair. I noticed as I discarded my shoes that there was a splash of something on the toe of one of them that might have been blood.

I sat down, brooding over a sentence of Renée's that I remembered:

"There was a list of names . . . thirty or forty prominent Spaniards . . . doomed to perish at his altar . . . De Garcia, Lopez, Manzanarez, Figuera . . .

And I had seen the knife with the owl handle sticking from the chest of a little, olive-featured man who bore one of those names! More than that, I believed that I had handled that very knife myself in Renée's suite at the New Venice barely an hour before the crime was committed!

An electric fire holds no pictures, nor indeed did I feel the want of them, for already my brain was full to overflowing . . . Juan Mitzakis, as Renée had so vividly described to me, appearing from the dead in the Gallia Palace at Nice . . . the dark eyes of Naia flashing defiance in Piccadilly . . . the dramatic recognition of a man stabbed outside the Haymarket Theatre . . . and, lurking behind it all, the great white bird, with eyes like green lanterns and a thirst for vengeance that was centuries old . . .!

Smoking there, with Susan on my knees and the civilized world around us oddly still, I began where Juan and I had prized up an iron door in the heart of Mexico and finished with the murder in the fog. A Spanish priest in the thirteenth century had driven the White Owl underground with the crucifix—and we, with our damnable curiosity, had seen fit to release it in the twentieth! Juan Mitzakis, who boasted Toltec blood, had disappeared with it into the bowels of the earth, and shortly afterwards Naia had crept into my tent with a prophecy which, in the light of recent events, appeared to have been fulfilled. Juan, always with the White Owl hovering near, had dropped a knife in Renée's room, followed her from the Riviera to London and snatched it back in the darkness; had set Naia to watch me when I emerged from the entrance of the New Venice, and had employed the owl-headed knife to murder a man who probably had never known his ancestor had fought with Cortes in Mexico and incurred the wrath of a heathen god!

To me at that moment, remembering the legend and the dramatic climax of a memorable adventure into the unknown, these events had a logical sequence. And it jarred somehow against everything I had been taught. If I went to Scotland Yard in the morning with my story, even with the additional testimony of Renée and Marie to back it up, the most I could hope for was to be regarded as a good-natured idiot. In this age of scientific marvels, when one flashed pictures from one side of the world to the other, when people who sang in Melbourne were heard through the medium of nicely polished cabinets and vibrating paper cones in London, when robots strolled in Oxford Street and opened exhibitions, a phenomenon without a formula cut no ice. Spiritualism was a game for cranks. To admit that a man roamed the universe killing people at the promptings of an evil spirit moving in the guise of a white bird would be ridiculous. It would be equally sensible to suppose that the coster monger who strangled his mistress in a common lodging-house in Shadwell was literally pitchforked into crime by a mediaeval devil with horns and a barbed tail!

And, in any case, my business was not with Scotland Yard, but with Juan Mitzakis himself. Manzanarez's fate had shocked me and I was sorry for him, but I was sorrier still for Juan, who was my friend.

A spirit of restlessness seized me and I began pacing the room.

Somehow or other I must find Juan, talk to him, reason with him, separate him from the dark-eyed creature who had become his constant companion, find some means of combating that grim white horror to which he had become a slave . . . On the face of it it was a colossal undertaking. I had not the least idea where in London he was staying, or under what name. Nor had I any guarantee that he would remain here long enough for me to trace him. There was just the chance however that he might come to see me, his companion on that last tragic expedition, the sole witness of his disappearance. Puzzling it out, it struck me as curious that he had not tried to see me before.

The clock on the mantelshelf struck three and I stretched myself and yawned.

"Bed, Susan!" I said aloud, addressing a throbbing mass of fur curled up in the place I had recently occupied. Susan, not bothered by the prospect of exchanging warm clothes for cold pyjamas and still colder sheets, blinked but said nothing. Actuated by force of habit, I poured myself out a nightcap and reached over for the siphon. At that moment the door-bell rang.

Some of the fluid in the glass spilled over as I set it down. I glanced up sharply, and the ring came again. I caught myself regarding my own reflection in the oval mirror over the fire.

"Better see who it is," I muttered, convinced by this time that, assisted by the lifting of the fog, a zealous constable had noticed my lighted window and suspected burglars. As I crossed to the door, a new sound drifted to my ears, an uncanny fluttering noise that appeared to come from the window itself. I hesitated and went back. Grasping a curtain in each hand, I flung them suddenly aside, and a vague, shadowy object, that had perched on the sill outside, uttered a shrill cry and pushed off clumsily into the night.

The sound of a door shutting brought me round.

Juan Mitzakis, tall, debonair, as handsome as ever, stood on the threshold, a section of dress-shirt showing beneath his unbuttoned coat, a silk hat held in his gloved fingers.

"*Juan!*" I ejaculated. "This is good. Renée told me she had seen you. How the deuce did you get in?"

He tossed a Yale key on to the little table by the decanter.

"You left this in the door!" he returned easily. "Damn' careless thing to do! D'you mind if I sit down?"

He removed his coat as he spoke, stuck it on a small chair, with the silk hat perched on top, and dropped into a corner of the chesterfield.

"Well, Dick!" he pursued, still in the same matter-of-fact tones, "here we are, you see!"

"I *do* see," I retorted. "But what an unearthly hour to call on a fellow!"

He drew a cigarette of prodigious length from a thin gold case and lit it from the flame of an automatic lighter. Suddenly his glance fell on the curtains and there was a suggestion of uneasiness in his voice when he next spoke.

"Draw those things, Dick, if you don't mind. Thanks! Been a beast of a night, hasn't it? I suppose it is a queer time to call, but I move around a good deal at night—and the only use I find for daylight is to sleep in—Pour me out about three fingers, there's a good chap. And for heaven's sake don't drown it!—I'm much obliged to you. Here's luck!"

"Chin-chin!" I answered and turned Susan out of my chair. She sat on the hearth-rug, eying me with evident disgust and washing all traces of my fingers from her fur, then sauntered over to resume her nap on the chesterfield. At sight of Juan, however, she arched her back, spat venomously and dived under the sideboard.

Mitzakis rested both arms on the back of the settee and laughed uproariously. And I sat there, watching him and wondering in what subtle way he had changed. Outwardly he was the same Juan Mitzakis I had always known. The drawling voice, the easy poise of his lithe body, certain characteristic mannerisms and poses . . . All these were there. And yet there was something lurking behind that I neither liked nor understood . . .

"I've a bone to pick with you," I declared after a long pause.

He raised his brows and whistled softly.

"Oh," he remarked, "only one! I should have thought there would have been several!"

"Confound you, you ungrateful blighter!" I retorted angrily. "I spent a whole fortnight looking for you once. Worked myself into a fever and had to crawl on half rations to the coast on your account. The least you could do was to come to see me when you got away. Where have you been?"

Mitzakis yawned again.

"At Giardino's Club," he replied. "Playing *chemin-de-fer.* Winning too, Dick; winning like blazes! Funny how you can win when money's of no particular consequence!"

I went over and shook him.

"I don't mean that," I cried. "I want to know what happened when you went down that hole—and what's happened to you since. How did you leave Mexico?"

His thin fingers described an airy gesture.

"Oh," he returned easily, "in the usual way, you know—in a boat." His brows had contracted until they almost met in a thin dark line over half-closed lids. His whole expression was mock-ing, exasperating. Looking down at him, my hands on my hips, a picture of Renée came to my mind, and I wanted to hit him.

"Is that your *bone,* Dick?" he added, "or only one of them?"

Without question Juan had changed—and for the worse. In the past eighteen months something vital had happened to him. He behaved like a man who had gone to the dogs—and reveled in it.

I bit my lip.

"Where are you stopping?" I demanded lamely.

A stream of smoke from his cigarette enveloped his face and through it the features of the devil incarnate mocked at me.

"At the Europa. I like it because it's quiet and select. There's no traffic there to speak of."

I moved to the mantelpiece and leaned against it.

"And—Naia, I imagine, stops there too?" I shot out.

The effect of my bombshell was extraordinary. He sprang to his feet, livid with fury and came right up to me, his fists clenched, the muscles of his face twitching.

"Naia!" he hissed. "How did you know her name? Who told you? I must get to the bottom of this!"

I met his gaze unflinchingly.

"My dear good chap," I retorted, "there's no earthly reason to be melodramatic. The lady and I are old acquaintances. We met, as it happens, in my tent in Mexico!"

"In your tent?" he stammered, and recoiled a step.

"And then," I resumed mercilessly, "we met again, as you know, in the West End some hours ago." I showed him my wrist. "You see that?"

The wild look had gone from his eyes and he dropped them un-til they focused upon the dull red marks where the girl had buried her teeth in her frenzy to get away.

"I didn't know," he answered presently. "She told me she had lost you in the fog."

He dropped into the chesterfield again and yawned. He had be-come suddenly dejected and tired and the fingers that fumbled for a second cigarette shook visibly. Something made me glance at the clock. It was five minutes to four.

"You see, Juan," I resumed, resolved to hammer sense into him while the mood lasted, "I know a deal more about this business than you imagine. I know, for example, that it was you who mur-dered Luiz Manzanarez in the Haymarket!"

Chapter 5

I HAD EXPECTED HIM to jump up again, but he didn't. Reaching across to the little table, he poured himself out a peg of neat spirits and drank it at a gulp. In an instant the suggestion of tiredness had vanished completely, and the old mocking look crept back.

"So you know that, do you?" he muttered between his teeth. "I imagined you'd hear all about it in the morning. That happens to be one of the reasons for my calling on you. Well, Dick, what do you propose doing about it?"

I shrugged my shoulders.

"So you admit it?" I said.

Juan Mitzakis laughed.

"Why not, since you know? I suppose I've acquired some of the Spanish-American characteristics since we last met. The fellow's face offended me—and I killed him. I've known men knifed for a lot less than that!"

I regarded him steadily.

"You are asking me to believe that the man was a complete stranger to you?"

He removed the cigarette from his lips.

"Absolutely."

"And yet you knew his name when I mentioned it!"

He laughed again.

"Lord, Dick! what a fine lawyer you would have made! I always said you'd missed your vocation! Let's see. What do I say to that? How did I know Luiz Manzanarez was—well—Luiz Manzanarez? I suppose you mean to have the truth. Where shall we begin?" He snapped his fingers. "Oh! I know. They were in the foyer between the acts. I'd been out for something—"

"I think I can help you there," I inserted icily. "You'd been to the New Venice, to Renée's suite—for a knife!"

He crossed his legs and eyed the glowing tip of his smoke.

"Very well. Have it your own way. There was a girl with him—quite a striking girl. Frankly, she fascinated me. I've always had a weakness for women, Dick, and she'd a trick of wrinkling her forehead when she smiled that made me think I'd like to know more about her. I asked the girl in the booking-office, but she couldn't enlighten me. I gave her a pound to buy chocolates with, and she interviewed the assistant manager on my behalf. I had a drink with him in the bar afterwards. He was quite a decent chap. He told me the girl was Margharita Manzanarez and that the little man was her uncle and a big pot at the Embassy."

I shook my head a trifle sadly.

"It's a good yarn," I told him, "but it won't wash."

He looked at me sideways.

"Why not?" he queried with a show of innocence. "Why not, Dick, if it's a good yarn?"

"Because I have certain information."

He swung his legs on to the upholstery and clasped both hands behind his head. His third yawn set me gaping too, but I could see there was no immediate prospect of his leaving me. To all appearances, he had settled down there for the remainder of the night.

"Information!" he interjected scornfully. "What information could you possibly have? Why, the chap's hardly cold yet! I did it on impulse, I tell you . . ."

"I haven't said that you didn't."

"And Margharita Manzanarez is a most charming girl."

"Agreed," I replied. "I saw that for myself."

He turned his head languidly in my direction.

"Oh, you were there, were you?"

"I arrived on the scene very shortly after you left. And it wasn't such an extraordinary coincidence either, because I was trailing Naia, and Naia, I shrewdly imagine, was looking for you. A policeman stopped me and I actually held up your victim while he took notes or something. Look here, Juan: Why not drop that cynical pose of yours and listen to reason? Confound it all, man! I'm your friend and the only man living who'll have any sympathy left for you by the time the morning papers come out. Put your cards on the table."

Juan reached for the decanter again.

"Don't nag me, Dick," he implored in a tone that made me hope that at least something of the old Mitzakis remained. "I've been through hell ever since I can remember, and I'm damn' tired."

A vague impulse carried me to the bureau. With a dim idea at the back of my mind of ramming my point home, I dug from a miscellany of papers and the usual junk bureau drawers seem constructed to hide the owl-headed knife he had given me on our last trip. I had barely touched it before he came at me from behind, breathing heavily, and snatched it away.

"By heaven!" he snarled. "You've no right to this. It's sacred, I tell you."

"Sacred fiddlesticks!" I retorted, licking the place where the blade had snicked me. "And anyway you gave it me yourself. Now, see here, Juan, I don't sleep all day like some people. I have to work for my living, and I'm hellish tired. I don't mind making a night of it, provided you keep your temper and drop all this tom-fool White Owl business. If you don't—I'm off to bed, and it's up to you whether you stay here or clear. You've behaved like a swine to Renée, and you know it. I'm not interested in the money side of the affair. It's the harm to her feelings I'm talking about. She saw you with Naia at Nice, I may tell you, and it damn' near broke her heart."

Juan Mitzakis stood very erect on the hearth-rug, holding the knife delicately with the fingers and thumbs of both hands, staring at it sullenly. He affected not to be listening, but I saw him wince when I mentioned Renée. The gold stud of his evening shirt had come adrift from a button-hole; there was white ash on his sleeve and one trouser-leg and the black bow-tie had got twisted side-ways. For the hundredth time in our acquaintance I told myself what a handsome figure he made, what a handsome pair he and Renée de Salis would make together.

An idea struck me, born of this reflection: I moved to where he stood and placed a hand on his shoulder.

"You're in a rotten mess, old son," I said.

He shrugged his shoulders.

"Well? What of it?"

"You've plenty of money still. You said so."

"Oh, yes; bags of it! Out of those blasted caves!"

"What?" I yelled. "You?"

He pushed my arm aside.

"Cut it out, Dick," he cried. "You're talking to me as if I were a decent law-abiding human—and I'm not—and you know it, if you'll only think! You pretend to yourself I'm a pitiful instru-ment—a poor idiot who's killed a man in his temper and I'll be arrested and hanged for it! Hanged! Oh, my faith, Dick, they can't hang *me!* They can't take me! You like Renée, don't you? You profess to have her interests at heart. And you're going to tell me to go abroad—go somewhere where your precious detectives can't find me, and get you to send her out to me! God, man! your job's to protect her from me, do you understand? I'm not a man, Dick. I'm not Juan Mitzakis. I'm a devil! I—"

He collapsed into a chair, his head buried in his hands and the knife reposing on the carpet between his patent boots. He was very limp now, limp and trembling, and big beads of sweat stood out on his temples.

Strangely moved by this sudden outburst, I bent over him.

"I know you are not to blame for what occurred tonight," I whispered. "It was because of that list—De Garcia, Figuera, Manzanarez and the rest of them."

He looked up sharply.

"Eh? Oh, it's that book. She's told you about it. I must destroy that somehow." A wild mood set in again. "But they deserve it, don't they, Dick? I mean —look what they did. But you can't do it properly in the streets. You haven't the time."

He began struggling into his coat.

"Stop here," I said. "I can give you a bed. I'll get Baines up to air it."

Juan shook his head.

"The dawn will be here soon," he muttered. "I'm afraid of myself in the dawn. Makes me talk too much. I've said more than I should already." He held out his hand, a cold, lifeless thing that chilled me as I took it. "Well, good-by, Dick. Glad to have seen you."

Still gripping his hand, I sought to detain him.

"Stop here," I insisted. "We'll face it out together. After all, it's partly my trouble. I shot at the thing."

He gave me a strange look.

"It was written in the stars," he said, and wrenched his hand free.

I got between him and the door.

"How long are you staying at the Europa?"

"No time at all. A matter of hours."

"And then?"

He was staring beyond me, at the window.

"Spain, I suppose. Barcelona, Madrid, Cadiz—I'm always moving."

"I'm going to follow you," I declared doggedly.

He seized both my arms and a look of fear crept into his eyes.

"Dick! You mustn't!"

He saw me maneuvering towards the knife, and he picked it up, slipping it into a pocket.

"I'm going to follow you," I said again.

He thrust an arm through mine and for a fleeting second I saw the old Mitzakis, boyish, impulsive, and this time his grip was warm.

"You spoke just now about listening to reason. Well, old son, it's your turn now. When a fellow commits some serious crime in this civilized community, you blame *him,* if your intellect's below the average. If it isn't, you blame heredity—some devilish impulse for which he has to thank his forbears. Somewhere back along the line I've an ancestress who was priestess at the shrine of—You can guess the rest. I've learnt a lot about her since we prized up that door. Get that book from Renée, read it, then burn it. You'll get a glimmering of my meaning from that. Practices, hideous practices that you've never heard of. It's beginning again, Dick. It's begun—"

The words faded from his lips as the flapping noise against the window began again.

"Don't stop me!" he shouted. "If you value your life, don't try to stop me!"

I folded my arms.

"Don't be a fool," I said. "I'm as strong as you are and ten times as obstinate. You're sleeping here, d'you understand?"

And then I gasped. Juan Mitzakis had changed into an unrecognizable fiend before my eyes. Two arms, swinging like flails, caught me and swung me into midair. I crashed on to the table, and glasses and decanter fell with me to the carpet. My head bit something that stunned me. Looking up after an interval that might have been years or only seconds, I felt the cool draught from the outer door fanning my cheeks. The room door was wide open and, framed in the opening, I saw Mitzakis, his silk hat set at a jaunty angle and a white owl, with vivid green eyes, perched on his shoulder. For fully a minute he paused there, a sinister smile playing on his lips, then turned abruptly on his heel and vanished.

Chapter 6

IT WAS TEN BY MY BEDROOM CLOCK when Baines roused me from my slumbers and set the familiar tray on a bedside table. As I blinked myself back to consciousness a miscellany of articles caught my eye—the morning tea, Baines's special brew, steaming and particularly welcome—a tumbler of clear water and an extra spoon—a square bottle of morning salts.

Baines in himself was a curio: he had been both an amateur and a professional light-weight, his ears were shapeless and clung close to his head, his nose had been flattened by much punishment. Such of him as was visible to the naked eye was repulsive. The strong cards in his suit were unswerving loyalty and a heart of gold. He picked up the square bottle in one hand and the tumbler in the other and eyed each in turn.

"Had a bit of a thick night, haven't you, sir?" he remarked.

I pushed myself up on my elbows.

"What the devil do you mean?" I queried.

He sucked his teeth—an action which irritated me at all times.

"Well, sir," he pursued, measuring out a liberal spoonful of white grains, "I was only judging by the state of the drawing-room. Looked as if an earthquake had struck it!" He tipped in the salts, stirred the fluid with a practiced hand and held it out to me.

"It did, did it?" I said.

Baines nodded emphatically.

"When Mrs. Baines first called me in to look at it, sir, the thought that come to me was that we'd had burglars. The bureau was open for one thing."

"I know," I returned, "I opened it."

"Then," continued Baines with much relish, "the other furniture looked as if it had been pitched all over the place—and there was half a decanter of good whisky spilled on the carpet, two broken glasses and the siphon rolled under the china-cabinet. There being no signs of anyone having broken in, I tried to wake you, but you was sleeping like a log."

"And so you thought I'd been drunk, eh?" I demanded, sitting upright and sipping my tea.

Baines, blinking under my gaze, endeavored to modify his original suggestion.

"Well, not exactly drunk, sir—"

"What would you call it?" I growled. "You don't suppose a man in his sober senses throws tables and siphons and decanters about, do you?"

He moved to the window and drew the curtains, and the added light set a curious pain behind my eyeballs throbbing again. It was dawning on me that I ached in every limb. There was a bump at the back of my skull like an egg, areas of more intense pain in my left arm and hip. I felt horribly, damnably ill. Gradually the events of the previous night came back to me. Renée's surprise call over the wire, the knife incident at the New Venice, the murder in the Haymarket and the culminating, nocturnal visit of an old friend. An old friend, eh? I wondered. I was suffering from his attentions now! Who was it I had entertained in those still night hours?—A devil masquerading as Juan Mitzakis, or Juan Mitzakis possessed of a devil?

"Phone the office, Baines," I said, "and tell them I shan't be there this morning."

He approached the bed again and stood at its foot, grinning over the figured mahogany end until I could have kicked him.

"I have done so already, sir," he announced.

"Oh! Anybody called?"

"No, sir. It's a bit early yet."

"Anybody rung?"

"Yes, sir. Miss de Salis. Asked if you got home safely—and if you wouldn't mind calling her up later."

I glanced up sharply.

"Miss de Salis, eh? How did she seem? Did she sound at all alarmed when she spoke?"

He shook his head.

"Not in the least, sir. Quite her old self, if I may be allowed to say so, sir. Asked after Mrs. Baines and the cat and hoped we was all quite well."

"I see. Well, get on to her as soon as possible, Baines, and ask her to lunch. Tell her it's important."

"Very good, sir."

He turned towards the door.

"And Baines!" I called after him.

"Yes, sir?"

"Ask Mrs. Baines, with my compliments, to do her utmost with that lunch. Tell her to send out for anything she wants."

"I will, sir."

Feeling more dead than alive, I crawled to the bathroom and shaved. A hot bath, treated liberally with ammonia from a rubber-corked bottle on the glass shelf, pulled me together wonderfully. The throbbing behind my eyes ceased, my manifold bruises seemed less apparent; I was able to think clearly. Dressing in leisurely fashion, I tried to decide what to do next. My duty as a law-abiding citizen was to go to the police with my story; my position as a close friend of the man who had committed that amazing crime was to shield him, provided always I was convinced that he was not a free agent. That was the point. No friendship on earth could stand up to cold-blooded, calculated murder. It wasn't to be expected. Remembering Mitzakis before his disappearance, I decided that the responsibility for the outrage rested, not with him, but upon some sinister influence—Something vaguely connected with that vile creature of the night whose green eyes had blinked at me from the living-room door. Working along those lines, two courses were open to me: to follow somehow and exert every effort to dissuade Juan from this career of wanton destruction—or to wash my hands of the affair altogether. The former presented untold difficulties; the latter held no difficulties at all. The police could not possibly suspect me of harboring the criminal and Juan's movements immediately before the Haymarket murder had been hidden in the fog. Unless I chose to enlighten her, Renée need never know what had transpired in the interval between leaving the New Venice and arriving home at my flat.

I settled myself down at my desk and tried to work, but concentration was impossible. Even in the broad light of day, my elegant visitor of the small hours haunted me. In departing after our tussle, he seemed to have left me with a definite moral obligation, embodied in sentences that stuck in my brain:

"God, man! your job's to protect her from me, do you understand? I'm not a man, Dick. I'm not Juan Mitzakis. I'm a devil!" . . .

I chartered a taxi and drove to the Europa.

Yesterday had seen London at its worst; today it was at its best. All the way to Bloomsbury I felt as if I had stepped from the realms of nightmare into a solid, matter-of-fact world. The sky was sapphire-blue. A wintry sun tempered the breeze, shining upon legions of shoppers, legions of men and women engaged in their daily duties. I caught myself surveying these multitudes in a detached kind of way—wondering what their particular problems were, wherein lay their thrills, and how in the world each eked out a livelihood. Beyond the shops and great multiple stores, where they bought at one price and sold at another, the frowning buildings and broad stone pavements revealed not a crumb of profit to the naked eye. And yet these seething, jostling hordes worked and played, laughed and cried, and somehow found a balance from which to pay rent and rates and taxes almost to infinity . . .! It was, and is, and ever will be one of the incomprehensible miracles of civilization.

The manager of the Europa, a little, stout man in scrupulous morning attire, received me in the privacy of his office. At all times he was respectful, deferential almost, although I could see that his interest in me depreciated a good fifty per cent from the moment he gathered I was not a prospective client!

At the mention of Mitzakis he shook his head.

"I am afraid I cannot help you," he told me. "We have nobody of that name on our books."

He went to the trouble of verifying this.

"My friend may be living here under an assumed name," I persisted. "You see, he called on me last night and gave me this address. I understand that he had arrived from Paris only yesterday."

His face brightened.

"From Paris, you say?"

"That was what I gathered. Just previous to that a lady of my acquaintance met him in Nice."

He dived through a glass door, returning after a brief interval with a large red-backed volume that I took to be the hotel register.

"A tall, dark man," he ventured, blinking at me. "Foreign appearance—somewhere around thirty?"

I nodded.

"That's it," I said. "Stopping here with a lady."

He closed the book with a snap.

"Mr. and Mrs. Julian Murray," he announced. "Rooms 41 and 42. Another gentleman with them—Señor Anton Valdao—room 47." He smiled faintly. "It seems as if you have had a wasted journey, Mr. Coombes. Your friends left for the Continent again this morning—traveling by air from Croydon."

I picked up my hat.

"They left no address?"

He shook his head.

"None whatever. They were only here one night. Just a chance visit, you see. They would hardly have given this address for letters."

He accompanied me to the door.

"I'm very much obliged to you," I said. "You've no idea, by any chance, where they were bound?"

"Paris, in the first instance," he declared after prolonged reflection. "After that, I understood they were leaving for Spain."

Chapter 7

RENÉE WAS WAITING FOR ME when I got back. She sat just where Juan had sat the night before, in a bright blue frock that suited her tremendously, reading the paper and stroking Susan.

"Hullo, Dick!" she greeted me. "How are you?"

We shook hands.

"I'm afraid I'm late," I said.

"Not in the least, my dear. I got bored at the hotel and drifted along here half-an-hour ago. Can you see any flour on me any-where? I've been in your kitchen—hindering Mrs. Baines." She passed me the paper, marking the place with her thumb. "Dick! Have you seen this?"

Sitting on the arm of the chesterfield, I read it through, conscious that Renée was watching me all the time. *"Haymarket Mystery"* it began. *"Well-known Foreign Diplomat Stabbed to Death. Owl-headed Knife."* . . . There followed a column and a half of fact and fiction skillfully welded together to form a story calculated to suit the readers' cravings for sensation.

I dropped it between us.

"Hm!" I commented. "Unpleasant—very!"

Renée de Salis faced me squarely.

"What's it all mean?" she demanded in a tone that left no doubt as to what *she* meant.

I shrugged my shoulders.

"Just what it says, I suppose; that an unfortunate though distinguished foreign gentleman met an untimely end in the Haymarket—in a fog."

She stamped her foot.

"Uncle Richard! I'm not an idiot!"

"I don't think I ever suggested you were."

"There are times, Dick, when I'd like to shake you. Don't you see? Of course you do, only you won't admit it—that Juan must have killed that man? Else why should he have come into my rooms for that knife?"

"Now you are dabbling," I interposed, "with what is commonly termed circumstantial evidence—and you want to hang poor Juan on it out of hand!"

Renée bridled.

"I don't want to do anything of the sort."

"I'll give you a case in point," I began. "Now, supposing a woman is found—where shall we say?—in Brixton, with her throat cut, and that medical evidence goes to show that the wound couldn't have been self-inflicted . . ."

"If you don't stop," interrupted Renée fiercely, "I shall scream!"

"But why?" I demanded. "I was merely endeavoring to show you—"

"I don't want to be shown, thanks. The whole thing's too absurd for words. This isn't a woman in Brixton. It's a man whose name was among those on that list I told you—murdered with an owl-handled knife that you and I were examining only a short time before. I ask you again—and I expect a sensible answer this time—what does it all mean?"

"I'm afraid I don't know," I retorted, hedging.

Renée sighed.

"I don't know how it is; but I somehow expected you to say that."

"What else could I say? I'm not clairvoyant!"

"No, but you might suggest a solution. You're fairly clever at that sort of thing when you choose." An appetizing odor drifted in from the kitchen and Renée de Salis sniffed. "You're preparing a most heavenly lunch for me, Uncle Richard. The sort of thing one pays for at hotels and never gets! And I really don't deserve it at all. If I'd stifled my fears and stayed on at the Gallia Palace, instead of running away, all this would never have happened!"

"I don't know why you should think that."

She shook her head.

"Nor do I, but I do."

"Juan could have recovered his knife just as easily from the Gallia Palace, and come to London afterwards."

The words slipped out before I could prevent them.

Renée pounced on them like a shot, turning them to her own advantage.

"So you do admit that it was Juan who killed him? Of course it was. It sounds a heartless thing to say, but I'm absolutely convinced. It only confirms what I told you last night. His sufferings have turned his brain—and he's over in Europe now, believing himself to be the avenging instrument of that ghastly cult. Poor Juan!"

I threw in my hand. There was nothing else for it. Renée's theory was refreshing. It explained why Juan had resorted to murder, constituted the sort of defense, in fact that in these days is the final plea of all criminal counsel. Guilty but insane. After all—and within certain limits—it was the only reasonable solution to the mystery. Judged by his treatment of me in that very room, Mitzakis was mad. From the moment he entered the door his manner had been strange, his conversation that of a lunatic subject to intervals of comparative sanity. And yet, acceptable as that theory was, it contained one serious flaw. It failed to explain the significance of the White Owl . . . Whence had it come? Granted that it was a tamed creature—a bizarre pet adopted by Mitzakis during his long incarceration—what instinct prompted it to seek out the window of the room he meditated visiting?

"I may as well make a clean breast of it," I said. "Juan did kill Manzanarez. I've know it for some hours—long before it got into the papers. He called here and told me so himself."

Renée gasped.

"He came here—to this flat—and you let him go away?"

"I did my best to stop him," I retorted, "and all but had my neck broken for my pains. I went round to his hotel this morning, trying to find him, but he'd left for Spain some hours before—by air." I gave her the whole story, from the time I left the New Venice until my departure by taxi for Bloomsbury, omitting merely those details that affected her relationship with Juan before his disappearance. She sat, with her hands in her lap, listening intently. Baines came in with *aperitifs* and went out again, closing the door after him.

"Dick," said Renée suddenly, breaking in on the end of my narrative, "supposing we begin at the beginning—I mean where you and Juan prized up that door . . ." She was upright now, pressing her finger-tips to her forehead, frowning a little as one does when confronting a baffling situation. "Supposing, when ages ago the Spaniards cemented down that door, there were living people inside."

I inclined my head.

"Burying alive was quite a popular form of punishment. I should think it highly probable."

She drew closer to me on the chesterfield.

"Well then, assuming that to be the case, assuming too that these people somehow managed to exist and—and breed . . . That's not quite the word I want, but you know what I mean . . . What do you imagine their present-day descendants would be like?"

"It depends a great deal on what their resources were below," I told her. "They must have had ventilation—or they couldn't have existed at all—"

"And," Renée put in quickly, "they must have had light—or their eyes wouldn't be much use to them now. And yet all you saw when you looked down was darkness and yellow fog . . . You see, I'm trying to account for Naia and this Anton Valdao—and for the fact of Juan's being alive at all. Somebody must have found him when he fell, and looked after him . . ."

"Naia, very probably. You remember it was she who visited my tent afterward."

She bit her lip.

"I hate that woman, Dick!"

"If we're going to theorize," I returned, switching back to the main issue, "why not argue on a reasonable basis. Let us assume, if you like, that the ancient religion and some of its adherents survived—not in the cavern we opened, but in an adjacent valley I and my men failed to discover. These twentieth-century Toltecs might have burrowed a way into the temple of the White Owl somewhere at the foot of the hill. Adhering to ancient custom, they kept priestesses at the shrine of their deity, and it was these—or one of these—that found Juan when he fell . . . *Naia,* quite conceivably was a general term applied to these vestal virgins—or whatever they were—signifying 'The Nameless One.' The fumes even might have originated in some gigantic, subterranean, sacrificial fire . . . Accepting all this, let us try to link it up with what is happening now. Until Mitzakis came to them they were a lost race, dwelling in a lost world, imbued with an inherited hatred of their Spanish oppressors. Juan, a virtual prisoner, pursuing his researches as soon as he was well enough, succeeded in discovering the vast treasures he had always believed to be there.—He admits now that his wealth came from those caves.—His one overwhelming desire, now that his end was attained, was to return to Europe—a continent of which his hosts had never heard."

Renée reached across me for a cigarette.

"I could have forgiven him almost anything," she interrupted in a low voice, "if he had left without that woman!"

"He may have found it impossible to escape without her. And in any case, you must remember, we are assuming he is insane."

She pondered this for some time, the blue smoke curling upwards between her fingers. When next she spoke there were tears in her eyes.

"We've got to get him back, Dick. Juan couldn't have killed Manzanarez of his own free will. It isn't in him to kill anybody. These creatures he has brought with him are using him—influencing him to do things against his will. We'll fight them, Dick, fight them with every penny I possess. The police won't know about this last crime—and we may be able to stop him harming anybody else . . . You'll find him for me and I'll talk to him. He'll listen to me."

I nodded gravely.

"And when you've separated him from his associates," I queried, "when you've brought him back to his sober senses—if ever you do—are you going to marry him?"

Renée shuddered.

"I don't know, Dick," she whispered. "I don't know, I'm sure."

"It'll be a tall order."

"Of course it will. I know that. I shall always remember Naia . . . I shall always remember it was Juan's hand killed Manzanarez."

The lunch bell rang and I came to my feet.

"We leave then for Spain on Monday?"

She caught both my hands.

"Tonight, Dick, if you can manage it," she said. "Tomorrow at latest. Is that a bargain?"

"Yes," I agreed, almost without reflection. "I suppose it is—provided you make it tomorrow and excuse me the moment lunch is over. As it is, I shall have my work cut out to get away."

I imagine every man living thinks himself indispensable in his own particular sphere. I found myself regretting my promise as soon as I had made it. Molehills were already becoming mountains. The moderate amount of business in my city office assumed mountainous proportions; the few small failings my chief clerk possessed multiplied alarmingly. I was going, principally because Renée had asked me and I had not the courage to refuse her, but I felt that on my return I should find myself in the bankruptcy court!

She stopped level with me as I held open the door.

"Why don't you say 'Damn the woman!' Uncle Richard?" she laughed. "I'm sure you're thinking it."

Chapter 8

WE FLEW TO PARIS, leaving Baines and Marie to follow by the normal route. Marie, whose religious scruples and physical fears coincided conveniently, definitely refused to set foot in an aeroplane, apparently preferring the martyrdom of a Channel crossing to the remote risk of breaking her neck. From Baines' depressed attitude when I gave him his final orders I guessed that Mrs. Baines had lectured him as to his future conduct (a) with Marie *en route,* (b) with any of those dark-eyed young things with which—according to Mrs. Baines's creed—Paris is exclusively inhabited. A glance at Renée's luggage in the vestibule of the New Venice convinced me as to the desirability of this arrangement. It comprised seven trunks of varying sizes, each painted with a green and yellow band to facilitate recognition, and I counted eleven hat-boxes!

Only four other passengers went with us—an American family of three, out for the thrill, and a stout, lethargic Dutchman who used this method of transport so frequently that he felt no thrill at all. I sat next Renée, who looked calm and self-possessed and miraculously turned-out—although she assured me afterward she felt as though she were going to be sick at any moment!—watching Croydon and Sanderstead dwindling into the haze behind us and wondering where the extraordinary adventure that had just begun was going to land us. Viewed in the broad light of day, it seemed hopeless. The necessities of the case demanded that we pursue our inquiries without outside assistance. Juan might be in Madrid by now, Bilbao, Barcelona, anywhere . . . Weeks could elapse before we could trace him, and by the time we had reached the town where he was last seen, he might be a hundred miles away . . .

"We'll begin," announced Renée suddenly bringing her lips close to my ear, "by inquiring at Le Bourget when we land. If they can't tell us anything we'll try the Carthagena—the hotel where Juan always used to stay when he was in Paris. These other people don't know Europe well; they're almost bound to depend on him as guide."

I regarded her in amazement. For a woman who had the reputation of never bothering her head about anything, Renée de Salis was uncommonly shrewd.

"And supposing he's left Paris when we get there?" I asked. "What then?"

She shrugged her shoulders.

"We'll have to try one of the towns he mentioned in Spain—in the order he gave, if you can remember it."

"I do," I said. "It was Barcelona first—then Madrid, then Cadiz."

It was raining in Paris when we climbed out. Our Dutchman stepped into an atmosphere of moist discomfort as if he were used to it—as I suspect he was. The Americans took it less philosophically. It gave me an inward glow of satisfaction at hearing Mrs. Cyrus Mullett, of Cincinnati, wishing aloud to her husband that she had stayed in London and cut out the Paris part of the program altogether! "If this is *'Gay Paree,'*" voiced Miss Mullett plaintively, "give me little old New York every time!" Altogether, you couldn't blame them. Personally, I wasn't disposed to blame them at all. Analyzing Mr. Cyrus Mullett, I decided he had been born under a lucky star. He seemed a nice, quiet, unassuming little man, belonging to the sort that deserve good fortune but rarely obtain it. His wife managed him—although she was the last person in the world to have admitted it—and Miss Virginia was as nice a little girl as one could find in two continents. "I can show you five things in that great city of yours," Cyrus had confided to me *en route,* "where you Englishmen have got us beaten to a frazzle . . ." What exactly those five things were is not important: it merely went to show the sort of man Cyrus Mullett was.

It transpired that they had reserved rooms at the Bristol. Not having the foggiest notion at that moment what our future movements were likely to be, I packed Renée off in the car along with them.

Things began to brisk up, in spite of the weather. It was officially recorded that a Mr. and Mrs. Julian Murray, accompanied by Señor Valdao had landed there the previous morning. In half an hour I had discovered the chauffeur who had driven them to their hotel. By a lucky chance, he was a Russian of good family, forced as so many like him had been to earn his living in the streets of the French capital. I had no difficulty in recognizing Juan from his description. His portrait of Naia was equally convincing. He referred to Valdao as "the little man with the green eyes."

One foot on the running board of his car, I pressed him further.

"Without a doubt, I should know him again, monsieur," he assured me. "One rarely sees such short men—even in France. Five feet in your measurement, I should say, sallow-complexioned, feet turned well out, and a thin, hooked nose—like a beak. He seemed half-asleep when they helped him into the car."

I thanked him and climbed in.

"And he had green eyes?" I queried, leaning out.

He paused, one hand on the gear-lever.

"Peculiarly green eyes, monsieur," he insisted. "I remember remarking on them to a colleague afterward. It was uncanny."

"Where did you take them?"

"To the Carthagena, monsieur," he answered promptly.

I requested him to drive me there and sat back in the cushions, satisfied that the morning's work had not been wasted. I caught myself reflecting on that mysterious quantity known as feminine intuition. Up to this point Renée was right. Juan, essentially a creature of habit, had taken his friends to his old haunt. I wondered if he had registered there as "Julian Murray" or whether he had clung to the name by which the management of the Carthagena had originally known him. It would be interesting to find out. However that might be, I was by no means relishing the prospect of a second encounter with Mitzakis. Remembering my threat, he might not be surprised to see me. I could hardly count on his being pleased . . . With Naia's attitude on learning the import of my mission to Paris, I was not particularly concerned. Valdao, as yet, was an unknown quantity. He might, as we had begun by assuming, belong to the lost Mexican tribe with which Juan had come in contact. On the other hand, there was no reason to suppose he was more than a casual friend, picked up on the journey to Europe. Looking back on it all, I believe that my sole object was to rid myself of an unpleasant duty and get back to London at the earliest possible moment. Had I known then what I know now, I am convinced I should have changed my destination to the Bristol, have picked up Renée and persuaded her to wash the entire business out.

And yet—it is difficult to say. Within a handful of moments of chatting with a family of decent, pleasure-seeking Americans, we were destined to be pitchforked into an adventure so fantastic, so thrilling, and yet so infinitely horrible that I find it hard now to persuade myself that it actually happened.

Gray suburbs gave way to the main streets and boulevards of the gay city. I saw dripping awnings, dripping trees, regiment upon regiment of moist umbrellas . . . We were threading our way through that extraordinary maze of traffic, moving in a series of rapid spurts, drawing up time and again with a back-breaking jerk before the passing hulk of a grotesque omnibus, a lorry or a gleaming limousine. Looked at through foreign eyes, it all seemed a desperate scramble for life, dependent on brake-linings and shrill motor-horns, and little, curiously composed gendarmes with white batons. Good fortune, skill on the part of my driver, a miracle if you like, twisted us from the main stream into the quiet backwater that held the Carthagena. I leaped out as the wheels scraped the pavement, requested the driver to wait for me and mounted the broad flight of steps.

Revolving doors admitted me to a comfortable, carpeted foyer. Here and there were little piles of luggage, here and there women, in twos and threes, sitting about near palm-trees in tubs. I interviewed an elegant young man, entrenched behind an equally elegant yellow counter. His English was irreproachable—his manner condescending.

"Monsieur desires—?"

I cleared my throat.

"I understand you have some friends of mine staying here—Mr. and Mrs. Julian Murray and a Spanish gentleman—Señor Valdao."

The telephone bell rang and he lifted the receiver by his elbow in a studiedly languid way. Apparently he had reduced the somewhat commonplace duty of telephoning in public to a fine art.

"I beg your pardon," he said at length. "I remember the party quite well—two gentlemen and a lady. Paris is full just now, you know—very full indeed. We are booked up here for weeks ahead. Yesterday, as it happened, some one had failed us. We were fortunate in being able to offer one single room to Señor Valdao. His two friends went elsewhere."

I produced my card-case, fingering it thoughtfully.

"And Señor Valdao," I hazarded, "is, of course, out at the moment?"

I hoped he would say that he was, partly because I figured that little would be gained from an interview with Juan's strange colleague, partly because I could hardly decline to see him now without explanation to this very superior young man.

He was telephoning again, screening his lips with his hand, as if he were passing a profound state secret along the line. He replaced the receiver and smiled.

"Señor Valdao is in his room at this moment. Number 83—on the third floor. The elevator is just over there—to the right, behind those palms. Good morning."

"Good morning," I responded weakly and stared where he had pointed. I was just making up my mind to take the main exit instead of the lift, when a hotel servant in blue and gold braid touched me deferentially on the arm.

"Your pardon, monsieur—the elevator is over there."

"Of course," I said. "How stupid of me!" He seemed determined that nothing should stand between me and the ordeal I was endeavoring to avoid. Beckoning at intervals, he preceded me to the lift, clanked to the metal trellis and called my attention to the fact that there was no smoking permitted. I removed my pipe from my mouth and held it behind me.

The man grinned.

"You English always smoking," he declared. I gave him a couple of cigarettes from my case. On the whole I preferred his frank geniality to the aloof air of the gentleman at the desk. His manner on accepting my humble offering suggested that these were the first English cigarettes he had ever received. He tried to spell out the maker's name—then gave it up with a despairing shrug and stuck one behind each ear. "Very good," was his final comment, "but too much opium!" I shook my head but declined to argue. It wasn't worth it.

On our way along the corridor we passed an elderly chambermaid manipulating a vacuum-cleaner. It was all very pleasant and up to date. My escort exchanged a word with her on passing, but I failed to catch what it was. We turned a corner and he tapped on a closed door.

"*Monsieur!*" he called loudly, then stooped to peer through the keyhole. Just above his head I read the number—83, in large black characters.

Suddenly I sniffed. The man sniffed, too, and recoiled a pace, his mustache bristling, his rugged face one big query-mark. From the cool, fresh atmosphere of that very modern caravanserai we had stepped into a zone of rank abomination—a belt of sickly odor that was vaguely and horribly reminiscent and yet to which I could not attach a name. A cog in my memory stirred and I started violently. Closing my eyes, I could see prickly-thorn, cactus and scrub . . . a vast, gaping chasm and yellow fumes pouring from the bowels of the earth!

"Nom de dieu!" exclaimed the porter. "What is it?"

He held his breath and tapped again. There was no answer.

"Monsieur!" he ventured, anxious no doubt to earn the tip he hoped was forthcoming; *"Monsieur! Monsieur Valdao!"*

He turned towards me, spreading out his arms in a sweeping gesture that was very eloquent.

I felt, too, that he was censuring me for possessing a friend who existed in an atmosphere like that!

"Very probably he's out," I ventured. "I—I'll call again later."

The man shook his head.

"No, no, monsieur; he is in. I asked Therese and she said so."

He tried the handle, muttering to himself as he did it.

"Locked? *Non, par dieu?* It is open—*Monsieur Valdao? Pardon?"* The door was fully open now, letting out whole waves of that extraordinary odor. It was dark inside, for the jalousies were shut. My companion had penetrated a couple of feet into the apartment, apparently with the object of acquainting Señor Valdao with the fact that I was there. Suddenly he let out a wild yell of terror, charged back into me, nearly bowling me over, then stampeded in a panic round the corner.

Curious to know what had startled him, I peered in. My handkerchief pressed to my nostrils, I made out the bright slits in the shutters opposite, a single bed that had never been slept in, a tall *armoire* with looking-glass front and, right in the foreground, so close to me that I could not imagine how I could have missed it at the outset, *an enormous white owl, perched on a table, watching me with vivid green eyes!*

Chapter 9

THE DOOR SLAMMED IN MY FACE.

For some seconds I remained there, rooted to the spot in astonishment, my senses more or less attuned to that ghastly odor. What, my reeling brain demanded, could it all mean? I had come there—partly against my will—to talk to Valdao—the man with the green eyes. And I had come face-to-face, for the third time in my life, with the White Owl!

It was incredible—inexplicable. I had the assurance of the man at the desk, of the chambermaid with the electric sweeper, that Valdao was actually in his room—and yet, when the porter had opened the door, there was nothing in view but the bird. Could it be possible that the tenant of No. 83 had slipped out unnoticed. If so, how was it he had omitted to lock his room, and what was the motive that had prompted him to leave so extraordinary a pet in charge? Any natural, reasonable solution to the mystery baffled me. Again against my will, I was forced to suspect some answer that bordered dangerously on the supernatural.

Un-natural, perhaps, was a better word to explain my chaos of disconnected reasoning. A year and a half ago Juan had disappeared, clinging to the wing of a white owl. Not an ordinary white owl, but a sinister deity in the existence of which he had partly believed before its dramatic reappearance on a Mexican hilltop . . . I had exerted every possible effort to find him—done everything, in fact, that was *humanly* possible. To all intents and purposes he was dead . . . It was not natural that he should have survived, that he should be in Europe at that moment, bent on a series of purposeless assassinations . . . And, beyond a shadow of doubt, that strange white bird represented the evil genius behind this career of crime . . .

I was on the point of departure when the door opened again and the head of a little, yellow-faced man was thrust through the aperture.

"Who are you?" he snapped in execrable French, "and what do you want with me?"

Before I could frame a suitable reply to this outburst the light of recognition dawned in those green eyes and I found myself held by them, astounded at their color, at the flames of livid fury that lurked behind. I sensed that the little man in that absurd, over-long dressing-gown knew me and detested me cordially—and yet, to my knowledge, I had never set eyes on him before.

The door swung wider and he began waving his arms in front of his face.

"Go away," he shrieked, "go away from here. I receive nobody—nobody, you understand." His mood changed in a flash. With a dramatic gesture, he wrenched back his gown and the pyjama-jacket beneath, revealing a section of chest that was uncannily white and a round, dark scar that a bullet might have made. At that instant I saw his nails—as long as a mandarin's and incredibly filthy. One of them pointed to the scar. "One would have been enough," he hissed, "but I can show you *three*—three, do you hear me?"

He leaned against the door-frame, yawning, as if a sudden drowsiness had overtaken him. His eyes closed and he opened them with an effort.

"One would have been enough!" I heard him mutter, half to himself. *"Valdao—never—forgets . . . The White Owl—never—forgets."*

There was an appreciable pause between each word—each syllable almost. He reeled back into the room and the door closed. I heard a noise from the far side as if he had fallen.

Other sounds echoed in the corridor . . . hurried footsteps and the voice of my porter, raised to falsetto, making the most of his adventure. He came into view around the corner, gesticulating violently, followed at a short interval by a little, stout, over-washed *maître d'hôtel,* the tall youth from the reception desk and the elderly chambermaid. The *maître d'hôtel* flashed a look at me and tapped authoritatively. Obtaining no response, he turned the handle and entered, falling headlong over the sleeping form of Señor Valdao. I squeezed in behind him. The jalousies were open now, bathing the apartment in bright sunlight. Apparently the rain-pall that had gripped the city had lifted since I left the street. It revealed an ample room, parquet-floored and well-furnished. Strange-looking luggage was scattered on all sides. The atmosphere was faintly odorous, but nothing more. There was no sign of the white owl anywhere.

Two of them, failing to awake Señor Valdao from his slumbers, carried him to the bed. The porter's fixed expression, now that his ghost had vanished into thin air, was distinctly humorous. I felt that I wanted to laugh. Slipping past the chambermaid, I made for the stairs unchallenged. Five minutes later I was back in the taxi, with my impassive Russian driver steering me through the main stream of traffic towards the Bristol. What exactly my thoughts were at that moment I do not remember. A sort of grim reaction had set in. I lolled there, limp and exhausted, numbed by the events of the morning that had comprised a flight from London, some brief investigations and an extraordinary, unsettling climax. And, at the back of it all, emblazoned on my mental horizon as vividly as any night-sign in Broadway or Piccadilly, hovered that half-veiled threat Valdao had breathed before he fell asleep: *"The White Owl never forgets!"*

I started and sat up. We were stationary now, held up by a policeman's baton at a spot where four roads met. Glancing upwards, I could see a stretch of blue sky. The sun was shining on wet roads and wet pavements; people were sitting out on chairs under the striped awning of the *brasserie* at the corner. Paris, dismal and drab an hour back, was full of color.

What was it the White Owl never forgot? That I had shot at it three times when it perched on that olive tree on that ill-fated excursion into the Mexican hinterland? And yet Valdao carried the scars! It appeared to suggest that the White Owl was a man—or Valdao the White Owl—I shrugged my shoulders and gave it up. It was an unhealthy business altogether. The hotel porter would be telling his wife and family when he got home *"Nom de dieu!* but it was exactly as I say. First there was that curious smell; then the bird. I tell you I opened the door and saw it. And then, afterward, when the manager and the rest came, there was nothing—only Monsieur Valdao!" And the family would all be duly impressed— or would tell him he was a liar or had been drinking too much *vin blanc.* As for myself, I was grateful for the fact that he had been there. Otherwise, I fancy, I should have come away believing the events of the past few days had turned my brain.

In some respects I was glad I had called at the Carthagena. That Valdao was merely a traveling acquaintance of Juan's was now an exploded theory. I had seen that peculiar being for myself, knew that I should know him when I saw him again. Somehow we must contrive to have the Carthagena carefully watched, so that we might trace Juan and Naia. Up to that point fortune had smiled on us; it would be fatal to let them elude us now. A further thought struck me: What was keeping them in Paris? Did they regard this break as a period of much-needed rest after their recent exertions—or had they some other victim in view? Both things were equally possible.

I spoke to Karolin, my intelligent Russian, before paying him off.

"You know the man with the green eyes," I said. "He is staying at the Carthagena now. There are good reasons why he should be watched. If you can arrange to hand your car over to a colleague for a time, hang outside that hotel and report to me here whenever he goes out or whenever either of his two friends calls to see him, there's an English pound-note a day for you."

Karolin thought the proposition over while he was counting out my change.

"Bien!" he agreed at length, "I think I could manage that."

"It should only be a question of days," I assured him. "Days—and nights. I was forgetting the nights. It's worth double my original offer to me to have him watched all the twenty-four hours."

I handed him back the change and my visiting-card, with "Hotel Bristol" scrawled on the back. In return, Karolin gave me his address, together with the assurance that I could count on him to serve me faithfully. There was always the understanding, of course, that I would supply him with my fresh address in the event of the Bristol's being full.

Renée was in the hall waiting for me.

"My dear!" she cried, springing up as I approached, "I thought you were never coming. The Mulletts have had their *dejeuner* and gone up to rest. I waited for you—and I'm simply famished." Her dark eyes searched my face. "Have you any news?" she whispered.

I nodded.

"Loads of it," I returned. "Find a table somewhere while I wash, and I'll tell you all about it."

"You've seen Juan?"

"No, but I've met Valdao."

"Oh!" she gasped, "what's he like?"

"A pretty nasty bit of work! How have you got on?"

Renée smiled.

"I've been chatting with Virginia mostly. We've been talking hats and things. She wants me to take her shopping. I've fixed up rooms, by the by. I hope that's right."

I hastened to assure her that it was.

"I think you'll like Virginia, Uncle Dick," she said when I joined her at the table. "She's so absolutely natural. When she says 'Will you do this—for me?' in that fascinating drawl of hers—you feel it'd be a crying shame if you refused!"

Chapter 10

KAROLIN RANG ME UP AT FOUR, to reassure me that he was at his post and that our quarry was still in residence. I went back to my room, where I had been resting all the afternoon, in a more contented frame of mind. A further visit to the Carthagena would be abortive. I had shifted my responsibilities on to Karolin and there was nothing left to do but rest and wait. From a business point of view, the arrangement suited me admirably. Instead of indulging in a break-neck journey to Barcelona, we were comfortably housed in Paris—within phoning-distance of London.

That enterprising plutocrat Cyrus Mullett had engaged a whole suite of rooms and we had tea there at five, at his invitation. Virginia had been to Lafayette's or the Louvre and had bought a frock, which she wore for our special edification. Cyrus related some of his back-home fishing adventures, I'm afraid slightly exaggerated. Mrs. Mullett did little but pour out tea and correct her husband whenever she thought he was breaking the bounds of credulity. Altogether it was an extremely pleasant interlude, particularly so in our case, because it kept us from thinking too much of the main object that had brought us there. It enabled us, too, to see the Mulletts, not as jaded travelers arriving in a rain-storm, but in the more intimate atmosphere of their own temporary home. Their sole desire was to be friendly. Nor did they once inquire the reason for our traveling together—although I fancy all of them suspected we were a runaway-couple and not altogether respectable! In any case, I can readily excuse them, if only on the grounds that Renée de Salis looked just the kind of girl with whom most men in their sober senses would want to run away!

For three whole days and nights, except for brief excursions into the street for my morning paper or tobacco, I remained within call of the telephone, afraid to move away from it for fear that in my absence the all-important message would arrive. For Renée it was a different matter. Reluctantly at first, she took my advice and "did" Paris with the Mulletts. She protested that circumstances might arise which would compel me to leave Paris at short notice, but I explained to her that the daily itineraries were usually fixed and that a messenger would find her. Her final argument was always that she would be bored to tears, which, oddly enough, she never was. Renée, who stopped in Paris more often than in London, discovered that she knew comparatively little concerning its accepted wonders. Without the least intention of becoming a tourist she had done so—and it was doing her all the good in the world.

Baines and Marie had turned up as directed and more or less in order on the evening of the day of our arrival—the former not the least unsettled by the journey, the latter limp and jaded. It said much for Baines that the seven trunks and eleven hat-boxes—to say nothing of sundry pieces of his own and mine—had arrived intact at their destination. As time wore on, I came to the conclusion that Mr. Baines was thoroughly enjoying this period of separation from his wife, looking upon it rather in the light of a new war! His war-time French had returned to him with astonishing fluency; he treated the hotel servants with superior reserve, as became a member of a superior race, and grew to know the district that separated the Carthagena from the Bristol almost as well as Karolin himself.

Towards the end of the third day I began to get anxious. Karolin rang me regularly, but there was always nothing to report. As far as he could gather, Valdao kept to his room; he had not set eyes on Juan or Naia again. Just after dinner on the third night a message was brought to me that Karolin was ill. The *grippe* had seized him and he had been unable to shake it off. He had secured a substitute—a very reliable Frenchman; but, of course, reliable as he was, he had never seen Valdao in the flesh. It was exceedingly unfortunate, but it couldn't be helped. I talked it over with Baines and we decided to undertake the night-watch together, the understanding being that once he had had an opportunity of seeing Valdao, we should split it up.

It was a fine, starry night when we set out. There was a suggestion of frost in the air, a wintry chill that was reflected in the faces that passed us—men in heavy overcoats from every country under the sun, elegant women peering from upturned fur collars at that fascinating, bizarre movie-reel of life—Paris after business hours. There was still that swift-moving traffic stream, still those grotesque, lumbering busses, but these were in the minority. Sports-cars, saloons, superior private-owned vehicles, intermingled with taxis of varying antiquity, flashed east and west in steady streams. Inside twenty minutes I had caught a dozen different languages— American, Spanish, Italian, Russian—strange-sounding accents from the Balkans—Turkish, Egyptian, Arabic. Two Siamese youths were chatting at a corner before a crowded, brightly-illuminated cafe. Laughter echoed in my ears, the clinking of glasses, people talking at the top of their voices in an effort to make themselves heard against that hubbub of horns and wheels and exhausts that never ceased.

Karolin's substitute—a slight, dark man in a threadbare coat and spats—met us by appointment in the American bar at the Carthagena at eleven. He might have been a gambler down on his luck—or a waiter out of a job. I was never quite satisfied which. He seemed intelligent enough and anxious to please, and Karolin had given him such a detailed description of the man he was required to shadow that I very much doubt if he would have missed him. I gave him a drink and a hundred-franc note and we parted on the distinct understanding he was to relieve us at six and to carry-on in any case, if we were not there. I suppose it was easy-money to him. The question whether we were blackmailers, confidence-tricksters or just engaged on some subtle intrigue in which a woman was involved did not disturb him one iota. He never even troubled to inquire. That is one of the outstanding differences between the French capital and our own. In England you would have to look far to find the ideal private detective or professional eaves-dropper; in Paris he lurks at every corner. This much our shabby-genteel investigator did for us before leaving: He ascertained in some mysterious way that Valdao was in and upstairs.

As soon as he had gone, I prepared to spend the night as comfortably as was possible in the circumstances. How Karolin and his colleague filled in their time without exciting suspicion I have never been able to discover. Baines and I sat in the vestibule by the palms until well after midnight, smoking and talking and trying to look as if we belonged there. One o'clock found us pacing the pavement opposite the hotel. Baines bored to death and distinctly mystified, myself thoroughly disgusted with the whole business. An hour passed and we were still strolling up and down, taking first one side of the road and then the other, to break the monotony.

"Who is this bloke we're looking for?" demanded Baines suddenly, pitching his cigarette-end into the gutter and fishing for its successor in a yellow packet.

I racked my brain for a plausible explanation.

"It's a queer affair altogether, Baines," I said, after prolonged deliberation. "Briefly, it concerns Miss de Salis, Mr. Mitzakis and myself . . . The man we are watching now is called Valdao. You know that already, of course. Miss de Salis and myself have reasons to believe that Mr. Mitzakis may be still alive and that this Valdao can tell us where he is to be found."

Baines whistled softly.

"Then Mr. Mitzakis wasn't killed in Mexico?"

"I don't know. That is really what I'm trying to find out."

He stared at me.

"Won't this Valdao say?"

I shook my head.

"These Mexicans are queer people, Baines. They're not like ourselves. They're very short-tempered for one thing—and rather handy with the knife for another. Señor Valdao is particularly short-tempered."

Baines yawned.

"I was driving a lorry once in Italy," he remarked reminiscently. "We was going up the mountains from Marostica. You know how them mountain-tracks wind. A couple of Arditi—those blokes that fight only with knives and hand-grenades—asked us for a lift, but we wouldn't stop. I suppose they cut across the rough ground while we was winding up the track. Anyway, at the next bend we sighted them again and, before you could say 'Jack Robinson!' there was a nasty-looking knife sticking in the lorry—just by my shoulder!"—He paused, sucking his teeth.—"We always stopped when we saw an Ardito after that," he added laconically, "stopped and took off our hats and asked if we might be honored by his presence in the old bus!"

"Well," I laughed, "you'll probably have a pretty fair idea by this time of the sort of chap Valdao is."

Baines stared hard at the broad entrance to the hotel.

"Whatever he is," he retorted, "he won't be moving out now."

"One would hardly think so," I agreed. I was answering at random, hardly conscious of what I was saying, intrigued by a new line of thought that had come to me suddenly from the night. I had been trying to give Baines a common-sense version of the story—when there wasn't one! I had told Karolin to watch a man, an elevator, a door—just normal things —when in reality I should have warned him against the abnormal happening. For the twentieth time that night we stopped at the corner of a dark passageway—a sort of private road leading to the back.

I touched his arm.

"Wait here," I said. "Move up and down, if you like, but keep your eyes glued on that door. I'm going down here."

Baines nodded.

"Right-o!" he agreed. "If you want me, just whistle."

Thirty yards brought me to the back of the Carthagena. I avoided a row of galvanized dust-bins, put out there for the morning, and stood in a wide deserted court, staring up at an immense rectangle of stonework—new and very American and rows upon rows of symmetrical, shuttered windows. I concentrated my gaze on the third floor, trying to decide the approximate position of Valdao's room. Metal fire-stairs zigzagged up the building at intervals—dizzy, openwork affairs, by any one of which Valdao could have made his exit.

The moonlight was very bright here. Standing in a patch of dense shadow, I lit my pipe. A lean black cat upset a dust-bin lid with a jarring sound that set me jumping—then streaked off past me out of sight. I was fumbling for the matches when a new sound broke upon my ears—a queer, *swishing* noise coming from the upper air. Looking upwards, gripped with a sudden sense of uneasiness, *I saw a great white bird, flapping across the vault of star-strewn heaven, swooping towards the windows.* I lost it and picked it up again—a vague white object against whiter walls. For a second it paused, hovering in mid-air—then alighted on a ledge and vanished through half-open jalousies into the room beyond.

Another brief pause and the figure of a man appeared, poised on a shallow balcony. For minutes on end he remained there, looking down, and I wondered if he could see me. The shutters closed again and he was gone.

My pipe was out, the matches still in my fingers. Deep in thought, I found my way to the road and picked up Baines.

"It's all right," I said. "We can go home now."

He gazed at me in astonishment.

"You've spotted him then?" he suggested, shuffling along beside me.

I inclined my head.

"Yes, I've seen him, Baines—seen him twice, for that matter. He has his own peculiar methods of getting in and out—and heaven knows how we are going to stop him!"

We found the Bristol and turned in. I was tired, worn out, dead to the wide—and yet for some reason sleep eluded me. I was wondering what this mysterious sortie of the White Owl signified—where it had been—and what ghastly tragedy it had left behind.

Chapter 11

IVAN KAROLIN REPORTED FOR DUTY on Monday. As it happened, I was alone when he called. I had persuaded Renée to join the Mulletts on a week-end excursion in their new car and had sent Baines to have his hair cut. I was writing at my table in the window when the telephone rang. Crossing the room, I picked up the instrument and lifted the receiver to my ear.

"Hullo?" I demanded, "who is it?"

"Karolin speaking."

"Good!" I said. "Come up. Are you better?"

A couple of minutes later he had tapped and was in the room, smiling, studiedly deferential as became an employee in the presence of his temporary employer. In spite of the privations he had undergone, the hall-mark of gentility was always in evidence, stamped as it were on his dapper, upright form, on honest blue eyes staring from a square, handsome face, evident in the honesty of purpose that had brought him from his bed when barely convalescent. He was so amazingly smart that I scarcely recognized him as the taxi-driver who had first driven me across Paris. A new gray overcoat hung easily on his shoulders, open in front to expose to advantage the new gray suit beneath. A gray soft hat, an American collar with pointed ends and the counterpart of a British regimental tie completed the picture.

"Sit down," I invited and pointed to a chair.

He removed his coat and complied, bending forward with his elbows on his knees, and still nursing his hat.

"I felt as weak as a rat when I got up this morning," he confessed, "but the sun was shining in at the window—and the call of duty was strong! Also, I had had an extraordinary piece of good luck and felt I just had to get out."

I raised my eyebrows. So that accounted for the transformation!

"Legacy?" I suggested.

He shook his head.

"Hardly that. The relatives I have been able to trace are as poor as I was. I have just posted a money-order to an aunt in Geneva. She was practically destitute. No, I bought a lottery ticket from a man who was down on his luck, and it happened to be the winning number! If I'd bought it direct from the people who run the thing I wouldn't have won a *centime*. I never do. As it was, I netted forty thousand francs!" He leaned back in his chair and laughed. "Just think of it! Forty thousand francs! How much is that in your money? About three hundred pounds, more or less. Nothing much to you. But to a poor devil who's been touting around Paris for a bare living! I tell you, it's a godsend!"

I passed him the cigarettes. Baines looked in, cropped and gleaming with brilliantine, and I told him to fetch us cocktails, realizing that this was an event in Ivan Karolin's checkered existence that must essentially be celebrated.

"Congratulations!" I murmured. "What are you going to do now?"

He shrugged his shoulders and laughed again—the laugh of a man who has suddenly discovered that life is worth living.

"Carry on, I suppose, and keep my eyes open for a better job. One has one's dreams, you know. Driving people from Le Bourget for example. It's more romantic than trains. Someday perhaps an American millionaire will drift down from thin air and offer me a private secretaryship. You never know. I could do a job like that. I speak five languages." He held his cigarette delicately, between the first and second fingers, watching the festoon of smoke it made in the steam-heated atmosphere. "But tonight will be a gala night for me. I shall go to Montmartre with a Russian who has not been so lucky—and we shall watch other people pretending to be happy! They pretend very well at Montmartre—and a bottle or two of good wine will help the illusion!—You would not care to join us?"

I shook my head.

"I should like to," I said, "but I'm afraid it's out of the question."

His face fell. I could see that he was genuinely disappointed. Quite suddenly it dawned upon me that I was one of his benefactors who had drifted down from the blue—a man who was worth two pounds a day to him while it lasted. The seedy opportunist who plied for hire grabbed at this unexpected windfall with both hands; the gentleman in him wanted to display his gratitude. I bit my lip. He was so high in the clouds this morning that I hated to have to bring him to earth. His colleague was still patrolling the Carthagena, relieved of his duties at intervals by Baines, but I had long realized that this type of espionage was wasted. Valdao came and went as he chose. It would be more profitable for me to bribe one of the hotel staff to advise me when the moment for his actual departure came.

Baines entered with the drinks and set them down between us.

"Miss de Salis is back, sir," he whispered in my ear and promptly effaced himself. As the door closed behind him, Karolin came to his feet, his blue eyes twinkling at me over his glass.

"Chin-chin!—as you say in your country," he laughed.

"Chin-chin!" I replied, taking his word for it, although I shrewdly suspected the younger generation said "bung-oh!" nowadays.

"This round ought to be on me," asserted Karolin. "After all, it's my celebration—not yours!"

"And these are my rooms," I retorted, "and not yours!"

He sat down again, his hands clasped over his knees, thoughtfully chewing the splinter of yellow wood with which he had recently impaled the cherry. For the twentieth time that morning I pinched myself and wondered if it was all a dream ... Karolin, who had gone to bed with the flu'—and got up again with a fortune! Karolin, whose cap, with the shiny peak, and oily trench-coat had been suddenly exchanged for such exquisite, well-fitting clothes! The habits of his old life of affluence were drifting back to him, helped no doubt by the suit, the surroundings and the cock-tail. Our contract apart, we met on equal terms, and I felt somehow that it would be a pity to lose sight of him. Mentally, I found myself running through the work at home, visualizing my staff and their respective salaries, wondering whether it would be policy to squeeze in somewhere a man who spoke five languages. Up to this juncture I must confess that sentiment played a big part in my calculations. I was not an American millionaire with money to burn, but a commonplace business man struggling to compete in the deflated markets of a post-war world. I hated to think how Karolin would feel when next he put on those clothes and climbed into the driving seat. Today he was like champagne, bubbling over with good spirits, effervescent. Tonight not improbably he would be drunk. Tomorrow he would be as flat as a pancake!

Still in a weak mood, I left him sitting there and went in search of Renée. Marie, informative to the fast degree, assured me that she was in her bath. I left a message and repaired to the sitting-room we shared with the Mulletts. Cyrus was there alone, writing postcards by the dozen.

"Say, Coombes," he bawled at sight of me, "but that surely is a wonderful car. Miss de Salis is just crazy about it. Virginia says she thinks of buying one like it."

"Good!" I commented. "Had a good time?"

"Fine!"

For twenty minutes I listened to Cyrus Mullett, expatiating on the car, the trip, the hotels, the exceptional weather, until my mind became a maze of pistons and cylinders, chateaux and scenery . . . When at length Renée fluttered in, as fresh and attractive as a butterfly out of its cocoon, I had all but forgotten the business that had brought me there.

"My dear!" she began, taking me by both hands, "I feel such a pig. I've had a most heavenly time. Haven't I, Mr. Mullett?"

Cyrus was sticking on stamps, hammering each one with his fist, as if mistrustful of any brand of gum manufactured outside the United States.

"I guess we all have," he agreed, and excused himself, migrating with his mass of correspondence towards the hall.

Renée pulled me down on to the couch beside her.

"Well?" she demanded; "any news?"

I shook my head.

"Precious little."

"Valdao's still at the Carthagena?"

"Still there. Looks as if he's dug himself in for the winter!"

"What about Juan—and that girl?"

"No trace of them yet. I've inquired at all the big hotels. There are millions of small ones, of course, that I haven't been able to tackle. It's going to be a big job, but I suppose we'll have to do it."

She caught my arm.

"You don't think they've left Valdao and gone somewhere else?"

"I think it's highly unlikely."

"Do you think they know we're here?"

"They're almost certain to," I returned. "Valdao saw and recognized me at his hotel. He'd be bound to tell the others. Perhaps that's why they're lying low."

There was a long silence in which Renée tucked her feet under her and sat like a child, not smoking for a wonder, staring into space. It struck me that she looked better than when we had met at the New Venice. Like Ivan Karolin, she had altered and generally speaking Renée de Salis with an object in view was preferable even to the same charming person with no one to consider but herself.

"I had a ghastly dream last night," she announced presently, "and please don't tell me it was due to indigestion, because for one thing it's vulgar and, for another, I've never had it."

"What was it about?" I asked.

"Yourself partly—"

"Then probably it was!"

She grimaced at me.

"I warned you that it was ghastly. Juan was in it and that horrible woman. The white owl was there too, sometimes perched on Juan's shoulder—as you saw it at your rooms; sometimes hovering in the sky above. It was all so real, too, so clear-cut, so logical . . . It seemed to have been going on all night. I awoke and found myself sitting bolt upright, shivering all over, and, somewhere up by the ceiling, I could still hear the fluttering of wings . . . Uncle Dick, I'm never going away with the Mulletts again."

I stared at her.

"But why on earth?"

"Because I've a conviction at the back of my mind that you shouldn't be left. Something terrible might happen to you while I'm away. Besides, I'm not pulling my weight. I'm leaving you to do everything. My dear Dick, that dream so impressed me that I ran straight to Baines when we got back—to see if you were still alive!"

I'm afraid I laughed.

"So I was dead in the dream, was I?"

She nodded emphatically.

"It began in the road, just outside this hotel. I suppose it was in the middle of the night, because there was nothing about and all the windows were darkened, except yours. I was by the tobacconist's on the other side, trying to nerve myself to cross the road to go to bed. For some reason, something held me, and I couldn't. I could see you up there, writing at your table. Suddenly a big white saloon crept up from the night and drew to a standstill outside. The roof-light was on. Juan was inside and the girl. The chauffeur got down and opened the door—and I knew in an instant it was Valdao, although his face was hidden by his collar. They wanted Juan to get out, but he wouldn't. The girl tried to pull him, and he shook her off. Valdao thrust a knife into his hand with a white handle. I saw him look at it and shudder, then stagger out on to the pavement. The next moment he was alone, looking up at you. I called to him and he saw me and smiled. He started to cross the road and the white owl swooped suddenly between us and settled on his shoulder. They went up the steps after that and through the revolving doors. The night-porter was there, sleeping—I suppose I followed, because we were in your room next."

"Most improper!" I commented under my breath, but she ignored the interruption.

"You were in bed," she pursued. "Juan was there with the owl-headed knife—and the bird itself hovered above everything, immense, horrible —and I felt that its green eyes were fixed: on me." She shuddered and turned very white. "Dick, I can't tell you what he did to you! I saw the knife and the blood and the owl perched on your bare chest, pecking savagely. There was red on its legs and wings—red on the sheets—and I knew you were still alive — and suffering! It was all dark after that. I could see two green eyes getting smaller and smaller, and hear wings flapping into the distance.—And then, I think, I woke up."

There was another pause.

"Nightmare," I suggested.

Renée nodded.

"I know, but it worried me; it still does. It made me wonder if they were stopping in Paris *to kill you.* "

"And yet," I ventured, "you had a perfectly heavenly time with the Mulletts!"

"Don't be a beast, Dick. That was merely common politeness. You couldn't expect me to tell them that I hadn't!"

Chapter 12

FRANKLY, I DIDN'T BELIEVE Juan and Valdao were stopping in
Paris to kill me, nor was I prone to pay any attention to dreams.
Renée's nightmare, in spite of her assertions to the contrary, had
its origin in lobster mayonnaise, helped by memories of the book
Juan Mitzakis had written, and memories of my adventure with
Baines outside the Carthagena. At any rate, Virginia assured me
afterwards they had had lobster mayonnaise on the night in question. The main fact that exercised my mind at that moment was
that Karolin was upstairs in my room, smoking my cigarettes and
wondering what in the name of everything was keeping me. I was
on the point of broaching the subject to Renée, when she jumped
from the abstract to the concrete—from spook-dreams to auto-
mobiles. And yet, as it happened, it wasn't such a jump either.

"Can you drive, Uncle Richard?" she queried suddenly. "Drive
anything, I mean?"

"Almost anything," I admitted. "I've owned a tidy few cars—
and I was a pilot in the war. Why do you ask?"

"Because Cyrus Mullett's new bus is a peach—and I'm seriously thinking of getting one like it."

"Because it's a peach?"

She shook her head.

"Because I fancy we shall need one very soon. They may leave
Paris at any moment, and we shall have to follow. If they decide to
go by train, we can find out where they've booked for and leave
the car here until we want it. On the other hand, if they escape by
road, bound for some unknown destination, we shall be in the
soup! You see that, don't you?"

I nodded.

"Even a car won't help us," I demurred, "if they get away without us knowing. There's more than one road out of Paris."

Renée frowned.

"I know that. Up to the moment, we've every reason to believe
they're going to Spain. That narrows it down a little, doesn't it?
Then the car they'll be using will be a white saloon. It was a white
saloon I saw Juan in at Nice and, whether you think it worth con-

sidering or not, I saw the same saloon in my dream. They couldn't have driven here when they followed me to England. The time was too short. They may have sent for it while they've been waiting here."

"They may have changed the color by this time."

"No, Uncle Richard, I don't think so. I don't pretend to know what really lies behind this white owl business, but I do believe the color has some meaning: The white owl, the white-handled knife, the car. Don't you think so yourself?"

I rose to my feet and bent over her.

"The truth is, my dear Renée," I told her, "that you've set your heart on having a car like Cyrus Mullett's and nothing this side of Hades is going to stop you. Mind you, I'm not saying it won't come in useful. Incidentally, too, it rather helps me out. I'm lifting the siege at the Carthagena and keeping in touch with Valdao's movements through other channels. That means, of course, that I'm contemplating paying off my spies. With your consent, I'm bringing into partnership a fellow you've heard a good deal of lately but never met—one Ivan Karolin. He's a good fellow and a gentleman and, as far as our present position is concerned, he knows Paris intimately. He's a taxi-driver for the nonce, but has his ambitions. Can we run to a chauffeur-secretary?"

Renée frowned again.

"I think, if you don't mind, Uncle Richard," she said, "I'd like to see him first."

I fetched Karolin down.

From the point of view of an undemonstrative Englishman, it was amusing to see him bend himself almost double before Renée and kiss her hand. Virginia and her mother looked in, dressed for out of doors. I apologized for monopolizing the room and introduced Karolin—and, of course, we had the hand-kissing business all over again. Renée, I surmised, was favorably impressed already; Mrs. Mullett's lips tightened under the ordeal, but I could almost hear Miss Virginia registering the thought that he was "just too cunning!" They departed, ostensibly to buy "candies," and we got down to business in earnest.

Karolin's history was interesting. He had been a junior subaltern just before the Russian revolution, taken prisoner and escaped, served with the British at Salonika. Before that he was a boy, the son of a prosperous financier who had lost his fortune and his life in the upheaval; after demobilization he had done most things from blacking shoes to casual labor at the docks. What he had saved from tips as a waiter in a third-rate restaurant had enabled him to buy his taxi.

"These things are good for one, in a way," he admitted, "provided, of course, that they lead to something better in the end. One always hopes for better things. One has one's dreams."

"So you believe in dreams, Monsieur Karolin," Renée shot at him from the sofa. His shoulders lifted a trifle. "Certainly, mademoiselle; but it depends on the dreams."

Her silent message, flashed through space to the table where I leaned, appeared to imply: "I wonder what he'd say if I told him *my* dream!" She turned to Karolin.

"Would you be prepared to leave Paris?—to travel anywhere at a moment's notice?" He fidgeted with his hat.

"In what capacity, mademoiselle?"

From that point I carried on, explaining that there would be a lot of driving and a minimum of correspondence. I guaranteed a year's employment, providing that he gave satisfaction, jotted down a sort of draft contract on a sheet of hotel notepaper. Renée and I retired to the window and hastily arrived at a figure calculated neither to depress Karolin nor raise his hopes unduly. In an hour it was finished and done with and we shook hands on the deal. Over a second round of cocktails our protégé became serious.

"You would rather I cut out Montmartre tonight?" he suggested.

His remark puzzled Renée until I explained:

"Monsieur Karolin has won forty thousand francs in a lottery and wants to get drunk on the strength of it."

He raised both hands in eloquent protest.

"Not drunk, monsieur; merely merry! I doubt if I shall get even as far as that now. One has to consider the dignity of one's position!"

Renée laughed.

"Oh, go to Montmartre, by all means, only don't wear that nice suit—or you'll get your pockets picked!"

Karolin flushed like a girl.

"You think it's a nice suit, do you? Well, I thought so myself when I bought it. The man who sold it me was a Jew. He told me it had been made for a prime minister—only the cutter had omitted to allow for His Excellency's having one shoulder higher than the other. I left him feeling I was half a shoulder better in every way than a prime minister!" He picked up his hat and bowed stiffly. "I report for duty, sober and in my right mind, at ten tomorrow. And now, with your permission, I will try to sell my car."

He paused in the doorway and looked at Renée.

"You asked me if I believed in dreams, mademoiselle. Well, I will tell you this. I have been driving people for seventeen months—some of the commonest people in existence—and some of the best. And all the time I have cherished one dream—that some one would emerge from the fuselage of a plane and offer me something better than I had already. Well, he has, you see—after seventeen months!"

"The obvious inference being," I returned, "that dreams can come true—provided you've the patience to wait for their fulfilment."

Renée rose from the couch.

"Those are not quite the sort of dreams I meant," she said. "You may not think very much of this one when you've been with us a while. Mr. Coombes hinted at danger when he spoke to you just now. I think it only fair to tell you that service with us may entail very great danger indeed. We have embarked on an extraordinary adventure, Monsieur Karolin, and there are strange people involved in it."

Ivan Karolin smiled.

"You forget, mademoiselle," he replied, "that I am by force of circumstance an incorrigible adventurer. And if our friend with the green eyes constitutes one of these dangers of which you speak, I shall be only too pleased to be at loggerheads with him. He omitted to tip me when I landed him at the Carthagena!"

With that he was gone, walking jauntily, humming to himself as if he felt he had come into two fortunes at least. Watching from the window, I saw him hail a taxi outside.

"A useful ally, I think," I remarked.

Renée nodded.

"At any rate, you'll have some one to work with that you like." A ripple of laughter escaped her. "It really is too absurd for words. We've engaged the chauffeur before we've bought the car—and now we've got to buy the car whether we like it or not! Come on, Dick. Let's put on our hats and go and look at it."

Chapter 13

ONE OF THE MOST PECULIAR FACTS of this life is that comparatively trivial incidents have sequences which none of us can possibly foresee. I had engaged Karolin mainly because I liked him,
partly because I thought him worthy of a better job, principally I
suppose because he knew each one of the trio we were seeking by
sight. Sentiment, a sense of sportsmanship, call it what you will,
had prevented us from standing in the way of his little flutter at
Montmartre. And yet, oddly enough, his presence at Montmartre
on that fatal evening was the one factor that enabled us to get in
touch once more with Mitzakis. Without it, we might have lost
sight of him altogether; with him, we were drawn into the grim net
Valdao was weaving, into an ocean of horror that was destined to
stagger and mystify humanity.

It was midnight and I was in bed. I woke with a start, conscious
that a noise like an alarm clock had been going on at my elbow for
some time. It had stopped when I woke. I sat up, rubbing my eyes,
wondering what it could have been. Nerves, windows wide open
because of the steam-heating, the shadowy outlines of furniture in
the intense blackness, combined to create a conviction that an echo
of Renée's dream had disturbed my own slumbers, and that I had
been disturbed by the flapping of imaginary wings. I fumbled for
the pear-shaped contrivance that dangled above me, found it,
switched it on with fingers that trembled so uncontrollably that I
was ashamed. Light, a tired yellow radiance that suggested nocturnal economy at the powerhouse, flooded the apartment, bringing with it a sense of security. There were no white owls, no green
eyes hovering by the ceiling, no lurking shadows wielding owl-
handled knives. In the shallow tiled recess below an oval mirror
one of the porcelain taps was dripping. The noise might have come
from there. I slipped out of bed and turned it off. As I did so, the
mystery resolved itself behind me—the telephone on the bedside
table rang.

I smiled at my own reflection in the full-length mirror. The next
moment I was sitting on the bed, nursing the instrument.

"Hullo!" I said softly. "Who is it?"

I waited patiently, but nobody answered. There came instead a confused medley of sounds like intense activity in a steel foundry and the constant going up and down of an elevator. Still holding the receiver to my ear, I hooked a cigarette from the tin and lit it, employing only the one hand.

"Hullo!" I cried again.

The noise faded out. A fresh sound, very sudden, very crisp, jarred my eardrum. Some one began speaking so loudly that he might have been shouting at me from the other side of the bed:

"Is that the Hotel Bristol?"

"Coombes here," I answered a trifle irritably. "D'you want the management?"

I heard the man at the other end gulp.

"Oh, it's you, Mr. Coombes. I've been trying to get you for the last quarter-of-an-hour. Karolin speaking, from the Étoile Bleu, Montmartre."

I caught my own reflection again in the glass, and the reflection and I exchanged glances full of deep meaning. Karolin, I thought, drunk as an owl, ringing up every number he could think of! Terrible people the Russians when they got soused! And yet, strangely enough, Karolin's voice didn't *sound* soused!

"It's you, is it?" I ventured. "What do you want?"

"Sorry if I've disturbed you," he said, "but one of your friends is here, and I thought I ought to tell you."

And even then the significance didn't dawn on me at once. I thought perhaps Cyrus had booked seats in a "Seeing-Montmartre Motor-Coach" and been trying conclusions with an Apache!

"What's the bother?" I asked. "Is he in trouble?"

A slight pause and then the voice came again:

"Not exactly, but he will be in a minute. He's had one row with a Spaniard and I fancy he's spoiling for another. They put him out once, but he's squeezed in again. It's the taller man I drove from the aerodrome."

My heart missed a beat and raced on again, rattling like kettle-drums.

"You're sure of that?"

"Absolutely. What do you want me to do?"

"Nothing," I said; "nothing at all. Wait there until I join you."

"Right," he agreed. "I wasn't moving yet, in any case. The *Étoile Bleu* . . . *Blue Star* . . . It's a pretty low-down place, but any taximan will bring you here. Rue Treille . . ."

He rang off.

I dressed hastily, shoved an automatic into my jacket, principally because there wasn't time to consider whether I should take
one or not, phoned them in the hall to knock up Baines and send
him down to me. Then I scrawled a hasty note to Renée and
pushed it under her door. There were two reasons why I was taking Baines; I wanted to show him Mitzakis and see what he
thought about it—and Baines was as reliable a customer in a
rough-house as I had ever known. I turned it over in my mind as I
waited for him. Juan had shown himself a hefty man to tackle, but
I calculated the three of us could manage him without trouble. By
the time we got there, the management would be wanting to re-
move him again. I could introduce myself as his friend—and we
would keep a taxi waiting. Juan, apparently, was alone. I was hoping that fact would make things a lot easier. If he had slipped out
by himself, and escaped for once the vigilance of Naia and the
White Owl, he should be in a mood to listen to reason. We would
bring him back to the hotel and get Renée up to talk to him.

Baines descended the stairs with his coat collar up and a purple
muffler twisted round and round his neck until it looked like a
hard lump. There was a smudge of whitewash where his hard hat
was dented in, which somehow suggested he had worn it in bed.
He sat down on the last step but three to tie up his shoelace.

"What's in the wind?" he queried huskily. "Another stunt at the
Carthagena?"

I explained that we were bound for a sort of nightclub, and his
face brightened.

"Nightclub, eh?" he muttered. The lace broke and he knotted it
skillfully. "That's the *emag!*"

"What's that?" I snapped.

His right hand concealed a yawn.

"Beg pardon, sir. I'm only half awake. 'Emag's' the back-slang
for 'game.' We use it in the ring. Funny how these things slip out
when you're not thinking!—I can't dance," he added, "if that's
what you want me to do."

I hastened to assure him that dancing was not necessarily a part
of the night's program. We passed through the hall together and
out into the road. The night-porter, a wrinkled septuagenarian who
looked as though he had never enjoyed a good night's rest in his
life, accompanied us through the doorway and watched us as we
went. At the corner a belated taxi-cab set down a woman in furs
and we climbed in. Paris dozes, but it never sleeps. There was still
traffic about, still the shrill tooting of horns, still knots of people

chatting at corners. During that journey Baines and I barely exchanged a word. We flopped in opposite corners, yawning and
smoking to keep ourselves awake. Baines, I thought, looked singularly bloodless, his cabbage-ear more prominent than ever. If we
had been prepared for the sortie it would have been different; this
crawling from a warm bed was the trouble. We were about to face
a delicate situation with leaden limbs.

Our taxi trundled us through a maze of narrow, sordid streets.
There were smells on the night air—mostly unpleasant. Strains of
indifferent dance-bands drifted from rooms with lighted windows.
A stocky gendarme, all mustache and cape, monopolized a corner
and a lamppost. Two bright-eyed girls, with no frocks to speak of
and ridiculously high heels, waved to us behind his back and
shouted something. A smooth-faced ruffian with no overcoat
lolled in a darkened doorway, picking his teeth. It was growing on
me, as we progressed, that this was not one of the show-quarters of
Montmartre, not that section of the underworld that catered for
sight-seeing Americans in char-à-bancs.

A fight was in progress somewhere. We heard screams and
hoarse voices shouting. Two men came at a jog-trot from a side-
street, split up and vanished in opposite directions. Our driver
glanced back at us and shrugged his shoulders. The screaming
continued. Windows were being opened, people issuing from
doorways. A couple of gendarmes hove into view, running side by
side in the road. Baines cleaned the glass with his sleeve and
peered out, his eyes sparkling, sucking at his teeth. There was
nothing he liked better than a street row or a street accident.

"Reminds me of Whitechapel," he announced suddenly. "I've
seen some queer things in Whitechapel; particularly on a Saturday
night. Broken bottles and knuckle-dusters. Hullo! More cops!"

Our taxi had stopped at a corner. The driver reached back and
opened the door.

"It's down there," he said; "the third door on the right, if you
still want it. It's no affair of mine, but if I were you I should keep
away."

An eloquent sweep of the arms took in an ever-increasing
throng of half-dressed figures, a sprinkling of women in tawdry
evening frocks, negro bandsmen in white shirts, a high hat or
two . . . night revelers, and those who battened on them, circling
like a swarm of bees around something that was certainly not
pleasant. Even as we paused there, watching over the bonnet of an
ancient Renault, the crowd developed a curious movement—like

waves, produced as far as we could gather by those who had seen the horror in the road wanting to get away, and those who had not yet seen wanting to get close. The police were arriving in force. They were not so considerate as our constables, but they seemed to know their job and the class of people they had to deal with. The waving movement changed. Whole chunks, whole sections of the crowd began scattering where the gendarmes were thickest and reforming again where they were not.

"What is it?" I asked the driver.

"Murder!" he returned with a firmness that sent a cold shiver down my spine. "Somebody stole somebody else's girl—and the knives got busy!" He spat on the pavement. *"Pardieu!* All that over a woman—and probably a bad woman! But, what would you? They're brought up on that sort of thing here!"

I gave him fifty francs.

"Wait here a moment," I told him. "We may want you again."

He laughed and climbed back to his seat.

"I'll wait at the next turning. It's healthier down there. And," he added significantly, "I don't think I shall have to wait long!"

Baines nudged me as we crossed the road.

"You keep close to me, sir. There's some tough cards about to-night." I nodded.

I had felt easy enough at the outset, mainly because of the two men who had run away. Now it was dawning upon me that these might be human jackals—light-fingered gentry who hovered around every scene of violence for what they could snatch and get away with. Mitzakis might be in this business—in it up to the hilt. He had been spoiling for trouble when Karolin phoned me. Baines, an expert where crowds were concerned, steered me into the thick of it. Raising on tip-toe, I saw that my worst fears were justified. The damning evidence was before me, conclusive, undeniable— Juan Mitzakis towered head and shoulders above the mob, his silk hat tilted to the back of his head, a long cigarette jutting from his lips. His face was white, as white as his shirt-front, and a faint smile flickered at the corners of his mouth. He stood in a restricted space in the very center, holding off a bunch of excited men with something I could not see. A fresh wave carried me forward, with Baines clinging to my arm like a male nurse in charge of a patient, knowing that if anything happened to me his job went too! A woman fainted and somebody picked her up. Somebody touched my free arm. It was Karolin.

"I saw you five minutes ago and lost you again," he panted. "It's been a fight to get to you. They threw the Spaniard out in the end—and your friend followed. You won't help him out of this trouble, I'm afraid. You see what he's done."

The line in front of us broke and we were there, staring down at the prone form of a man mutilated beyond recognition, weltering in a dark pool that filled the hollows in the road and left the other dry.

"Vendetta!" suggested Karolin in a whisper, and shuddered.

I shook my head.

"It's not quite that," I said. "I'll tell you about it later."

I could see the owl-headed knife now—in Juan's hand. The handle was discolored, dark stains showed on the wash-leather gloves he wore; but the blade glinted clean as if it had been freshly wiped. The police closed in on him, driving us back. He threw away the knife and went at them with his hands, sweeping them aside like so many skittles. A bearded man in plain clothes called to him in authoritative voice to surrender. He presented a revolver and Juan threw back his head and laughed. We were twenty yards away, back numbers; people were jostling us, treading on our toes. I backed against an ambulance that had come up unnoticed in the excitement. From the running-board I saw official caps and heads and Juan still struggling, but less violently. A ghastly depression seized me. The fog had helped him on that other occasion; this time he was doomed. They didn't often employ the guillotine in France but its grim blade hung over Juan's neck and nothing I could do could save him. People didn't believe in Toltec rites, familiar spirits, things that came from the bowels of the earth and wrought havoc. You couldn't expect It.

And then, into that bizarre scene of murder and police and vulgar sight-seers there drifted a miracle from the heavens themselves. It damped the spirits of Ivan Karolin, reduced Baines to shivering pulp. Above the muffled ticking-over of waiting cars, I heard the wings of the White Owl! Immense, savage as a vulture, it swooped between the houses, scattering gendarmes, populace, everything. In the panic that followed a tall figure brushed past me and was gone, running like the wind. It was Juan Mitzakis, minus his hat, his overcoat flapping behind.

I smote Baines with my fist.

"Come on!" I cried. "Pull yourself together! We've got to catch him!"

I heard revolver shots at the next corner. They were doing what I had done in Mexico—firing at the White Owl. I hoped that they had had better luck.

Chapter 14

WE EMERGED INTO BETTER THOROUGHFARES. From the November gloom I picked up monuments I knew, familiar buildings, famous multiple stores. Juan had stopped running, satisfied apparently that he had made his getaway, satisfied that the three men
who followed at a discreet distance had no interest in his movements. Perhaps even he had forgotten us entirely, for after the first
five minutes he never once glanced behind him. Bare-headed,
striding along with a queer, jaunty gait, he crossed the Avenue de
l'Opera, taking a short cut to the Rue de la Paix. This was interesting, I thought. He was making for the Carthagena. In that
case, his lodging must be quite close to Valdao's. It puzzled me
that neither Baines, nor Karolin had ever encountered him.

Presently the hotel itself loomed up, slumbering in its quiet
backwater.

Baines touched my arm.

"He's turned in there," he said, "turned in where you went that
night."

Karolin nodded confirmation.

In two minutes we were at the corner ourselves loitering in the
shadows, wondering what we should do next.

I looked at Karolin and rubbed my chin. The lane was a dead-
end, as far as I remembered, a cul-de-sac, a convenient way in for
staff and way out for garbage. There could be only one reason for
Juan's going there.

"We must look into this," I muttered.

Leaving Baines as a sort of rear guard, we pushed ahead,
Karolin on the one side and myself on the other, moving softly and
examining every patch of blackness we encountered. The same
dust-bins showed up, and I believe the same cat, hunched up and
feeding on fish-bones . . . The back of the Carthagena was several
degrees less savory than its interior! On the whole, it was as well
its distinguished clientele only knew the main entrance! We met
by a jutting wall that screened a row of lock-ups from the road.

"No luck yet!" Karolin whispered. His blue eyes scanned the building and I saw him start. "There's something moving up there."

Following the direction of his pointing finger, I picked up a crouching figure at the third bend in the fire-stairs. It reached over and tapped on the shutters of Valdao's room . . . the sound drifted down to us in the stillness. Another sound, familiar, significant, blotted it out.

"The White Owl!" I confided to my companion. "It's coming home."

The form on the stairs became erect. It was Juan Mitzakis, beyond question, his dark hair uncovered, his white face staring upwards. The shutters behind him opened stealthily and a faint light appeared beyond. At that instant the White Owl fluttered from the mist on to his shoulder and perched there. The great wings closed slowly; it moved from side to side and became still.

"There's nothing much of it," said Karolin. "It's all wings—like an eagle. Wonder how he trained it?" Karolin only knew half the story; barely that. He little guessed what I knew—or thought I knew. I felt for my pipe, hoping subconsciously that a smoke would help me out with the fresh problem that was revolving in my brain. In the past few days I had taken a course, as it were, in Supernatural Science and Black Art. My experiences in Mexico had added weight to the wrong side of the scale. Because I could find no logical explanation for what I had witnessed, I had grown to believe that Valdao and the White Owl were two personalities, if one could call them so, interchangeable at will. Which, as Euclid and the rest of reasoning humanity would have said, was absurd! Tonight's evidence made it doubly absurd—*because somebody had opened those shutters for Mitzakis!*

He passed through as we waited, the white bird still perching there. The jalousies had closed again, the curtain fallen on yet another act in this extraordinary drama. I pressed in tobacco with a trembling finger. There was a curious sense of finality about those shutters, as if an orchestra was playing "God Save the King"—and we were all expected to rise and go home. But going home was out of the question. We had picked up the trail at last; at all costs we must keep it.

I turned to Karolin.

"Find Baines," I said, "and tell him to watch the main entrance. If he sees Mitzakis he must follow him wherever he goes and keep in touch with Miss de Salis or myself by telephone. If he doesn't show up, it'll mean we've interviewed him already." I looked at my watch: It was twenty minutes to two. "Tell him he needn't wait after four."

The Russian nodded and hurried off. In three minutes he was back again. I caught the glowing end of his cigar, a luxury no doubt bought for his celebration at the Étoile Bleu. He stood by me, eyeing the building.

"It wanted a bit of nerve," he mused aloud, "stepping from those stairs on to that balcony. It looks easy enough from here, but you try it!"

"I mean to," I returned.

Karolin stared at me.

"Is that fellow a friend of yours—really?" he demanded.

"Yes, I suppose so. At least, he was once."

"And yet he murdered a man in Montmartre tonight—" he spoke softly, between his teeth—"cut off his ears, hacked him about so that he died slowly—in agony!"

"I know," I retorted. "He killed a man in London—just over a week ago."

"He must be mad!"

I inclined my head.

"That's precisely what I fear—what I'm hoping. I came to Paris to try to stop him killing any more people. You see, Karolin, Miss de Salis was engaged to him once. We were all three of us very great friends. He was supposed to have died in Mexico. Eighteen months later he turned up at Nice with a native girl, called Naia. His real name is Juan Mitzakis, but he travels as 'Julian Murray.' The man with the green eyes is Valdao, a Mexican of sorts."

He brushed the ash from his cigar with his little finger.

"And the White Owl?" he queried; "where did he pick up that?"

"In Mexico, too, I believe. There's a queer story attached to that, but it's too involved to tell now. Out of fairness to yourself, I'm being as frank as I can. There are only two explanations for what you saw tonight: Either, as you suggested just now, Mitzakis is a homicidal maniac—or he's being influenced by the people he's with. It's our job to find out which. I'm afraid I'm not up in French law. In England, if they caught him, the verdict would be 'guilty but insane.' "

Karolin puffed for some moments in silence. Presently he said:

"It would be roughly the same over here, provided he had a smart counsel to defend him—and provided, of course, he is insane. As to outside influence,"—He shrugged his shoulders—"that is a very different matter. I should imagine it would be difficult to prove."

We remained there for a quarter of an hour, smoking, talking quietly, watching the shutters that hid the man whose fate we were discussing, a pock-faced Mexican and an owl . . . Frost sparkled the paving-stones, glittering in stray rays of light; the mist was increasing in density, swathing the building in a veil of mystery. The ends of my toes felt dead. Karolin had hit the right nail on the head. The defense of outside influence wouldn't stand. A jury would laugh at it; it could put no barrier between Juan and the rope—or the guillotine. Had there been a woman in the trouble, it might have been different. The French had a notorious weakness for the *crime passionnel,* acting doubtless on the time-honored belief that woman was the root of all evil . . . But murder, mutilation, unprovoked assault—! I shook my head at the darkness.

"No, Karolin, we've got to see this fellow, talk with him, thrash the matter out for ourselves. If he's crazy, he must be put away; if he's not, we must separate him from the other two and ship him somewhere where neither they nor the police are likely to find him. Miss de Salis bought a car this morning. It's an expensive one and they promised delivery in the morning. We must get Mitzakis somehow, hold him until it's ready and drive him out of Paris—out of France, if possible."

He shook his head.

"The French detectives are pretty thorough," he reminded me. "All the frontiers will be closely watched." The cigar had gone out. He threw it away from him. "Pau is a good spot—in the Pyrenees quite close to Spain. I worked there once as 'boots' in a swell hotel. Lots of English people go there for the winter. Then there's the Swiss frontier and winter sports . . . You don't want a quiet place; criminals often make that mistake. In quiet places people only read papers and gossip. You want somewhere where they're used to strangers. Disguise him a bit, keep him out of sight until the excitement blows over. That's what I should do."

"It'll have to be something like that," I agreed. "I doubt if you could cross the Swiss mountains in a car at this time of year. They were making for Spain in any case."

Plans for the future petered out; we discussed the present emergency, viewing it from all sides. Skirting the courtyard, we made for the fire-stairs, mounted them, clinging to the crazy openwork structure that was painfully cold to the touch. There was a door where we had last seen Juan, but it was fastened on the inside. As Karolin had predicted, the gap between the iron landing and the balcony presented difficulties. A steeple-jack or a mountaineer might not have noticed it; to us it yawned like a vast chasm, with a thirty-foot drop beneath. And yet Juan, with the bird on his shoulder, had taken it in his stride! I paused, leaning over, grateful for that pall of gray mist that must have screened our movements from any prowling night-watchman, suddenly aroused from his sleep by a sense of duty. There was only room for one of us on that shallow balcony, and little to be gained by crossing there at all. The jalousies were closed; forcing them was out of the question. If those inside heard us and opened them, it was ninety-nine chances to one we should be at their mercy. And thirty feet was a nasty drop! If, on the other hand, they didn't open, our only prospect was a cold and hazardous journey back—a sort of inglorious as-you-were.

Karolin's mouth came close to my ear.

"Stumped, eh?" he diagnosed. "Well, there is a way out." His face wore an aggravating smile. "Leave me here and go round to the front and call—"

"What?" I gasped. "At this time of the morning?"

"Why not? You're the bearer of an important message. Pitch 'em any yarn you like. They won't be any the wiser. Your pals'll open to an hotel servant. Wait till they do, push in with your gun and hold 'em up."

I bit my lip. It certainly sounded feasible.

"What about you?"

"I'll have got over by that time and be waiting. Before they've tumbled to what's afoot, you could slip round and open the shutters."

I measured the gap again with my eye, gauged for a second time the strategic value of that balcony. Karolin's plan was better. One had always to bank on its not working, but our present scheme had the same weakness aggravated a thousand times.

"We'll try it," I whispered.

I had turned to go when he pulled me back and pointed to the window.

"Listen to that!"

A strange noise had set up, the sound of an unearthly chanting coming from Valdao's room. Soft, low-pitched, weirdly melodious, it filled the night, infusing us both with a vague superstitious dread.

Karolin caught my eye.

"What's it mean?" he stammered.

"I don't know."

"Nice for anybody sleeping in the next room! They'll turn him out for that in the morning."

I nodded. It was a mystery to me the management hadn't done so before. The weird incantation ceased. There was a tense silence. A peal of laughter followed, mad, hysterical stuff which somehow expressed exultation. Another silence and the single *tinging* of a bell. We were both by the hand-rail now, craning over, listening. Some one was telephoning in French. I recognized Juan's voice:

"Is that—" (I didn't catch the name.) "Murray speaking . . . About our car . . . Eh? Oh, not now . . . at eight this evening . . . Rue Solferino . . . by the Quai d'Orsay. Will that be all right? Oh, and fill her up . . . petrol, oil, water, everything . . . And look at her tires. You've got all that? Good night."

We descended to the courtyard in silence, picked up Baines, set our faces towards the Bristol. The message had been lucid, to the point, illuminating indeed—it hardly suggested that Mitzakis was mad. And yet I fancied the laugh was his too. The Rue Solferino— at eight! The problem had worked itself out very pleasantly. I would find Karolin a bed somewhere, scribble another note to Renée and turn in.

Baines's hands were deep in his pockets, his brow furrowed with thought. The "Yellow Peril" between his lips had a dejected droop. It perked up suddenly and he spoke:

"I suppose it'll all be in the papers by breakfast-time."

"Bound to be," said Karolin.

"Mr. Mitzakis too! I'd never have believed it. If you'd told me—"

I swung on him sternly.

"The best thing you can do," I advised, "is to wipe it clean out of your mind. Forget it, you understand, and keep your mouth shut."

Baines blinked and began sucking his teeth.

Chapter 15

BAINES WAS RIGHT. The papers had it in flaring headlines, the *Matin,* the *Figaro,* the *Petit Parisien,* and all the rest of them. He bought a selection of them and dumped them beside me with my *petit déjeuner.* Also he handed me a note from Renée, in answer to my two:

Dear Uncle Richard,

Glad you got back safely. So nice of you to think of me. I found the letters on the mat before Marie came. I tell you they gave me quite a thrill! It's an age since a man pushed letters under my door!

Don't stop in bed *too long,* there's a dear. I'm aching to hear the news.

Renée.

I heaved a sigh of relief. It was obvious from the tone of her letter that she didn't know yet. Baines apparently had kept his mouth shut, as I'd told him. Renée rarely bothered herself about papers before eleven. I gave Baines further instructions—to see Marie immediately and make sure that none of these lurid descriptions got to her before I'd had time to give her my version.

He hovered in the doorway.

"What time would you like your bath, sir?"

I looked at my watch.

"In ten minutes' time; as soon as you're back, in fact."

"You'll be wearing the blue suit?"

"Oh, yes; I suppose so."

The blue suit was a weakness of Baines's. He wore blue suits himself when off duty—Admiralty serge that a petty-officer cousin sent up from Portsmouth. To Baines, blue serge was an emblem of respectability.

"What tie, sir?"

"Oh, any tie. I'm not particular."

He hovered a bit longer, grasping the lapels of his jacket with both hands. I could see he was turning over something in his mind.

"If we are—er—leaving tonight, oughtn't I to commence packing?"

"One suitcase for myself," I returned, "and as little as you can possibly do with. We'll have to arrange for the rest to be sent on when we know where we're stopping. I'll talk to you about that later.—Is Mr. Karolin up?"

Baines nodded.

"I met him on the stairs not five minutes ago."

"Good! Tell him I'd like to see him."

He effaced himself, leaving me to digest my breakfast and the efforts of French reporters reveling in the sensation of the moment. There were columns upon columns of it; the murder in the Rue Treille, the quarrel in the restaurant that had preceded it, the knife, the crowd, the dramatic intervention of a strange bird. I scanned the first report to the end, jumping whole paragraphs, turning eventually to the stop-press news. Satisfied that no arrest had yet been made, I drank some coffee, that astounding beverage that is served in a myriad of pleasant ways from Stamboul to Dunkirk, but has never succeeded in crossing the English Channel! It was odd, that. I wondered if the projected tunnel would make any difference. Buttering a *croissant,* I examined three different descriptions of the assassin. They varied in minor details, but in general they were good. Monsieur Pelot, the most prominent of French detectives, had charge of the case. The knife and a silk hat were in his possession. The hat bore the name of a London maker. They all stressed this, living apparently in the hope that an interview with a Regent Street hatter would produce the wanted man. The White Owl baffled them. Two gendarmes were in hospital, suffering from its attentions. It had been fired at, as I knew already, and missed. It had swooped, created a panic, interrupted operations with uncanny prescience for sufficient time for the murderer to make good his escape, then flapped away into the night from which it had come. People were already putting two and two together—and making five of it. What bearing, one leader-writer asked, had the owl on the knife—or the knife on the owl? Like Karolin, others dwelt on vendetta—Corsica—Sicily—suggested some echo of the Mafia.

Baines came back, and I was still reading. I heard him muttering to himself in the bathroom, turning on taps, whistling. The smell of ammonia drifted in. Baines's infallible remedy for a late night was ammonia in the bath!—the famous concoction of a gentleman whose very name implied baths and washing!

I was wondering at what hour Juan had left Valdao's room, if indeed he had left it at all; and under what roof in this cosmopolitan city Naia was waiting for him. Other thoughts came to me: Where had he disposed of the blood-stained gloves, the stained clothes so dear to the criminologist? Rooms in modern hotels offered few facilities for burning clothes. It would be risky to dump them in one of that row of bins, or bribe the furnaceman to get rid of them. Perhaps he had changed into another suit at Valdao's — and thrown a parcel into the Seine on his way home.

My second cup of coffee was cold, cold and syrupy with those dominoes of sugar they pack in little packets with blue printing, two at a time. I slid from the bed and groped for my slippers, drawn by a cloud of steam and the odor of Baines's confounded ammonia . . . Soaping myself in an atmosphere of white tiles and porcelain fittings, I decided that Juan had a sporting chance of eluding Monsieur Pelot, the guiding star of the Sûreté. If it had been London, it would have been different: Juan was noticeable in England with his dark eyes and his olive skin. In Paris so many people had dark eyes and olive complexions. Men looked very different, too, in evening and morning dress. Nobody at the Etoile Bleu had remembered seeing him before. The Gay City was used to late hours. What was irregular or shocking in England, in Paris was just the normal course of events. Juan had stopped out all night, it was true; but if the police intended interviewing all the dark-eyed gentlemen in Paris who had been guilty of infidelity or passionate adventure on that fatal evening, they would have their work cut out with a vengeance! I recognized just one flaw: If Juan had been seen going out in one suit and returning clad in another. In that case, his landlord might unburden his suspicions at Police Headquarters.

I interviewed Karolin in my dressing-gown. I felt I knew him sufficiently to entrust him with what inside knowledge I had. He listened to the end, leaning against the bed, his blue eyes fixed on my face. His comments on my narrative came as I dressed. They were backed by the sound common sense inherited partly, I imagined, from the financier his father, part of it acquired from the hard life he had been forced to lead.

"We Russians," he said, "are reputed to be superstitious. It is absurd, of course. Our peasants are superstitious, but all Russians are not peasants. Rasputin, true enough, inspired a sort of superstitious fear in people of most classes. It took him as far as the Kremlin, but that was at a time when half the civilized world was hysterical. You and I look upon the supernatural as a thing apart. Spirits may be hovering all around us in the ether, but they don't come into our everyday lives any more than we interfere with theirs."

"Meaning," I interrupted, "that the White Owl is just a white owl?"

"Precisely. I contend that, if you hadn't seen this Mitzakis clinging to a bird when he tripped at that hole in the ground, no doubts to the contrary would have crossed your mind. The story of his dreams is curious, but to me it suggests one of two things: Either he had read of Naia, the Owl God and the altars weltering in blood in the hieroglyphics he translated in Guatemala—or he had been to that spot in Mexico before."

I shook my head.

"Your first explanation is quite feasible," I said. "As to the other, I think it's out of the question. If he had been there before, he would have told me. He told me everything."

He passed a hand through his hair.

"You told me just now that you believed 'Naia' was a general name given to priestesses of the cult, a name that might have been handed down through generations. That strengthens my theory that the dreams were direct fruits of his explorations, of something he had read and knew already.—He fell down that hole, was picked up by natives, patched up and permitted to survive. The girl may have had decent instincts of sorts and have gone to your tent of her own accord. The 'twenty moons' she spoke of was a pure coincidence. Apparently he had been in Europe some time before you saw him. So much for the past. Valdao is not the White Owl. He has inhabited caves, subterranean tunnels, lived in these places where white owls breed. Possibly since the days of Spanish persecution people like Valdao have been living like that, handing down from generation to generation a tendency to hide by day and emerge by night. To put it more simply, they have reversed the clock. Mitzakis spent over a year with them—and he has learnt to reverse the clock too . . . He talked to you about heredity. There, I think, you have it in a nutshell. Toltec blood, a bit of Greek . . . And Greeks can be the very devil when they like! . . . This mania for exploring, dissecting, deciphering . . . Mr. Coombes, I cling to the belief that your friend is as normal in most respects as you or I, only"—and he shot out a stubby finger in my direction—"he has his moments of stark, raving insanity. A bump on the head may have helped it. He takes the wrongs of the ancient Toltecs to heart. He kills as they killed. If he were as invulnerable as he boasted in

your flat, he would stop still and defy the world. But he isn't because, you see, *he runs away!"*

I flopped down in my shirt-sleeves on the nearest chair and
stared at him. Ivan Karolin was a genius, a genuine "find," an astonishing fellow altogether. It did me the world of good to listen to
him.

"You think he is human in every respect?"

"Of course; don't *you?* And the White Owl is a trained creature—marvelously trained, I admit—that looked after Valdao
once, in the wilds, and now performs a similar service for them
both. Supernatural, my friend? Not a bit of it! They use trains,
aeroplanes, cars—just like us! They wear clothes, carry luggage,
live in hotels! Don't tell me they pay their bills with spirit-money.
They'd have their baggage impounded in five minutes!"

"And Manzanarez?" I stammered weakly.

Karolin smiled.

"I'm afraid I'm doing all the talking. You are sure you are not
offended?"

"Not in the least. Quite on the contrary."

"Then I will proceed to draw on my imagination a little further.
Mitzakis met fifty Spaniards, eighty, a hundred perhaps—before
he admired Margharita in the foyer of the Haymarket. The sound
of her surname reminded him of the writings, the book he had
partly finished . . . Manzanarez! It upset the balance. How do you
say it? He saw *red*—and killed, but first he had to find the knife—
and Miss de Salis had it, comparatively close at hand, at the New
Venice."

A telephone message came to say that the new car had arrived
and we went down. Renée was there already, talking to an enthu-
siastic young salesman in tortoise-shell-rimmed glasses. The bonnet was open, its gleaming internal workings exposed to view, but
I could see from the expression on her face that the mere mention
of cam-shafts or overhead valves left her utterly and entirely cold.
Her gaze wandered as he talked, pausing lovingly on its cellulose
finish of crimson and gold, crimson leather upholstery and those
little glistening et ceteras that feature in the catalogues as "refine-
ments." But it was good to read the appreciation in Karolin's eye.
In him, at least, the young man who had driven her round found a
sympathetic listener.

Our Russian whistled softly.

"A *Morbizon* eight-cylinder! That's something, that is!" He began fidgeting all around it, poking his head through the front win-

dow and back under the bonnet again. I could see that he was just itching to drive it.

The salesman pulled on his lemon-colored gloves. He turned to Renée.

"I fancy you'll find it quite in order, mademoiselle. If you experience any difficulty, please ring us and we'll send some one round immediately. But I don't think you will. It's a most reliable car. We've never had a complaint yet." I had taken an instinctive dislike to that young man. He was so thoroughly pleased with himself, so full of his own importance. The next minute I hated him cordially. "Nasty business—that White Owl Murder," he added, smirking at Renée. "The papers are full of it this morning. I had the latest as I left the showroom: they've caught the fellow. Pelot arrested him at the Gare d'Orleans. Wonderful chap, Pelot— *Bonjour, mademoiselle; bonjour, messieurs!"*

He clapped on his hat and was gone.

Chapter 16

I DON'T QUITE KNOW WHAT I expected Renée to do, but she didn't do it. She merely opened the back door of the saloon, sat down in its luxurious interior and beckoned to me to do the same. Karolin, aroused from his inspection by the closing of the door, fastened down the bonnet, treating it with far more consideration than just an ordinary chauffeur would have used. He paused on the pavement outside, his heels close together, his body slightly bent, a little undecided apparently as to what the correct attitude should be. It was the first time I had seen him at a loss.

"Do you wish me to drive you somewhere?" he inquired at length, and he looked at Renée.

"Can you drive it yet?" she asked.

Karolin flushed.

"Oh, yes, mademoiselle—surely."

"It's quite a new machine."

"But I'm quite an old hand, you know. Where would you like to go?"

"Corinne's, in the Rue de la Paix—number 27 *bis*. I want to call there. After that we might drive out to the Bois de Boulogne. That would be nice, wouldn't it, Dick?"

"Delightful," I agreed, and Karolin took the wheel.

The gear snicked in and the Morbizon "eight" took the road smoothly. Without question, it was a wonderful car and Karolin handled her well. From time to time I caught glimpses of his reflection in the windscreen, and on every occasion he appeared to be smiling. If he were conscious of the "pull" of that powerful engine, he must also have been conscious of the steady sucking of that "tide in the affairs of men which, taken at the flood, leads on to fortune." . . . From greasy oilskins to the suit made for a prime minister! From a decrepit *Citroen* to the driving-seat of one of the three best makes in existence! He had had his dream, of course, but had never banked on its turning out as it had. Wherefore, Ivan Karolin smiled!

On the way to Corinne's, Rue de la Paix—the designer of frocks who was as big as Carpentier and had been gassed in the war—I was conscious of Renée's gaze. Whenever I met it, she would look away, and I felt that she was silently reproaching me for keeping her so long in the dark. She got out at Corinne's, having uttered only three sentences all the way, and those devoted entirely to the comfort and efficiency of her new toy. As soon as she was out of sight, I slipped to the corner and bought a paper, opening it at the kiosk and searching through it in a guilty, self-conscious sort of way, although there were at least three other people doing exactly the same thing. Under the searching gaze of the hawk-faced old woman in the black shawl, who presided there in solitary state, I felt that the secret was written on my forehead—that I, Richard Coombes, was the one person in all Paris who could supply Monsieur Pelot with all the information he was seeking, the true identity of the assassin, his history, his probable motives!

It was cold and a trifle damp underfoot, but the sun shone and the pavements were alive with people. A little bearded man in a tight-fitting black overcoat and broad-brimmed hat was arguing at the top of his voice with another who was stout and clean-shaven and wore a cape. They were talking about the murder. The two smartly-dressed women by the curb were talking about it; everybody was talking about it to everybody else . . . I could hear what the big and the little men were saying—and it was all so absurdly adrift that I wanted to butt in and put them right. Again I was struggling through endless columns, smudged printing on paper of an appalling quality, seeking the answer to a question that the newspaper-woman would have given me for the asking, had I but had the courage to inquire. I lit upon the name of the murdered man—Ramon Garcia. There had been something like it in the list in Juan's book . . . Suddenly I started. I had unearthed it at last—at the very foot of the page:

RUE TREILLE MURDER

The police visited an *hôtel des voyageurs* near the Gare d'Orleans at eight this morning and arrested a man who was stopping there. He will be brought before the examining magistrate this morning.

And that was all. No name, no description, nothing; just that. I folded the paper and thrust it into my coat. One sentence hovered in my brain—a fragment of Juan's telephone message to the place

where he garaged his car; *Rue Solferino—by the Quai d'Orsay.*
And the house where the suspect had been arrested must have
been a stone's-throw from there! Filling my pipe, one eye on 27
bis, where Renée had disappeared, I turned over that item of stop-
press news, endeavoring to read between the lines. Monsieur Pelot
had a reputation; there were people in Paris who believed him infallible. Supposing the efforts of that uncanny bird had been un-
availing—and Pelot had traced Juan to his lodgings and captured
him? In that case our wanderings were at an end. We would find
out what lawyer Juan was employing, introduce ourselves as his
friends and try to persuade the court that all this had arisen through
the accident he had had in Mexico. It was on the cards that I
should have to give evidence. There was still the chance, however,
that the police had made a mistake. The Gare d'Orleans was on the
Quai d'Orsay—the normal station for anyone arriving from or setting out for Spain. A Spaniard might well have been suspected,
some acquaintance of the dead man, someone with whom he
might have quarreled. I was in two minds at that moment, assailed
by two conflicting points of view: To have Juan at large, murder-
ing at random, was the last thing in the world that I desired; nor
did I want him caught and dealt with under foreign jurisdiction,
although, to all intents and purposes, he was a foreigner. If
Karolin's theory held water and this extraordinary sequence of
events owed nothing to the supernatural, he was bound to be
brought to book sooner or later, if not in France, in Portugal, Italy
or Spain. The popular notion that a special Providence looks after
babies, lunatics and drunkards had been exploded time and again.
Granted that a lunatic had cunning, there must be times when a
person subject to fits of lunacy was off his guard. Juan Mitzakis,
from the general point of view at least, was a pariah, an outcast, a
fugitive from justice. To get hold of him, as we planned, reason
with him, harbor him for any length of time, would certainly be a
risky undertaking . . . Quite suddenly I saw a flaw in Karolin's
argument: He had not attempted to explain the connection between
the bullet-wound Valdao had shown me in his frenzy and the
rounds I had blazed off at the White Owl!

I turned back towards the car.

As I did so, a gloved hand fell on my sleeve.

"Señor Coombes," a soft voice breathed in my ear. I looked
round, a little surprised that any one in Paris should have recognized me and remembered my name. And then I caught my breath.
I was inhaling that same mysterious fragrance that had come to me

once in a tent in Mexico, in fog-bound Piccadilly—looking into
dark eyes that were tear-filmed and unquestionably friendly.

"Naia!" I said, "or is it Mrs. Mitzakis?"

She shook her head slowly from side to side.

"Still Naia." She glanced back half-nervously over one shoulder. "Listen: There are things I must tell you . . . strange things
that even you may not understand." She was speaking in Spanish,
not the Spanish of those little yellow books that tourists buy, but a
kind of patois that the *leperos* used on that one eventful expedition
I had made into the Mexican hinterland. "It is dangerous here: You
must tell me some place where I can come to you."

Instinctively my glance drifted to the Morbizon, glistening in
the sunlight, with Ivan Karolin in sole possession. This unexpected
meeting with Naia was little short of providential. I felt that we
should learn something at last. I caught her arm.

"I am stopping at the Bristol," I said. "We'll drive there now.
You can tell me in the car."

She hesitated, her small fingers fidgeting with her bag, and in
that brief interval Renée emerged from a doorway, crossed the
pavement and climbed in. I saw Naia's lips tighten.

"That woman," she demanded; "does she belong to you?"

I shook my head.

"I am not married." I tried to draw her towards the car, but she
shook herself free, displaying a trace of that wildness I had noticed
on our last meeting. She spoke between her teeth:

"Then it is she . . . the other woman . . . the girl he speaks of in
his dreams! It was because of her I came to you. You must take
her away."

"Why?" I asked.

The fingers of both her hands touched my coat and a strange
sensation swept through me, queer, inexplicable, as if, out of
streets and boulevards vibrant with life, something had touched me
in which no real life stirred!

"Because," she assured me solemnly, "the things of the past are
not good for him. He feels them. They drive away the Spirit—and
he slips back. After that, the Spirit becomes angry and seeks to
destroy. You are a strange man, Señor Coombes. Once already it
has tried to kill you—and yet you have come to Paris, seeking it."
Her voice grew more shrill. "You must go, I tell you—go right
away from here. The Spirit is angry."

I nodded grimly. It sounded like a confession of weakness. I
thought I saw why they wanted us out of the way.

"The White Owl, you mean?" I suggested.

Her hands slipped from me, crossing themselves at her breast. The dark eyes closed.

"It commands," she whispered, "and I obey."

Looking round, I saw Karolin signaling to me.

"Where is Juan now?" I inquired.

"Asleep."

"In his room?—Near here?"

She inclined her head.

I bit my lip.

"If you are afraid of meeting Miss de Salis," I said, "come to see me this evening between five and six."

She surveyed me thoughtfully.

"You will be alone?"

I gave her my promise.

"Very well; I will come."

She turned abruptly and hurried off. I watched her cross and enter a building, followed at a discrete distance and noted down the number. By the time I reached the car, Renée was bristling with curiosity.

"A strange woman, Uncle Richard!" she greeted me with. "It seems I can't let you out of my sight!"

Slamming the door, I sat down beside her, reflecting upon the extraordinary uncertainty of life in general. I had combed Paris for more than a week and found no trace of Juan until Karolin showed him to me in Montmartre. I had set out to try a new car with Renée—and it had stopped within a hundred yards of Juan's hiding-place!

"Hardly a strange woman," I returned easily. "As a matter of fact, it was your *bête-noire*—the girl you saw with Juan at Nice. For some reason I can't fathom, she's anxious to speak to me and is coming to the Bristol tonight. The police haven't caught Juan, by the way. It must be some other poor devil. Juan's in bed. Apparently Naia left him there to talk to me."

Chapter 17

WE DROVE TO THE BOIS DE BOULOGNE, left Karolin by the road-side to resume his inspection of the inner mysteries of the Mor-bizon "eight" and strolled for a while on the moist earth under the trees. Presently Renée took my arm. "I've been behaving like a beast this morning, Dick," she admitted. "I can't imagine what you must be thinking of me."

"Moods?" I suggested, contriving to appear sympathetic.

She shook her head.

"I don't think so. Just ordinary bad temper! It was that little beast in the wash-leather gloves. You remember what he said to me just before he left? Quite unnecessary too. His employers had sent him there to deliver a car, not to discuss current topics with its owner. But he did discuss them, Uncle Richard, and it served to remind me that I was the one person in Paris who didn't know Juan had run amok again. I felt as though I were being treated like a child."

"It was my fault," I said. "I'm frightfully sorry."

"You needn't be. I suppose I ask for it. I've been treated like that ever since I can remember. My father always did when he was alive. Juan began where he left off, and as for Marie—"

A convenient tree-trunk, uprooted in the last storm, barred our progress. We sat down on it, our feet in a carpet of dead leaves. A lone robin, its red breast accentuated against a background of somber hues, fluttered to within three yards of us and surveyed us with studied indifference, unaffected by the sound of our voices or the swift passing of cars along the adjacent thoroughfare.

"I wanted to tell you myself," I ventured. "I had not the slightest intention of concealing anything. When I wrote you that first note, Karolin had just telephoned from Montmartre, saying that he had seen Juan. I took Baines with me and went. It never occurred to me that you would want to come—"

"Did you think I would be frightened?"

"I don't know what I thought. I had an inkling that something pretty ghastly might happen—which, of course, it did . . ."

"I know. I read it all in the papers at Corinne's." I saw her shudder. "They don't leave much to the imagination nowadays! Did you see it happen?"

"No. Apparently it had happened just before we arrived. But I saw the police and the Owl and Juan running away. Karolin joined us in the crowd and we followed him to Valdao's room at the Carthagena. The police had lost track of him by this time. We overheard a telephone conversation to the effect that their car was to be prepared for a long journey and brought to the Rue Solferino at eight tonight."

"Which looks as if they're leaving Paris for good."

"Yes."

Renée sighed.

"I shall be sorry to lose sight of the Mulletts; but I suppose it can't be helped. They're going to Biarritz in any case next week. You've told the hotel people?"

"Baines has. If we do go this evening, they'll have to keep the bulk of our luggage until we send for it. I'll explain all that to them when we get back. Unless you propose leaving Baines and Marie behind as well—"

She stared at me. "But of course we're going. We must!"

"Quite so," I agreed; "unless I succeed in getting information from Naia that will insure us getting into touch with Juan here. There's always that possibility, you see. Unless I'm very much mistaken, Naia should prove an extremely useful ally."

She shrugged her shoulders and looked away.

"What do you suppose she wants to see you about?"

"About *you,* principally."

Renée jumped. "Why *me?*"

"I haven't quite got the hang of it yet," I confessed. "She told me a lot of rigmarole about spirits and danger, and the past interfering with the present. Her main idea, apparently, is to get us both to go back to England. I'm wondering whether it wouldn't be a good plan to pack her off to her own country by the next boat. She's obviously disgruntled about something, and a threat of setting the police on her track should help. I don't mind putting up the fare."

She gave a little vicious jab at the carpet of leaves with her heel, and the robin retreated hastily, flying on to a bare branch overhead.

"My dear Dick, why should you?"

"I don't know; it might be policy."

She was silent for a time. I could see that she was annoyed at

something, and thought I could guess what it was. The mere mention of Naia was like a red rag to a bull to Renée. She could find a
hundred and one excuses for Juan, whose abominable crimes were
public property; yet she wouldn't admit in Naia's case the existence of a single decent motive. It was natural, I supposed, but an-
noying. Naia, from an entity that might or might not be influencing Mitzakis in his career of violence, had become a vital factor in
our problem. Humored, she might divulge a wealth of useful information.

"Why should you go out of your way to help that woman?"

I shrugged my shoulders. Slowly, persuasively, I stated my
case. And all the time she looked away from me, staring into the
blue haze between the trees, affecting not to be listening. I talked
for ten minutes, addressing my remarks to a green pull-on hat and
the delightful curve of neck that showed above a green leather mo-
toring-coat. At length my patience grew exhausted.

"The truth is, my dear Renée," I declared, "you're hopelessly
and horribly jealous!"

"I am," she admitted, not turning her head; "Damnably!"

"And purely because Naia is associating with Juan."

"I didn't say so."

"No, but it's true nevertheless. Why not let me pack her off to
South America by the next boat? You won't feel so bad about it
then. You couldn't."

"Oh, couldn't I!"

"Well, could you?"

She turned suddenly, moist-eyed and repentant. A warm hand
fell on my knee and she favored me with an expression that I was
at a loss to understand.

"Poor old Uncle Richard! I'm being an awful trial to you, aren't
I? I cavil at you because you don't take me into your confidence
immediately—and when you do, I refuse to listen to reason! And
yet what woman in the position I'm in now would listen to reason—where a woman like Naia is concerned?"

"After all," I protested, "she may be harmless enough. Juan
may have brought her across to Europe against her will."

She shook her head firmly.

"No; that I do not believe."

"You're allowing yourself to be influenced by that absurd
dream of yours."

"Oh, no, I'm not. I saw her quite clearly in Nice; I knew perfectly well who she was this morning when I saw her talking to

you. You men are all the same; you'll persist until the crack of doom in believing a woman's everything but what she really is— so long as she's pretty and fascinating! She is pretty, isn't she?"

"Yes," I said; "I suppose she is."

"And fascinating?"

"Undoubtedly."

She clapped her hands.

"Well, there you are! So of course, to your male eye, Uncle Richard, she's a poor modest vestal virgin, dragged from the temple of the White Owl by Juan, a scoundrel of the deepest dye! Your private opinion is that Juan should be horse-whipped. But you don't mind according her an interview yourself, alone, at your hotel this evening!"

I sprang to my feet, flushed I suppose; certainly very angry. The insinuation was unwarranted, unpardonable . . .

"Renée! I—"

"Why should she want to see you alone, do you suppose? Why shouldn't some third party be present? Why not Monsieur Karolin —or even myself?"

"For two very excellent reasons: She doesn't know Karolin— and she's as jealous of you as you are of her. More so, if possible; Juan talks about you in his sleep."

She patted the tree-trunk with her hand.

"Do sit down, Dick, and be sensible. I didn't mean to make you angry, but the temptation was irresistible. Besides, you're always so calm and philosophical that it's a pleasant change to see you properly roused! No, Dick, you must cut out the 'sinned against' notion and face facts. Naia's fascinating. You admitted that yourself. And most fascinating women are dangerous when it suits them. She fascinated Juan at the outset. He would have been content to go on poking about in musty tombs, collecting data for his unfinished book. Probably she knew where the treasure was hidden and led him to it. Possibly she had heard Juan speak of big cities across the water, of shops and hats . . . Even unsophisticated vestal virgins sometimes think of clothes, Uncle Richard!" A shadow crossed her face, and she made a small concession. "She may have been fond of him, of course."

"Well," I said, "what then?"

"Her meeting with you this morning wasn't an accident. It was much too coincidental for that."

I bit my lip.

"You think she followed us in the Morbizon?"

"Of course. And there must have been some better reason for her following than that she was jealous. Jealous women cling to their possessions, Dick; they don't leave them! Do you remember what she said to you when you saw her in your tent? *'The White Owl commands,'* wasn't it?— *'and I obey.'* That was before all this happened, when Juan was lying unconscious in the cave. When she followed you in the fog in London it might have been at the orders of the White Owl too—or of Valdao."

I sprang to my feet for a second time.

"Good Lord!" I exclaimed, astounded at the infinite possibilities of this fresh theory. "Then you think—"

"I think, Dick, that this business of this morning is a trap, and that if you keep your appointment alone, you will be extremely unwise."

The thing was so absurd that I burst out laughing.

"But what on earth could happen to me at the Bristol?"

She caught both my hands and drew me down beside her.

"Don't keep it, Dick," she implored, "for my sake, if you like. So many things have happened already that we can't explain. See her if she comes, of course, but have Karolin and Baines hidden somewhere in the room—and armed. Promise me?"

I nodded.

A cloud must have obscured the sun, for it had suddenly become very dark. A chill wind shook the forest, and leaves began falling, twirling as they came. Renée shivered and buttoned up her coat.

"Let's get back to the car," she whispered, "Monsieur Karolin will think we're dead!"

And then she screamed and clung to me tightly. I caught the direction of her gaze and followed it, seeking the cause of her agitation. Thirty yards from us, striking an attitude at the far end of the glade, I saw Juan Mitzakis! He wore a gray overcoat, something like Karolin's, and the peak of a gray cap was pulled over his eyes. The inevitable cigarette was there. As I stared at him, filled with amazement, he threw back his head and laughed.

"Juan!"

The cry came from Renée. She had left my side and was hurrying towards him, both arms outstretched. She called again and Mitzakis vanished, possibly into the trees, apparently like a gray wraith into thin air. I overtook her and held her firmly, while from the depths of the silent forest there drifted to us the shrill screeching of an owl.

Chapter 18

KAROLIN HAD HEARD THE OWL TOO, but he did not remember that spell of darkness, nor had he seen Mitzakis entering or leaving the wood. But then, of course, there were countless places by which he could have come and gone. All the way back to the city I tried to puzzle out his motive—a hopeless sort of task, considering that I believed Juan to be mad, and madmen could hardly be credited with sane motives! If Renée were right and Naia's projected visit to me was a trap, this continued dogging must be part of the plot and, in appearing so dramatically before us, Juan had risked giving it away . . . And yet, in his sane moments before the disaster, he had always had an exaggerated sense of the dramatic, the bizarre. I paused in the midst of my efforts, staring at Karolin's broad back and the regular pattern of the herringbone tweed that covered it. Juan had actually been there. There was no question about that, for we had both seen him simultaneously.

My thoughts darted off at a tangent. An entire audience, fifty people perhaps, I remembered, had been deceived by the famous Indian rope-trick. They had seen the rope stiffen and straighten out in the air, the boy climb it, the man with the knife in his teeth climb after him. Heard the cries, seen the blood, been convinced that a brutal murder had been committed in their midst. And yet the lens of a camera, opened at judicious intervals, had revealed that the whole thing was a magnificent hoax—and that the actors in that time-honored drama had remained absolutely stationary!

That opened up an interesting point: Was Valdao an accomplished hypnotist? Had he the power to convince an audience, providing they were in the right frame of mind, that things were happening which, in effect, never happened at all?

I decided to debate it with Karolin and hear his views.

Pending further evidence to the contrary, however, Juan had actually been in the forest, had let us know that he was there, and walked away. There were the impressions of heels in the soft earth where he had stood, although, as Renée had pointed out at the time, they might have been mine, made as I passed a few minutes before. We had embarked upon a half-hearted search, but found nothing.

Ever since his visit to my flat in London Juan had left us severely alone, and now he was showing intense interest in our movements. Why? Because Karolin, Baines and I had followed him home in the early hours? I thought not. Because he knew we were on his track and feared we might go to Monsieur Pelot with information that might lead to his arrest? I bit on that. Remembering the details of his last crime, he might have suspected the bonds of friendship were wearing perilously thin. And then, prompted by a memory of his curious laughter in the glade, I hit upon another solution that sent a hot sensation traveling all over me. Jealousy! Totally unfounded jealousy of myself! Naia had implied a revival of his interest in Renée.

I mopped my forehead and sat up. My gaze sought Renée. She evidently was thinking too. I hoped along different lines.

"Daylight, Dick?" she whispered from her corner.

"I don't know. Do you remember how we were standing when he saw us?" She frowned.

"When I saw him I was clinging to you, because I was afraid. Why?"

"I was only thinking. And just before that you were holding my hands and trying to make me promise not to see Naia alone."

"Yes, I remember that quite clearly. What on earth are you driving at, Uncle Richard?"

I shrugged my shoulders.

"I knew it," I said. "We seem to be wading in jealousy this morning! Naia, yourself, and now Juan. Jealous women cling to their possessions, don't they, Renée? I'm not sufficiently versed in the subject to know if jealous men do the same. If they do, we should be seeing a lot more of Juan Mitzakis in the near future!"

The frown vanished from her face. An expression of genuine horror took its place.

"Dick! You don't seriously imagine he thought that you and I—?"

"Why not? Figure it out for yourself. We were together at the New Venice when he blew in for that knife; we flew from London together; we've been more or less in each other's company ever since. You and I know that Juan himself is responsible for the situation—and that everything's square and above-board. But I'll bet you anything you like the Mullets have their suspicions, decent people that they are. And Juan, in his present state of mind, may be imagining anything."

"But how perfectly ghastly!"

"Of course. But it's a reasonable possibility—and we've got to face it."

She colored a little and laughed.

"How absurd! As if you cared two hoots for me!"

"The trouble is that quite probably I do."

She shuffled closer.

"Now look here, Uncle Richard, I positively refuse to allow you to flirt with me in my own car! Besides, I know you too well. You'd let almost any woman inveigle you into a promise of matrimony rather than hurt her feelings. Now, wouldn't you? Uncle Richard, you're blushing!"

"So are you!"

She unfastened the flap of her bag and consulted the mirror that was concealed there for confirmation. A shake of her powder-puff set a myriad of pink motes dancing in the sunshine and a pleasing perfume scenting the air. She applied it to her face, eying me all the time.

"You're not looking what you're doing," I reminded her.

She consulted the glass again and removed a superabundance of the indispensable commodity from the sides of her nose.

"Is that better?" she demanded, holding up her face for inspection.

"Perfect!" I replied.

"Now you're laughing at me—and I hate you! You've spoiled what might have been an interesting morning. But, seriously, Dick, I don't like the look of things at all. If Juan is really jealous, he might do anything . . . I've suspected from the first that, sooner or later, he would turn his attentions to you. Not because of me, but because you were interfering with his plans. Dick!"

"Well?"

"Let's go back."

The suggestion staggered me.

"Back?" I echoed. "Back to England, d'you mean?"

Renée nodded.

"I'd far rather do that than anything dreadful happen to you."

"Nothing dreadful is going to happen to me."

"You don't know."

I faced her squarely.

"Now, look here, young woman," I retorted firmly, "I want you to understand this: Nothing is going to happen to either of us, as long as we keep our heads and refuse to allow ourselves to be led away by wild theories. The only people up to now that Juan's succeeding in harming are those whose names annoy him—quite innocent persons, in fact, who hadn't the faintest idea what was working in his brain. Which, by the way, only goes to show that ignorance and bliss don't always combine! Murder's a comparatively simple matter, provided you're in the mood and the other fellow wholly unsuspicious. A homicidal maniac would have no trouble in selecting a certain victim on Victoria Station during the rush hour, on the Embankment, in any movie-theater anywhere. With you and me it's different. We know his motives and his methods."

The frown was there again, clear-marked and singularly attractive.

"His methods have baffled the police in two countries already."

"Admitted. But in London he chose a fog that would have baffled anybody, and last night it was only the timely intervention of the White Owl that saved him. You can't blame the police for that. Nobody could have suspected he kept a highly trained bird in readiness somewhere, to be whistled down when he wanted it."

She regarded me steadily.

"A highly trained bird! What put that idea into your head?"

"Karolin, as a matter of fact; but I've come to much the same conclusion myself. You see, it's the obvious solution to the mystery, and it explains everything. Generally speaking, Juan only goes out at night and this queer bird of his follows him like his shadow. Marie saw it in Nice, I saw it three times in London—outside your suite, on my own window-sill and perched on Juan's shoulder after we had that scrap. For some reason, Valdao looks after it in the daytime, much as the goat-master of the Welch Regiment looks after the regimental pet."

She gave me a wistful smile.

"Still making up fairy tales for the edification of the very young, Uncle Richard?"

"Not in the least."

"Then perhaps you'll explain how it was you couldn't kill the White Owl in Mexico—and why the police failed to shoot it last night. You're a good shot, Dick. Juan always said so, and I imagine the French gendarmes have revolver-practice some times."

We were back in Paris, passing with amazing smoothness through broad, somber streets. Renée stopped Karolin, slipped out before I realized what she was doing and bought a paper. Renée was used to foreign newspapers. With an instinct that to me was uncanny she hit on the spot in an instant, marking it with a beautifully manicured thumb nail. The suspected man had been examined and discharged. Prompt work for the French that! But Monsieur Pelot was a live wire. He never believed in wasting time. The police were working along fresh lines, so the writer assured us; information had come to them from an utterly unsuspected quarter, and interesting developments were expected.

Renée looked at me.

"Is that just 'Journalese,' Uncle Richard, or does it mean anything?"

I lit my pipe.

"The usual newspaper optimism," I assured her. "It's a sound policy. It makes people buy the next edition."

The match I was holding burnt my finger. I threw it away with a muffled exclamation, prompted partly by the pain, partly by the fresh thought that had come to me, inspired by those few lines of print. "Information—from an unexpected quarter . . .!'"

I felt myself going cold.

A picture crossed my brain of a little, scandalized hotel-employee with bristling mustaches staggering back from an open doorway—and the green eyes of the White Owl! In the excitement I had forgotten that man, forgotten that incident entirely. Nobody, with the exception of that superannuated bell-boy and myself, had seen the Owl in Valdao's room. Up to this morning, he must have believed it was hallucination. After the first editions were out, it would have returned to him with all its vividness. He was the type of man who welcomed notoriety. It was ten chances to one he would have gone to the police at the first opportunity. The "interesting developments" that were expected, would include an interview with Valdao, the fat manager, the chambermaid, the clerk at the desk. Through them they would learn of Juan and Naia. I clasped my forehead. They would hear of me too—the mysterious caller, who had visited the room and disappeared!

I leaned over and spoke to Karolin.

"The Hotel Carthagena," I said huskily. "Don't stop there. Just drive past—very slowly."

He touched his hat to show that he had heard.

"Something new?" asked Renée at my side.

I inclined my head.

"Just an unpleasant suspicion," I answered. "One of those flashes of intuition that women believe in—and we lesser mortals experience once in a blue moon!"

The Morbizon "eight" forged ahead.

Chapter 19

IVAN KAROLIN HAD NOT BEEN A TAXI-DRIVER FOR NOTHING. He knew his Paris. We entered the street where the Carthagena lay by the other end—the end I had never explored. There was a gendarme at the corner, small, erect, as efficient in his particular sphere as his taller London prototype was in his. His presence there probably signified nothing, just an habitual pause on an habitual round, but it filled me with a vague apprehension. In an endeavor not to look what I felt, I glanced over Karolin's shoulder at the speedometer. We had dropped to barely five miles an hour, running as easily and smoothly as if we had been doing fifty. I was as proud of it as if it had been my own—prouder perhaps, because I had gone to some trouble in obtaining a genuine "demonstration model," a car that had been carefully "run-in," tested on the road, refurbished and fitted with new tires. I had recognized from the first that, without that, it would be useless for our purpose.

I stared through the window, gleaning confirmation every minute that my suspicions had been justified. The backwater was still quiet enough, quiet in a queer ominous sort of way. I noticed a score of men, police quite obviously, plain-clothes men posing unsuccessfully as just ordinary civilians, split up into groups of two and three, lurking in doorways, in the road itself, patrolling the narrow pavement on either side. A hundred yards from the hotel a tall, lean man, with eyes like gimlets and a harsh voice crossed the thoroughfare and stopped us. He opened the nearside door and leaned in.

"Your pardon, madame; are you going to the Carthagena?"

Renée shook her head.

His gaze traveled round the interior, resting for a matter of seconds on each of us in turn. "English?—You have your passports?" It was like the preliminaries to a customs examination all over again! Renée opened her bag, I felt in my pocket; Karolin produced his *carte d'identité* and handed it over. Presently the inspector, or whatever he was, returned the documents with a bow, slammed the door with an air of finality that induced a pleasant sense of relief, and spoke to us through the open window.

"I must apologize if I have caused you annoyance, but one has one's orders, you know." The veil of suspicion was lifted, I gathered, and once more we were respectable citizens! "Would it inconvenience you to pull into the side and wait, say, a matter of ten minutes? No? I am much obliged."

He watched Karolin pull in, raised his hat, and made off, pausing at each of the little groups in turn. Observing through the glass at the back, I deduced that the raid was at an end. The plainclothes men were losing their attitude of expectancy and not a little of their dignity. Cigarettes were lit, most of them were laughing, talking in that excited, high-pitched manner that invariably suggests to the uninitiated foreigner that a quarrel is being indulged in on a large scale. They reminded me of schoolboys at the morning "break."

I turned back and saw Renée looking at me.

"Quite an adventure!" she sighed. "Did you expect all this, Uncle Richard?"

I nodded.

"More or less, although I hardly counted on our being stopped. That newspaper report gave me the idea. It's probably been going on for an hour or more, and we've arrived at the tag-end."

Her eyes were wide open, her cheeks slightly pale.

"They're on the track then!"

"It looks like it."

"Juan wouldn't be here. We saw him in the *Bois.*"

I shook my head.

"Nor the Owl apparently," I added. "They've come here for Valdao."

Renée started.

"How did they know? Who told them?"

"The little attendant who took me to his room on the morning when we flew from London. You remember. I told you about it. He saw the White Owl when he opened the door. I'd forgotten that—until I read that notice. When the papers came out this morning, it would be the first thing that would come into his mind. That sort of people live for publicity; it gives them a leg-up, as it were, where they live. Probably there's money in it too."

Karolin leaned back.

"As likely as not," he said, "he'll make his fortune out of it. The newspapers will be on him like a shot. He'll sign his name to 'exclusive articles' he hasn't written a word of—draw quite a handsome sum in remuneration, and buy an *estaminet* with the proceeds. If the criminal remains at large long enough, he may even run to a small hotel! When your Frenchman becomes a capitalist he doesn't waste his money; he looks round a sound opportunity to make it more! If he hasn't business acumen, it's a thousand to one his wife has. And think of his unique position! The only man in Paris, barring yourself of course, who has actually seen the White Owl off-duty, so to speak! A strange species of white owl in Paris in November! There couldn't be two of them."

Renée clutched my arm.

"Did you leave your card when you called on Valdao?" she demanded.

I tried to think.

"No," I returned. "I fancy not. I remember taking out my case, but I don't think I left a card. Very probably I gave my name to the man at the desk. We'll hope he's forgotten it by this time."

Another car passed us, a biscuit-colored Hispano with a built-in luggage affair at the back. It was stopped outside the hotel, examined as we had been and instructed to park. Karolin, after the fidgety manner of all taxi-drivers, had been stealing yards all the time, keeping his engine running, apparently oblivious of the fact that the Morbizon was heavy on "juice." He stole a whole chunk this time, bringing us opposite that little side-turning that had produced two strange adventures already. He switched off here and studied the pleasing lines of the Hispano, just in front. His action irritated me at first. I feared we were in for a second passport examination when I noticed a square label stuck on the wind-screen, flapping slightly in the breeze. I guessed it as a sort of clearance certificate, a guarantee against further annoyance.

The bearded man I had noticed in the Rue Treille came down the steps of the Carthagena, accompanied by the fat manager and the elderly bell-boy, who carried his cap in his hand. I remarked for the first time that he was as bald as an egg! As if conscious of his own importance, he swaggered a little, talked at random. He seemed to be all wrinkles from his square, badly-shaven chin to the summit of that polished dome! There was a lot of arm-waving and shrugging . . . Monsieur Pelot—I had persuaded myself by this time that the bearded man was Monsieur Pelot—shook hands with both gentlemen, walked away a dozen yards, turned, came back, and commenced talking all over again. I thought somehow that he looked the reverse of pleased. I hoped there had been a hitch somewhere.

"Don't sit so far forward," whispered Renée. "They may recognize you."

I drew back.

"That's my attendant," I told her, "and the fat chap's a manager of sorts."

"I know," she said. "I guessed that from the descriptions you gave me. Who's the third, a detective?"

"Pelot, I fancy, of the Sûreté. He was on the scene last night. Valdao's beaten them, I think."

Four other men pushed through the swing doors and down the steps. Three of them raised their hats to Pelot and joined in the conference on the pavement; the fourth—stout, almost German-looking, in a green felt hat that looked too small and big rimless spectacles, remained apart, his hands clasped behind him, studying the building up and down. He glanced at the others and moved off towards the back. I lost him behind the jutting wall that sheltered the lock-ups, picked him up again at the far end of the courtyard. He appeared to be conducting a minute examination of a vast area, moving ponderously, stooping, crouching, gazing up at the fire-stairs . . . Something would attract his attention and he would walk rapidly, stop and look down. He actually scaled the stairs that Karolin and I had used, tried the door, measured the distance between the flight and the balcony, and came down again.

And Pelot was still talking!

For some reason or another, I was beginning to be more afraid of this new investigator than of the great Pelot himself. He seemed a man of action, rather than words. There was something of the bloodhound about him, smelling away there around service entrances and garbage dumps. Probably a round half-dozen of his colleagues had examined that same patch already. Probably it had been scoured from wall to wall, from fire-stairs to garages. And yet this fact did not seem to disturb him one iota. He buttonholed a chef in a tall white hat, white overalls and loud check trousers. Quite a pleasant interview apparently, for I saw the chef laugh. The white hat disappeared and our investigator came slowly towards the road, sucking at a long black cigar.

He paused by the row of galvanized bins, his hands still behind him, as if counting them over and over again. I saw him move to the end and lift up a lid, peer in and close it again; lift a second and go through the same performance—a third, a fourth. The fifth receptacle had a heap of rubbish all around it, as if it had been carelessly tipped. An enormous rat, emerging unexpectedly from the heap, ran over his toes. Our detective didn't jump; he picked up a convenient half brick and heaved it after it. I heard Karolin laughing.

And then tragedy, grim, stark, so silent that it was lost on the group in front, happened before our eyes. The fifth lid lifted by itself! An arm and a knife came out, swept downwards and struck. I saw the stout man stagger away and fall, struggle to rise and fall again, rolling from side to side. Valdao came out of the bin, sprang out like some grotesque jack-in-the-box, drew a cap from his pocket and clapped it on, then bent for a brief space over his victim.

The stout man sprawled on his side. He was very still now. Valdao had no overcoat. The blue suit he wore was dusty and soiled. I saw him struggling with the other, turning him by main force, pulling at a sleeve. The coat came free and he drew it on, exchanged his cap for the detective's green hat, appropriated the glasses. The next moment he had emerged boldly from the turning, passed Pelot and the others and sauntered, with amazing effrontery, between the halted Hispano and ourselves.

Shielded from the group, he began to run. He had barely reached the corner when Karolin sprang through the door without a word, and was after him.

Renée was clinging to me, white as a ghost. I heard the shrill alarm raised across the road and looked in time to see the group break up.

Chapter 20

SHEER, COLD-BLOODED MURDER!

Drama, the trend of modern literature, the movie reel—all these had robbed it of half its terrors, at least, one would have imagined so. And yet the fate of the stout detective in the hotel yard affected me so deeply that I could almost feel the six inches of supple blade cutting through flesh and sinew.

It was the first murder I'd had ever witnessed. I had seen the immediate results of Juan's homicidal adventures, but the mischief in each case had been accomplished before I had arrived. Here I had seen the fat man in the rimless spectacles scouring the court-yard, climbing and descending the stairs, poking about among the bins where Valdao lay hidden—seen Valdao, curiously like the rat that had run across the detective's shoe, making a bold bid for freedom in a borrowed overcoat that was several sizes too large and a green felt hat worn back to front! Well, the rat was gone and the dogs were after him and nobody seem particularly interested in our car.

The driver of the Hispano, a languid youth in a fur collar, crawled out to talk to us.

"Curious that," he said in French, nodding towards the corner. "Did you see him running? I suppose that was the man they were after." The entrance to the yard came within the scope of his vision. Two men were bending over the dead detective. The chef in the white hat was there, a tradesman came round in his shirt-sleeves, followed by two women; a boy on a bicycle stopped whistling and left his machine to obtain a closer view.

"Murder!" pursued the languid youth. "My mother mustn't see this!"

He climbed back and started his car.

I looked at Renée. She was all right now, wonder fully calm considering.

"I suppose the funny little man was Valdao?"

"Yes, that's right."

I slid over the back of the seat in front and took possession of Karolin's wheel. A touch of my shoe set the self-starter going.

Snicking in a gear, I piloted the Morbizon round the corner, drove it fifty yards or so and stopped.

"You think Karolin will find us here?" she queried from the back.

"Almost bound to, I think. If he doesn't come ten minutes, we'll push off. He'll guess we've gone home. We're clear of the Carthagena anyway. That place was getting on my nerves."

"Extraordinary that he should have left us like that," commented Renée suddenly. "Did you tell him to go, Dick?"

I shook my head.

"No, but somebody had to, and you can't chase a fugitive through Paris in a car. There's too much traffic. I might have gone, but I suppose Karolin's still sore about that tip Cacao never gave him. Things are beginning to move now, Renée, and alter. I doubt if Naia will call at the Bristol this evening; I doubt too if the white saloon will show up in the Rue Solferino at eight. If it does, it'll be a miracle if the whole party boards it. Valdao's a marked man. Very likely they'll have taken him by then. If they haven't, he'll be spotted the first time he shows himself."

"One certainly would imagine so."

There was a long pause. We watched people passing, scanned the street at intervals hoping to see Karolin's gray overcoat standing out against the more somber coatings of business men.

"How are you feeling now?" I asked.

"Extraordinarily well, thank you, Uncle Richard. I feel I've what Virginia would call 'graduated' this morning. Seeing that poor man killed in cold blood was pretty horrible, of course, but no worse in a way than what a nurse has to undergo in an operating theater. And it wasn't a closeup, don't you see. One didn't hear things. It might have been two people rehearsing for the pictures. You saw far worse things than that in the war."

I screwed up my eyes.

"I did, but it was different somehow. You expected death there, waited for it, inflicted it yourself. I can't say that I like these street affairs even now." I looked at my watch; it was five minutes past one. "Here!" I cried, welcoming an opportunity to change the subject, "we must get back. It's after one."

I drove to the Bristol with a deal less confidence than Karolin had displayed. I hadn't handled a car of any sort for months and I'm never driven in Paris in my life. Keeping to the right was peculiar at first, overtaking on the left seemed all wrong. I parked the car outside the hotel with a distinct feeling of relief and went up the steps with Renée.

In the elevator on the way to our rooms she patted my shoulder and smiled.

"A truly wonderful performance, Dick! I don't know how you managed it."

"And," I returned, "to tell you the honest, unvarnished truth, nor do I!"

We had the dining-room almost to ourselves lunching by the window while, at a table in the center of the room, as if marooned on a lonely island, a fat Frenchman with serviette tucked into his collar consumed roast duck and peas with evident enjoyment, not to say *abandon!* A small regiment of waiters stood about like the lifeless models in clothiers' shops. Virginia came down presently and yarned to us in her fascinating American drawl. She had heard from Marie that we might be going, and was really quite depressed about it. She had come armed with notebook and pencil and was bound on collecting addresses.

"We're going to Biarritz next. Pop told you that, I guess. Mother's seen pictures of Nice, so we shall go there too. What's the climate like on the Riviera, Renée? More like Miami, Florida?"

"It's very nice," said Renée; "I like it. But I've never been to Florida."

"Oh, but you should; it's just perfect! Big comfortable hotels and palm trees. You seem to meet everybody there you've ever known. I'm crazy to go there again. We'll visit Monte Carlo, of course. Pop saw a man last night who said he'd won forty thousand dollars there in a week. That's a lot of money. Have you ever been to Monte Carlo, Mr. Coombes?"

"Yes," I told her, "but I've never won forty thousand dollars. The man your father met was probably a fisherman or a golfer!"

Virginia laughed.

"Really?" she demanded in her engaging way, "do you really think that? But people *have* won a whole lot of money at the tables."

"Quite so, but most people lose consistently. That's why the Prince of Monaco is such a wealthy man. He doesn't keep his casino open for any philanthropic reason."

"And if you're cleaned up, do they pay your fare home?"

"Something of the sort, I believe. I've never tested it for myself. Quite a number of unfortunate speculators 'say it with re-

volvers!' I'm told there's a cemetery packed exclusively with people who thought they were going to win forty thousand dollars in a
week!"

Miss Virginia went limp with laughing. She dropped her pencil
and I groped for it under the table.

"You're a terrible man, Mr. Coombes!" she protested. "You
make me almost scared to go there at all. Can I have your address
in London, please. We'll be going there in the Spring. *If* we've any
money left after Monte Carlo, we'll be stopping off at Adelboden
for the winter sports. Would you like us to call on you in London?"

"I should be charmed." She shot a side-glance at Renée.
"D'you think he really means that? I never know when he's talking seriously."

"He means," said Renée, "that he'll be delighted, but that he
quite expects you to break your neck in a bob-sleigh at Adelboden!"

I left them talking "dress" and went out, interviewing the management on the way. This mention of Nice, Monte Carlo, Adelboden had unsettled me; it reminded me that I was a businessman
with work to attend to, not a sybarite like Renée nor a wealthy
American seeing Europe in the winter. I made with determined
steps for the Rue de la Paix, for the entranceway through which
Naia had disappeared that morning. For the past hour or more a
notion had been building itself in my brain. There was just the
sporting chance I should find Juan there. He had admitted to me
that he was never at his best in the daytime. If I could get him by
himself and talk to him, I might yet save this wild journey to some
unknown destination. If he proved reasonable, I could phone
Renée and bring her along. It intrigued me, as I walked, to reflect
on the marked change that had come over Renée in the course of a
single morning. The murder at the Carthagena, ghastly as it was,
had acted as a tonic. She had seen Valdao caught, just as any normal criminal might be caught, in a corner; she had seen him bor-
row clothes to disguise himself, and run. A normal occurrence, in
a way, but it had knocked on the head all those vague superstitious
theories in which she had half believed. Valdao had run for his
life; whereas, if our original formula had been in any sense correct, he should have taken to his wings—*and flown!* The White
Owl, obviously a distinct and separate entity, hadn't put in an appearance. Valdao had been left to his own resources—to a knife

and his own legs. I wondered where they had taken him and Karolin, and why Karolin was so long in showing up.

The number I had noted down resolved itself into a select set of residential chambers, with wide stairs and a tiny, self-operated elevator, and a middle-aged *concierge* on duty in a glass box in the hall.

"Monsieur Julian Murray?" I demanded—and the *concierge* all but fell off his stool.

"Ma foi!" he stammered, absence of teeth making his speech increasingly difficult to understand; "Everybody asks for him—and what can I say?"

"You can say whether he is in or out," I suggested.

He bobbed out of his box and came round to me, gesticulating wildly.

"I tell you he is out—gone—*disparu!* The week before last he came to me with a story. The hotels were all full and he wanted rooms . . . I explained that I had nothing. He was a charming gentleman and his lady was very beautiful."

"And so you found them an apartment," I put in.

"I found them an apartment because it was raining—and I had not the heart to turn them out. The people at number three were away in Egypt. They had let their rooms two years ago; this time they had said nothing."

"And he paid you pretty handsomely, I presume?"

The fellow blinked.

"Monsieur Murray was a gentleman." He spread out his arms in a sweeping gesture that was meant to imply that undeniable gentility formed an excuse for everything. "An hour ago the police were here, inquiring for him. I myself went in with them. It was empty; there was nobody there—nothing. I remembered then that, shortly after eleven, the lady had sent me out for theater tickets and I had been away half-an-hour. In that half-hour, monsieur, they must have departed."

I swore softly. This business was full of deadends, Juan was as elusive as an eel. I thought I could see through the trap now: He had sent out Naia to intercept me, to arrange an appointment that she would never keep. It was not a scheme for inflicting injury on myself, but a move to keep me inactive for a matter of hours. Jealousy pure and simple had drawn him from the trees, where he was spying on us. He had realized his mistake there, and expedited his departure so that there should be no chance of our encountering him. Some clue, something found at the Carthagena perhaps, had brought the police to that address.

I gave the fellow a note, resolving to clear out before they came again. Last night's murder was hardly a thing to be mixed up in; the very last thing I wanted was an interview with the redoubtable Pelot.

"It is of no consequence," I murmured. "You need not mention that I called."

He pocketed my note.

"And then," he said, continuing the story where he had left off, "two other people came—an Englishman like yourself and a lady. The Englishman said he was a detective from London. He showed me some papers, which meant nothing to me, you will understand, because I do not understand your tongue."

A bell rang and I saw that uncanny lift going up by itself.

The *concierge* moved to the gates and stared upwards.

"They should be coming down now," he added.

Curiosity and an inborn dislike of appearing to run away held me there. Besides, I had nothing to fear. Nobody in England had any reason to connect me with the man who had committed the Haymarket Murder. The lift stopped and two people got out— a little, clean-shaven man with a face like a ferret and gray hair showing under the brim of a hard felt hat and a tall, dark woman in black whose face was somehow familiar. The man handed the *concierge* a key and a note. It was of a large denomination, and the *concierge* was all smiles. The woman walked right up to me, stared, gasped, then held out her hand with a little cry of surprise.

"Mr. Burnett," she called back to her companion, speaking Spanish, "isn't it extraordinary? I know this gentleman. He helped the police on that dreadful night. I've been hoping to meet him ever since and thank him for what he did. I am deeply grateful to you, Señor," she whispered to me. "Perhaps you will tell me your name."

It was Margharita Manzanarez!

Chapter 21

MR. BURNETT SHOOK HANDS.

The Señorita Manzanarez was laughing, excited, prone to take this sudden encounter as merely a pleasant coincidence. Her companion, on the other hand, was not. The look he gave me as we gained the street together expressed "What the deuce are *you* doing here?—and how much do you know about this extraordinary affair anyway?"

And, of course, he had every excuse. A man had been killed in peculiar circumstances in London—and I had emerged from the fog and lent a hand. There was nothing to arouse suspicion in that. But coupling that fact with the other—my being in the immediate vicinity of Juan's flat when they had come there in search of him—formed a whole that was distinctly compromising, to say the least of it. I led them through the Rue Daunou to a cafe I knew in the Avenue de l'Opera, saying little, reviewing my position as best I could. Whether Burnett was a detective or not, the same danger existed. Any friend of Miss Manzanarez could hardly refrain from divulging to the police the slightest clue that might lead to the apprehension of her father's assassin.

It was distinctly chilly, but we sat down at one of those little tables with which the pavements of Paris are littered. A waiter came out and took our orders, a couple sat down at an adjacent table . . . fashionably dressed people passed to and fro. Burnett said something and I answered at random. I was still thinking. Either I had to face the examining magistrate—the one thing I wished to avoid at the moment—or it was a question of cards on the table. I would have preferred to have talked it over with Renée, but that was impossible.

Margharita, amazingly attractive in her black, was relating the circumstances that had led up to her being there, explaining everything, including Burnett. "You see," she said, "I had only come to England for a holiday. I am studying music at the Conservatoire. After my poor father's tragic death I came back. My mother has been dead for some years, and my father had a house at Clichy and other property in France about which I had to see the lawyers. The man who stabbed my father was a complete stranger to me. He spoke to me earlier in the evening in the vestibule of the theater and, of course, I remembered quite clearly what he was like. I gave his description to the police in England before I left. I supposed he was still there, in hiding somewhere. Imagine my surprise, señor, when I ran into him yesterday evening in the Boulevard des Italiens! He was there, I assure you, his hands in his pockets, staring into a shop where they sold knives, señor." Her handkerchief went to her eyes and I looked away. "I did not let him see me. Choking down my fear, I followed him to the house where we met just now . . . I spoke to the *concierge* and reassured myself that he was actually living there. I got his name—Julian Murray—went to the house of a friend and put through a call to London. My friend at the Embassy did not wish to trouble the police until we were quite certain. I was certain, you see, but he was afraid I might have been mistaken. So he went to this gentleman, who very kindly left at once by the night boat."

She paused there and Burnett cleared his throat. It was coming! I could feel it!

"And now, Mr. Coombes," he rasped, "perhaps you'll be good enough to tell us what *you* were doing there?"

I smiled.

"It so happens," I returned, "that I knew Mr. Murray very well indeed some years ago. We were at Cambridge together and close friends afterwards. The last I saw of him before that unfortunate business in the Haymarket was in the backwoods of Mexico. He fell through a hole into some old ruins and, although we searched for several days, nothing was seen of him again. We left him for dead and came home. On the fatal night—I suppose we must call it that—I had just learned that he was alive and in London. I—er—traced him to the Haymarket Theater and arrived just in time to assist the police. Miss de Salis, by the way, who was engaged to Murray before his disappearance, is actually here in Paris with me. There were certain features connected with the crime that led us to believe that he had committed it. We formed several theories, I must explain, but what we had at the back of our minds was that he was mad. We wanted to make sure of this and, eventually, to get hold of him and have him put away. I traced him to the Hotel Europe and, finally, to Paris. Miss de Salis and I flew across and have spent the past nine or ten days looking for him here. This morning I saw a woman, who has been his companion recently, entering the building where he rented an apartment. I called there

after lunch, hoping to find him, and met you. And there," I con-
cluded, "with the exception of some details which I shall be
pleased to give you later, you have the entire yarn."

Burnett fingered his glass.

"I'm much obliged to you, Mr. Coombes," he said. "You must
forgive me if I appeared suspicious, but you'll admit, I think, that
finding you there when we did was most extraordinary."

"Most!" I agreed. "I gather you are a detective?"

He inclined his head.

"I'm a retired member of the C.I.D. and I do a bit of private
work from time to time. Señor Ballester, the Señorita's friend in
London, has put business in my way on many occasions. Natu-
rally, when she phoned him last night, he sent for me." He bent
forward across the table. "You've heard what happened last night,
of course?"

"Oh, yes."

"A nasty business, Mr. Coombes! An extremely nasty business.
Now, mind you, I'm not implying that the fellow isn't mad, but
there are certain peculiar facts connected with the case, with both
these cases, that need a lot of explaining. The same weapon was
employed—a knife with a white owl carved on the handle; and
here, so I read in the papers, a real white owl actually took a
prominent part. That is," he added, "if one can take the reports to
be correct. The French are a funny race, quite different to ourselves. When you cross the Channel it's like stepping into another
world. They're more excitable than we are, more superstitious.
Also they've great faith in this Monsieur Pelot. A criminal being
helped out of a tight corner by a white owl takes some swallowing.
I take it you agree with me there? It might—mind you, I'm only
saying it might—be a cock-and-bull story invented to excuse the
police from making a mess of their job. Liquor might play some
part in it. There's a deal of liquor flying about in the early hours in
Montmartre. I've been there, and I know."

"I think I can help you there," I put in quietly. "I've been trying
your job while I've been here, though not with any great measure
of success. Somebody rang me from the Étoile Bleu last night, a
fellow who was in my pay. He had seen Murray and his victim
quarreling, and guessed that more serious trouble was imminent. I
took my man and a taxi and got to the spot as quickly as I could.
The trouble had happened before I arrived, but I saw the police at
work—and I saw the white owl!"

Margharita uttered a faint cry and stared at me in astonishment. Burnett stuck both hands in his pockets and leaned back in his chair. "So you saw it, did you?" he remarked, though more as a soliloquy than anything else. "Any idea how it got there?"

"No," I said. "That is to say, not exactly. I have my private views on the matter, of course—"

"And those are, Mr. Coombes—?"

Somewhere about this time it dawned on me that, if we hoped to continue our investigations unhampered by the police, we must do our utmost to prevent Burnett interviewing Pelot. I determined to invite him to the Bristol, introduce him to Renée and the Mulletts—at all costs keep him interested. Karolin's theory of the White Owl wouldn't do. I felt that my own, vague as it was, was better . . .

I cleared my throat.

"The White Owl," I returned in a low voice, "has no lucid explanation, except perhaps to Spiritualists. It appeared to Murray and myself under mysterious circumstances in Mexico. Its arrival in Europe coincided with Murray's reappearance. I am inclined to believe that this creature exerts an extraordinary influence over my friend, transmitted in some strange manner through two other people—mediums, if you like. If the Señorita and yourself will dine with me at six-thirty, I will endeavor to explain myself more fully."

I hailed a taxi and drove them to the Bristol then and there. The Mulletts were out in their car. By a fortunate chance, Renée had declined an invitation to join them and was superintending Marie's packing of her clothes for the journey. We foregathered in the sitting-room and I gave them the promised details, from the ill-fated expedition eighteen months before to its bearing on Juan's recent activities. Margharita's English was only fair. I translated for her whenever I saw she was at a loss. Burnett was much impressed. By degrees an extraordinary compact was formed, a sort of fusing together of two forces. Baines and Marie once more were to remain behind, to follow with the luggage if necessary. Margharita and Burnett were to squeeze into the Morbizon with us. Provided, of course, that the journey was necessary at all. Looking at those two women, both beautiful in their own particular way, I began to wonder how they would hit it off. Renée was all sympathy at the moment, attracted to the other because of her recent loss. But Renée was a spoiled child, accustomed to be admired, accustomed too to a lot of attention. I hoped, when her present mood wore down, there would be no sparks flying!

Our guests departed presently, to turn up to dinner with two commendably small suitcases. My own luggage was reduced to a minimum: Renée's comprised a case to be housed in the container at the back and a dressing-case to be squeezed inside. On the whole, it was a great concession, not to say a sacrifice, when one remembered the seven trunks and eleven hatboxes! It astounded me how she had managed it!

Seven-thirty arrived—and still no news of Karolin. The hitch was explained to the others, and everyone became jumpy. Taking it all round, dinner was rather a tragic repast. I settled our bill, made provision for the servants and embarked upon that ghastly round of *pourboires*—a problem that has yet to be successfully solved! I remember being conscious of an uncomfortable feeling inside. Failing Karolin, I would have to drive the Morbizon, and felt I would rather have known a little more about it. Leaving the others in the hall, I went out to fetch it—and there it was, large and unmistakable, drawn across the entrance!

I stared at it in amazement. Ivan Karolin was at the wheel and, strapped to the carrier behind the container, there reposed an enormous wooden trunk! If that was Karolin's contribution to the kit, he most certainly would have to think again!

He climbed out and saluted me, grinning like a hyena.

"All correct, I think," he murmured.

I pointed to the trunk.

"Why on earth didn't you report before," I demanded sternly; "and what the devil have you got in there?—clothes?"

His head came closer.

"Not clothes," he whispered and then went off into paroxysms of laughter. *"I've got Valdao in there.* You wanted him, didn't you?"

Chapter 22

"OH, HE'S A POOR SORT OF CREATURE—this little man of yours with the green eyes," said Karolin, still wiping his own.

I had dragged him into a deserted corner of the vestibule and cautioned him to speak quietly.

"I tell you I've had the time of my life with that fellow. He caught a bus at the first corner—and I all but broke my neck getting it. In less than half a kilometer he was off again, walking very quickly, his shoulders down and that extraordinary overcoat flaping around his ankles. He crossed the river by the Pont Alexandre III, took the coat into a dry-cleaner's and came out without it. A little farther on he bought a hat; I didn't see what he did with the other. At the Invalides he hailed a taxi and boarded it from the pavement side, just as anybody would. I sprinted and swung in by the other. We both sat down together. It was very funny. He was shivering all over with the cold and a touch of fear too, I imagine. As soon as he saw me, he tried to get away, but I held on to him and showed him in a half-a-dozen words that it would be stupid to play hanky-panky with me. He calmed down after that and I told the driver to take us to my old lodgings in the Quartier Malakoff. As it happened, I knew the driver and made him promise, if the police made any inquiries, to keep his mouth shut."

He paused, his eyes tight closed, as if endeavoring to pick up the details of a busy day in their chronological order.

"Well, I pulled him up the stairs, pushed him into a chair and locked the door. Then I gave him a taste of what the police would have done if they'd caught him instead of me. I made him turn out his pockets, put everything he had into a parcel, and tied it up. That wasn't a long job because, beside his passport and a wallet of notes, there wasn't very much."

He drew the packet from his pocket and passed it over. I thrust it into my coat and glanced at my watch. Time was going.

"Why didn't you phone me?" I asked.

Karolin shrugged his shoulders.

"For two very excellent reasons: There wasn't an instrument in the place—and I didn't dare give Valdao the chance to slip me

again. It was lucky, by the way, I understood a few languages, because he had only half-a-dozen sentences of English in his vo-
cabulary and his French was almost as bad. We jogged along with
signs and dog-Spanish. He's a queer beast this Valdao! More like
an animal than a human being, and incredibly dirty! He knew
enough to understand that murder in a civilized community was
looked upon in a serious light, but I couldn't persuade him he had
done wrong in knifing the detective: The man had interfered with
him when he wanted to get away. That was his attitude. In Mexico, apparently, when one is faced with a contingency like that,
there is only one answer—the knife!"

"In some parts of Mexico," I murmured.

Karolin nodded.

"In the part where he comes from, at any rate. His yarn was that
he was your friend's servant, and that he was paid to do what he
was told. His proper name was Valdatli or Valdatil. I had the
devil's own job with him, because he kept dropping off to sleep.

"He wouldn't admit much, except that Mitzakis was waiting for
him somewhere or other and he thought they were leaving for
Spain. When I mentioned the White Owl, he began raving like a
lunatic. Well, I gave him some food but he wouldn't touch it.
About three this afternoon he fell into a deep sleep, and nothing I
could do would rouse him. I got a brace and bored some holes in
an old trunk, threw some clothes in the bottom and lifted him in.
Then I locked it, got somebody to help me carry it down, strapped
it on a friend's car, found the Morbizon and transferred the trunk
to our luggage-grid."

"I suppose he's all right in there?" I queried anxiously.

Karolin grinned.

"As right as he deserves to be."

"You're sure he can breathe?"

"Perfectly."

I had no experience of the luggage-grid of the Morbizon, but it
seemed to have held up all right up to now. In any case, it was an
ingenious way of getting our prisoner clear of Paris. What we
should do with him after that would have to be decided later. We
collected the remainder of our party, sorted ourselves out in the
Morbizon and drove to the Quai d'Orsay station. Parking there,
clear of the taxis, Burnett and I strolled to the corner of the Rue
Solferino.

There had been an appreciable rise in temperature since the
afternoon, and rain was falling, a gentle moisture that stood on our

overcoats in little beads and showed in a thin spray against the light of every street lamp. The roads were treacherous! I saw a sports-car skid badly coming round from the Solferino Bridge. They were effecting road repairs opposite the station; the red warning-lamps, hung on their trestles, looked oddly bright. The lights along the river looked bright. The entire city seemed clothed in an aura of radiance; the open cafe-fronts seemed inviting.

I caught my breath.

The white saloon was there right enough, drawn in to one side, a mechanic in a blue raincoat and check cap pacing up and down on the pavement, stopping every now and again to scan the street in search of Mitzakis. The clock at the station showed three minutes past the hour. Burnett spoke.

"Our friends are late," he said. We strolled past it, keeping step, trying to appear unconcerned. A hundred yards convinced me that we were not the only people on the lookout for the owner of the white saloon. There were the same detached groups of loiterers as I had noticed in the street where the Carthagena lay, the same preposterous disguises, the same curious air of expectancy. I thought I recognized the inspector who had stopped our car; the trim beard of Monsieur Pelot was conspicuous by its absence.

"Police!" I whispered in Burnett's ear.

"Yes," he agreed, "I thought so too. But it's not badly done—for the French! I've seen worse on our side of the Channel, though not lately. The new Commissioner's gingered them up!"

We turned and walked back. I felt a deal more confident, now that I had Burnett with me. If I were questioned I could refer them to Burnett—and he, of course, had satisfactory credentials. He had been employed by reputable people in London to act on behalf of Sefiorita Manzanarez; there could be no suggestion that he was a friend of Juan's. The big hand of the clock had reached the quarter. It chimed —and we exchanged glances full of significance. "A wash-out!" suggested Burnett.

I rather thought so too. It was impossible at this juncture to say how much Mitzakis knew. If Valdao's appointment with him had been here, at the car, he might still come. On the other hand, his failure to meet him some time earlier in the day would have aroused his suspicions. He could have gleaned little from the papers. Since the morning they had been singularly reticent; there had been nothing about the raid at the Carthagena or the murder of the detective. One presumed that Pelot was exercising a temporary censorship. It was also very evident that he and his men had been busy. The mere fact that they were here at all suggested uncommonly good staff-work, as Burnett would have put it, "for the French," Burnett's attitude being that there was little real detective efficiency outside Scotland Yard!

At the Quai d'Orsay corner we turned again, a lot wetter than when we started, a trifle dejected. My companion was perhaps the more disconsolate, seeing that I had not yet let him into the secret of the trunk on the back of the Morbizon. We were halfway back to the saloon when Juan Mitzakis, dropping in like a bolt from the blue, brought off one of the most astounding feats of colossal impudence I have ever witnessed. So effective was it, so accurately timed, that it left one breathless and impotent. And yet one felt that the cunning of a maniac was behind it all.

From the back of a porch not ten paces from the car a tall man in evening dress emerged, followed by a woman blazing in diamonds. The man had a white beard and, across his immaculate shirt-front, there stretched a broad crimson ribbon; his silk hat was poised slightly to one side, his cape hung over one arm. He brushed past the two detectives who were sheltering there, held out a thin white hand to see if it were still raining, bent down and said something to the woman, whose black veil fell like a flimsy portcullis over the upper half of her face. I saw her help him on with his cloak. The light from a street lamp fell across her features—and in that instant I saw through the ruse. The face was Naia's; I would have known her anywhere.

"Burnett," I whispered, "there's something wrong here. Nip back to the *gare* and fetch Karolin and the car. Walk to the end of the road, and then run. If you start running now, they'll scent something." He nodded grimly.

"Got you!" he returned—and went.

Good chap—Burnett, I thought. He hadn't served in the C.I.D. for nothing! My eyes were glued on the girl and the man whom I now recognized, in spite of his disguise. The sheer audacity of it staggered me. They were pottering there on the pavement, apparently in search of a taxi—and presently they were going to steal that white saloon under the very noses of a score of picked gendarmes! I wondered . . . The psychology was sound . . . A beggar, a business man even, might well have been stopped and questioned, but the crimson scarf suggested diplomatic immunity, the whole get-up of possibly the two most conspicuous people in Paris almost guaranteed them safe passage.

Mitzakis spoke to one of the detectives, who directed him to the corner. At that instant and with dramatic suddenness, the White Owl flew down from the roof above, perching itself on the radiator like a gigantic mascot!

The mechanic let out a wild yell and bolted; men shot out on to the pavement, cannoning into one another in the excitement. The bird left its perch and wheeled in a big circle. I saw Naia slip into the car—then Juan. The door slammed—the self-starter whirred and functioned. Shouts rent the air, a revolver shot; police were swarming on to the scene from everywhere. A detective sprang in front of the saloon as it swerved outwards. The buffer flung him aside. I heard the *thud* as his head hit the curb. Another was on the running-board when it streaked down the road in a cloud of exhaust. The Owl flying with incredible rapidity, flapped at him and he fell, rolling over and over in the thoroughfare. The bird vanished through the window—and the white saloon was gone.

A horn tooted at my elbow and set me jumping a mile. I looked round and saw the Morbizon.

Chapter 23

To THIS DAY I AM AT A LOSS to explain how Juan got clear of
Paris, and equally at a loss to explain how Karolin followed. We
sighted him first in the Boulevard du Montparnasse, hung on to
him across the Place d'Italie, saw him bear left into the Avenue
d'Ivry, across the bridge and out.

The thundering of that white machine sent cars, cycles, trades-
men's vans converging towards the pavement. Half-a-dozen attempts, some half-hearted, some desperate, were made to stop
him, but he sailed through it all, driving with consummate skill
and a daring that Karolin could not be said to have equaled, seeing
that he merely skimmed through in the other's wake. Rules of the
road were lost on Juan. He chose the side that was clearest and at
one corner he actually drove clean across the pavement itself, scattering customers seated at tables outside a *brasserie*. Accidents
directly contributable to the lunatic ahead happened on all sides.
Two police-cars collided head-on at a crossroad with a crash that
could be heard half a mile away. Karolin had to swerve to avoid
the debris. I was sitting by his side and I caught the little shuddering scream Margharita gave when she looked. Tall buildings gave
way to suburban villas, suburban villas to more isolated dwellings,
tall rows of poplars dripping moisture and fields. I looked at the
speedometer. We were doing seventy! I worked it out from kilometers into miles. We were keeping pace with the white saloon;
there was barely a hundred yards between us.

"It's madness," growled Burnett from the rear seat. "One of us
is bound to hit something soon."

I did not answer. I was thinking of Valdao on the grid at the
back, wondering if he were awake or dead, or if we had jolted him
off in Paris! Right in front of Karolin's face the automatic screen-
wiper was swinging to and fro with a precision that reminded one
of a clock. It was raining harder now, blurring my vision. I looked
back. There were lights on the road, far, far behind; we had out-
distanced motor-cyclists, police-cars, everything. We flashed
through a village. Dogs shot out and barked at us, tried to pace us
and were lost. We overtook lorries, lumbering steam-wagons,

road-transport trailing from a great metropolis to the outlying districts, Orleans, Bourges, Tours, anywhere . . . met great high-seated vehicles loaded with wine-barrels . . . Headlights loomed up in the night, dazzled us and passed . . . There were long periods when we scarcely met anything.

The adventure had its thrills, its hairbreadth escapes, its amusing side. It amazed me, too, that the Morbizon maintained its speed, considering the magnitude of its load. Three men and two women inside—and one unfortunate traveler bumping about on the grid! It was colossal! And the extraordinary thing about it all was that we had not the remotest idea where we were bound. I presumed Juan knew, although that was by no means an established fact. He seemed to be picking his road, avoiding large towns, choosing stretches of rough surface that tested tires and springs to their utmost limits, in a manner that suggested long experience of the route, or days of study with a map and pencil. There was a certain consolation in the reflection that he couldn't go on forever; it was just a question of tank capacity and petrol consumption. Two hundred miles at the outside would bring a halt. Consulting our own map, I calculated that would land us somewhere short of Limoges. As the crow flies, the Spanish frontier was some two hundred and fifty miles farther on. The array of instruments on the board, red and black figures ticking over, slender hands on white dials, worked overtime, registering gradients, oil-pressure, kilometers, time. We had been driving for more than two hours, averaging roughly fifty! Barring compulsory stoppage, all other things being equal, it was on the cards that midnight would bring about an encounter with our quarry.

What, I wondered, would the nature of that encounter be? I tried to picture a roadside petrol-station, some ramshackle village affair perhaps, with the two cars drawing up in the night. What would happen then? It would be Juan's policy to fill up first, hold us up by some means, while water, oil, petrol, all these three essentials were being poured in. That would insure him a good start, a possibility of escaping us altogether. He might resort to violence, to that same type of diabolical cunning in which he had proved himself a past master, to bluff . . .

Karolin seemed to have read my thoughts, although his own must have been roughly the same.

"We can beat him for juice," he announced, his eyes never leaving the road. "I knew a man once who had that sort of car. It may do sixteen, if it's properly tuned-up; not more. They may squeeze ten gallons into the tank; no, more than that, twelve . . . We carry quite that, and I checked it as it went in." He was speaking in English terms, for my particular benefit. "I reckon we can carry on another twenty miles when he's empty."

Through the smeared pane I saw that the road was dead straight. Karolin pressed the accelerator and the poplars by the roadside seemed to merge into one. He was demonstrating how much we had in reserve. The red light of Juan's car appeared to be backing towards us with the speed of an express train. I held my breath just as a crash seemed imminent. His foot lifted a fraction and the danger passed—another fraction and the distance between us increased perceptibly. A front tire sent a flint *pinging* off into the bushes.

Karolin shot a glance at me.

"It's a car!" he remarked laconically.

I nodded.

A voice spoke to me from the back—Renée's:

"Where are we going, Uncle Richard?"

I turned and looked at her. It was a tense little group back there; Burnett, with Renée's case between his feet, Renée and Margharita on either side of him.

"Ask me another!"

My expression must have amused her, for she laughed.

"Rather thrilling, isn't it?"

"Yes."

"Bit too thrilling for me," confessed Burnett. His collar was turned up, his hard hat rammed on tight. I noticed he was biting on the stem of an empty pipe. "That driver of yours is a good chap. Notice how he missed that lorry at that turning? I thought we were 'for it' then!"

I nodded again, although the incident was lost to me. It was difficult to separate one hair-raising happening from a whole succession.

"He'll get rid of that car somewhere," he pursued staring ahead. "The police all over France must be looking for a white saloon by this time. They'll have the make and number. He'll be looking out for something fast and less conspicuous."

"He'll be lucky if he finds anything," I said, "at this time of night."

I consulted the instruments again, glowing in an oval of ghostly white. We were getting on. Karolin looked cool as a cucumber. I imagined he was happy to be leaving Paris behind, to exchange his ancient Citroen for this silky, eight-cylindered marvel. We negotiated an "S" bend, a sharp corner beyond and emerged on to another stretch of straight. Conversation had become general at the back of me. Renée and Burnett were talking, with Margharita Manzanarez chiming in. The atmosphere of excitement seemed to have lulled.

Burnett reached over and touched my arm. "If we hadn't these ladies here," he told me, "d'you know what I'd recommend?"

I shook my head.

"Why, pull ahead, turn into the side and force an accident."

Renée sat bolt upright.

"Oh!" she exclaimed, "and what about my car?"

Burnett fingered his chin.

"There is that, of course," he admitted. "Pity we didn't hire one for the job; it would have been better. You see," he continued, reverting to his original theme, "if we got ahead of him and slowed gradually, he'd be bound to slow too. The smash needn't be terrific, if it's properly managed. I've tried it on myself with car-thieves and it's worked wonderfully. As soon as we got him into the hedge, we'd jump out and have him covered before he'd have time to extricate himself from behind the wheel." He rubbed the window and peered out. "It's a good spot for it here now. Suggest it to the driver and see what he thinks."

"What about the ladies?" I asked. "Do we drop them first?" I added a rider: "And, supposing the plan doesn't work, do we pick 'em up again and risk losing the other car?—or do we just leave them behind?"

And there, I flatter myself, were our difficulties in a nut-shell. The maximum speed of the car ahead was still an unknown quantity, the skill and resource of its driver infinite . . . The road was not over-wide. Juan might let us catch up with him. He had done so once already. But overtaking was a different matter. To insure success we had to maneuver our car into a certain position; it could easily take us a couple of miles to do that, if ever we achieved it at all. And the girls would be waiting where we had dropped them. Nor, in the present circumstances, was I so optimistic about the nature of the crash as Burnett. He had seen Juan ride rough-shod over the traffic south of the Seine, but he had no conception yet as to the lengths Juan Mitzakis could go. *"I'm not a man, Dick,"* he had confessed to me in my flat, *"I'm a devil!"* And, in that lay the explanation of everything. It was the strength of a devil that had pitched me across my own room on that eventful night when Manzanarez had died—it was the luck of the devil that had got him out of Paris unscathed.

And, I imagined, Juan was not just sitting at his wheel doing nothing. That queer, warped brain of his, unassisted by outside advice, was working all the while. He was planning too, planning how to thwart us, considering not only counter-moves, but cunning, full-blooded schemes of his own. Time was invaluable to him, freedom to act, breathing-space . . . As Burnett had said, he must exchange the white saloon for another, assume some fresh disguise, send Naia across the frontier first perhaps, and then bluff his way through himself . . . His task was difficult in any case, with us on his trail it was a virtual impossibility.

While we were discussing it, threshing out Burnett's suggestion and the three or four others that arose from the first, Juan Mitzakis played his ace. On the last stretch of that straight run, with a pale moon sailing between watery clouds and a clustering hamlet in sight, the White Owl came like a bird of ill omen, pursuing its unwieldy flight along the hedgerow.

I saw it first and pointed, nudging Karolin as I did so.

"Look out!" I yelled.

He had picked it up too, but barely in time. His foot slid from the accelerator to the foot brake. All his limbs seemed to be working, his whole body, as the grim menace swooped at us from the night, its enormous spank of wing blotting out everything.

The next second disaster was upon us. Magnified in the headlights until it assumed incredible proportions, the White Owl enveloped the whole world. It was past the lights, a ghostly, vampire thing; a savage, nightmare creation that was all eyes—terrifying green spheres . . . I heard Burnett's cry of consternation, Margharita's shrill scream. A sickening jolt indicated that we had left the road. Contact with the roof rammed my hat over my eyes. The car heeled over, poised as if about to fall altogether, slid twenty yards and stuck fast, its engine still racing.

There came a pause in which the five of us exchanged glances, as if we were all astounded to find ourselves still living. Karolin muttered something in Russian and switched off. Burnett began fumbling with a window. I opened mine and peered out. We were an appreciable distance from the road, axle-deep in mud and ooze. I could see the track we had made between two belts of tall rushes.

Karolin folded his arms and sat back. Presently he fumbled for a cigarette, lit it and tossed the match outside.

"That settles it!" he declared. "We're here for the night!"

I clutched at him and pointed again.

The white saloon had turned and come back. I heard its brakes as it stopped. A door opened and a tall figure emerged. It was Juan Mitzakis. The pale light of the moon fell on him, bathing him in an unearthly radiance. His cloak still hung from his shoulders, but the hat and the broad band across the shirt-front were gone. His beard had been removed too, but the long cigarette was there—a sort of indispensable part of his make-up. He strolled to the edge of the morass, and the White Owl flew from the darkness where it had lurked on to his shoulder. *"A Dios!"* he shouted across the divide. A peal of insane laughter echoed in the stillness and faded out. The car trailed off, backed into a cart-track a hundred yards back, and flashed past again. It turned for a second time lower down and came back more slowly, as if its driver were looking for something he had lost. Karolin leaned through the window and fired, in a desperate attempt to burst a tire. Burnett and I followed suit. Mitzakis reversed into the cart-track once more, accelerated, and flashed through our zone of fire at a good forty. An arm waved to us from a window—and he was gone. The rear-light dwindled into the night, became a tiny pin-point of red—and vanished. A belt of white mist arose from the water-lands like steam.

Chapter 24

MORE SILENCE FOLLOWED, and then everybody began talking at once. The fact that Juan had outwitted us and escaped, the sheer miraculousness of our immunity from injury, even the horror the dramatic appearance of the White Owl had inspired in every one of us—all this was blotted out by the discomfort of our present situation. The Morbizon wallowed in a bleak wilderness of ooze and reeds, tilted, bogged, hopelessly stuck . . . Cold, clammy and penetrating, set our teeth chattering. I passed my flask over to Renée and closed the window; she unscrewed the top and handed it across Burnett to Margharita.

"My dear!" she queried, "what on earth are we going to do now?"

"We don't appear to have sunk any farther in," I said. "We shall have to try to wade through this mess—and carry you. We'll take anything removable from the car and beat it for the village inn."

"Supposing there isn't a village inn?"

"There's almost bound to be. If there isn't, we shall have to persuade one of the inhabitants to take pity on you, while we decide what's to be done. I imagine a local contractor and a lorry will be our first objective, though I doubt if we shall get any one to stir out until the morning."

I got out and tested the mire with one foot. It was an unpleasant process, but it assured me that a comparatively firm footing was possible.

"Do be careful," advised Renée. "Don't get sucked in."

"I don't mean to," I replied. "It's all right here."

She shivered.

"It must be frightfully cold!"

"It is!"

Slamming the door after me, I waded round to the back. And then I whistled softly. Two broken straps dangled from the grid. The trunk that had contained Valdao had vanished!

I looked about me, chilled to the marrow, my nostrils assailed by the nauseating miasma that hung everywhere. Presently I unfastened the luggage-container, pulled out a case and prepared to make my first journey to the road. Karolin barged into me, still smoking, and possessed himself of the other. We squelched in silence, feeling our way through the mist. We found the trunk. Karolin fell over it and came up a mess of swearing filth. Leaving it where it was we pressed onward. We struck the road ultimately, dumped our burdens and looked at one another.

"Well, Karolin," I laughed, "what price the dream?"

He was removing his overcoat, handling it deliberately, as if the accumulation of a little more mud on his fingers mattered. His expression was irresistible.

"Hell!" he retorted. "Don't talk to me about dreams! Look at this!"

The gray overcoat was no longer a thing of beauty. He spread it out on the low bushes and regarded the nether ends of trousers that had been made for a prime minister, wiped his hands on them and found another cigarette to replace the one that had been extinguished during his partial immersion. Bereft of his coat, his condition was not much worse than my own. He completed a sort of rough toilet with his handkerchief and began wading back. I followed. Forgetting Valdao and his precious trunk, we splashed back to the car, meeting Burnett who had become an amphibian too . . .

"What's it like?" he asked.

"Not too bad," I assured him. "It might be worse."

The question now arose how the girls were to be carried. Renée, who under the guise of a lady of fashion carried the heart of an adventuress, was all for removing her shoes and stockings and wading it like the rest of us. Margharita had less of the venturesome spirit. She looked at the oily mess and shuddered.

"It's comfortable in here," she suggested. "Can't we stop until somebody comes with a boat or something?"

"Nonsense!" said Renée, and unfastened a stocking. "Don't look, Uncle Richard!"

"I'm not," I retorted, "but you needn't bother about those. I'm going to carry you picka-back."

"How do you know what I'm doing, or undoing, if you're not looking? Besides, I love paddling."

"You won't," I told her, "in this. You'll want a bath afterwards and, from what I know of French villages, there won't be one. Karolin's had a bath already—and found it distinctly unwholesome!" Renée surrendered.

"You can't make it a 'flying angel,' Dick? I used to love those."

"Nothing doing!" I declared. "Hold on."

After all, there's a great deal to be said for short skirts! There's something to be said, too, for a whimsical outlook on life's little adversities. Renée looked on the funny side, and somehow the funny side prevailed. Karolin forgot the ruin of a new suit, the derelict overcoat spread on the bushes: Margharita forgot her fears. I heard Burnett telling her about a flooded tunnel in the Ypres sector . . . Five minutes later Renée and I were alone in the mist, her arms clasped around my neck and my arms encircling two delightfully shaped legs.

"You're sure we're going right?" she whispered.

I was following the trail the car had made from the road.

"Yes, I think so."

"Aren't you cold?"

"A bit."

"What happened to the flask? Did we leave it in the car?"

"I suppose so. Miss Manzanarez had it when I saw it last."

I squelched another twenty yards and sighted Valdao's box again. A corner of it was in the water, the corner that Karolin tripped over; the rest of it was propped up in the reeds. It occurred to me that it had fallen very lightly for a trunk with a man inside. Renée didn't know yet. I hadn't had time to tell her.

"Is that one of ours, Dick?" she shrilled.

"It's Karolin's."

"Oh!—Won't he be annoyed?"

I laughed.

"I don't think he cares much what happens to it. Valdao's in there. He pushed him in this afternoon, when he was asleep, and tied him to our luggage-grid just before we started."

Renée gasped.

"And he's been there all the time?"

"Yes. Must have been darned uncomfortable!"

I stepped up on to something solid, lowered her carefully and stretched my arms.

"Was I so very heavy, Uncle Richard?"

"Not too bad!"

"What do we do now? Stop here and wait for the others?"

"You can," I said. "I'm going back for some of the luggage."

"Wait a little while," she pleaded.

"Why?" I demanded. "Are you frightened?"

She shook her head.

"Not exactly, but I want you to stop with me all the same. It's nice to have you to myself. Just think of it, Dick; we started out, just the two of us. When was it? The week before last? It seems like years! And now we're a charabanc-party!"

She sat on the cleaner of the two suitcases and sighed.

"I thought you were enjoying yourself."

"Not altogether. If you and I had been stranded in a marsh in some remote part of the Continent it might have been amusing—romantic even! But this is like a railway accident. It's so communal!"

"You don't like our friends?" I hazarded. "I've hardly had time to know them yet, but the Morbizon was rather like the second-class compartment of almost any night train running from the Gare de Lyon."

"How do you know? You've never been in one."

"No, but I've looked in several—on the way to the restaurant-car. They're always full of nice people who can't afford first—and unpleasant people who oughtn't to be able to afford second! You see what I mean, Dick; the nice people have had the others thrust upon them, whether they like it or not. I felt rather like that to-night."

"But," I objected, "Miss Manzanarez *is* first-class."

"I know, and she's very pretty, and that's why you stand up for her. But Burnett is a retired police-constable or something. He couldn't help it, poor dear, but he made me feel as if Margharita and I were two female criminals under escort!—You're rather a dear, aren't you, Dick?"

"Quite probably; but what's that got to do with it—with Margharita and Burnett, I mean?"

"I don't know. Contrast, I suppose. Give me a cigarette—or are they all oozy?"

"No. That part of me's tolerably dry."

I handed her my case and lit up for her. The flame from the match illuminated her face. She sat on that suitcase knock-kneed, pigeon-toed—anyhow. Her frock was a long way above her knees, the leather coat unbuttoned and open in front. She had changed her hat since the morning and it didn't match the coat. It was close-fitting and black—rather Mephistophelian. When she smiled up at me, it make her look incredibly wicked!

She blew out the match.

"I expect I look a fright!" she said.

"You don't; you look delightful."

She puffed out a wreath of smoke.

"Worth running away with, Dick?"

The tone of the question staggered me. I eyed her narrowly, wondering what she was driving at.

"Of course; why?"

"Let's run!"

"Renée!"

She stood up suddenly, facing me . . . Very close, her arms apart. Something seemed to snap inside me and I caught her to me. I was mad, I suppose. It was the situation, her mood, the hat. "I would, Dick," she whispered, "really." Her eyes, dark and very close to mine, spoke volumes. Our lips met. I heard Burnett floundering about somewhere and started back. And still she clung to me, her whole body pressed against me.

"Steady on!" I muttered.

Her arms slipped down and she stole back to the case. "Oughtn't we to do something for that poor man?" she said very loudly. "Valdao, I mean; he must be stifled."

"We can't," I told her. "Karolin's got the key."

Burnett deposited Margharita on the road.

"Lord!' he muttered; "what a business! I missed the track in the fog. Seem to have been wandering about for hours."

Renée's voice chimed out again, entirely self-composed: "We thought you'd been rather a long time."

Margharita was really frightened now; she was clinging to Renée and I fancy she was crying. Burnett had proved himself an unreliable mount! He began telling me all about it, explaining where he thought he had gone adrift, excusing himself . . . Smells apparently affected him; they always had—ever since he was a child. When he was fighting in Flanders he always carried a bottle of Eau-de-Cologne. The odor of the swamp must have blotted out his other senses. I endeavored to lend a sympathetic ear, obsessed as I was with a sense of guilt, of faithlessness somehow to Juan, of a myriad of other conflicting sensations that I wanted to be alone to analyze.

Karolin called from the mist:

"Mr. Coombes! Can you hear me?"

"Hullo!" I cried, "I'm coming now."

I stepped down gingerly. The stuff was up to my knees again. One shoe had worked loose and I had a bother to keep it on.

"Here I am," he said almost at my elbow.

I bore right and found him, white-faced and shivering, staring into an open trunk—and the still, curled-up form of Valdao! The stench from the box was horrible, reminiscent of that one morning at the Carthagena. Choking down a feeling of nausea, I touched it; it was stone-cold! I swung round on Karolin.

"My God!" I muttered. "He's dead!"

Karolin gulped.

"I know," he said. "Awkward, isn't it? I made the holes big enough, too . . . and scarcely any water got in. It was fright, I suppose—or the jolting." He clasped his forehead with a muddy hand. *"Diable!"* he exclaimed suddenly, as if momentarily inspired: "Perhaps that accounts for it—"

"For what?" I demanded testily.

"For the way that big bird came back. Did you see the fury in its eyes? It was terrible!" His own eyes stared into mine, wide-open with excitement. "Valdao was the link between your friend and the White Owl . . . the *human* link . . . or perhaps only partly human. It knew we had killed Valdao—and flew at us to avenge him!"

This fresh theory staggered me, but I could frame no words to refute it; it coincided so closely with another of my own.

"Mitzakis thought we had Valdao somewhere," pursued Karolin. "That's why he passed us slowly that time. He was trying to see how many of us there were."

I shook myself. Emphasized by the grim trophy in the box, the whole business seemed unhealthy.

"What are we going to do with this?" I asked.

Karolin spread out his hands.

"Dump it in the swamp somewhere," he suggested. "He's a felon anyway. If we keep our mouths shut, the police will suppose Mitzakis pitched him there. It's the only way."

I saw he was right. We carried Valdao a matter of seventy yards from the trunk and dropped him. It was an unpleasant business. Karolin pressed the hunched-up form beneath the surface with his boot.

"There," he said, "that's done." There was a touch of bravado in his tone, but I could see he didn't like it.

Chapter 25

THE PLOT DEVELOPED AS WE WADED BACK. A mystery had to be evolved here, some plausible explanation to satisfy Renée until a more suitable opportunity arose for telling her the truth. I was annoyed now to think that I had told her about the contents of the box at all. It would have sufficed to have said simply that it was Karolin's.

We found the trunk again and Karolin slammed the lid.

"Phew!" he muttered; "it reeks!" He spat into the morass. "I've a suit of clothes in there at the bottom. It's an unpleasant thought, but presently I shall have to nerve myself to get into them. They'll be drier than these—and both are equally unwholesome! You can't stick at sentiment, can you? We couldn't in the war." I ran my eye over the trunk, examining the holes made by brace and bit . . . nice, clean-cut circles, roughly an inch and a half in diameter, running in an irregular line all round the top. I tried one of them with a couple of fingers, and got them badly jammed at the second joint. Whatever had been the cause of Valdao's death, it most certainly wasn't suffocation. I wondered if his heart was groggy. That run from the police might have started the trouble, and the bumping on the grid proved the last straw.

"Listen," I said presently. "Miss de Salis knows what was in there. I told her just now. What are we going to do about it?"

Karolin rubbed his chin.

"Tell her there was nothing inside when we un-roped it. She'll think Mitzakis released him while I was talking to you at the hotel. If the police begin to ask awkward questions, we know nothing about Valdao. Shutting him in there was merely a mad-brained scheme of my own. If we told them the truth, they're not likely to believe us."

I pondered it over and eventually agreed; there seemed nothing else for it.

"Don't say anything to Burnett," I enjoined. "We may enlighten him later, but not now."

We carried the trunk to the road. Renée and Margharita were standing close together; Burnett was walking up and down, trying to get warm. I reminded him there was still some luggage in the car and he made for it reluctantly, holding a handkerchief to his nose. Karolin sat down on the trunk. I saw him produce a clasp-knife and begin scraping off mud.

"I'll buy you a new suit," I laughed, "when we get to the next town."

He replied, without looking up:

"Thanks. It'll have to be a grand duke's misfit this time!" He stood up and lifted the lid. Presently he unearthed some of his own belongings. "We'll see how these go when they're aired," he muttered. The article to which he referred was a pair of blue serge trousers, frayed at the turn-ups. Hitching them over one arm, he trudged off into the night.

Renée came over to me.

"Why don't you get something out of your case and change?"

I shrugged my shoulders.

"I will, as soon as we get to the village."

"You might catch your death of cold by then." Her eyes sought the trunk. "Where is he?" she whispered.

I looked away from her.

"Gone, I'm afraid."

"Gone? Disappeared, you mean?"

"Yes."

"Since we've been here?"

I shook my head.

"In Paris, I fancy. He was inside when Karolin strapped it on the Morbizon. When he opened it just now, he wasn't there . . ."

She wrinkled her forehead.

"But, how funny!"

Karolin came back in his dry garments, whistling. Burnett scrambled from the morass with the last of the baggage. I managed to warn Renée to say nothing yet about Valdao. Burnett had discovered the flask. All of us, except Margharita, had a pick-me-up. Splitting up the bags between us, we headed for the village.

Three-quarters of a mile brought us to the door of the hoped-for inn—an unpretentious-looking establishment, with a farm-cart parked on one side and an ancient fountain immediately in front. By this time it was past midnight and the place was in darkness. Karolin hammered on the door. A window upstairs opened and a head looked out. Karolin spoke to the head and it disappeared. There was a long wait—and then a light showed behind the broad window-front. A short, unshaven man, his braces over his nightshirt, interrogated us; a tall, angular woman joined in from behind. Karolin explained and we were admitted. There was a bar inside, a gleaming coffee-machine, bare boards and a host of chairs stacked on small tables. We hooked five of them down and sat in a pathetic little semicircle in the midst of our hand-luggage . . .

I had not paid particular attention to what had been said, but I gathered that our reception at the Estaminet of the Three Swallows had been, to say the least of it, frigid! It was perfectly understandable: We were not on the main route to anywhere and these people resented being knocked up in the dead of night to attend to five chance travelers. Karolin was prowling about, perfectly at his ease now, ordering hot drinks and something to eat. He mentioned the bar in the bog, and immediately afterward our hosts began to thaw. Madame worked to a point of vantage from which to examine our luggage, our general appearance, the girls' frocks. A pretty girl of sixteen or so, the daughter of the house apparently, came in by a far doorway. The entire family retired to the background and held a consultation. Presently Madame advanced towards us, rather in the guise of the emissary of an erstwhile hostile power bearing a flag of truce. She had evidently sorted us out as two married couples and the chauffeur. She had three rooms she could offer—two doubles and a single. The double rooms were on the first floor, the single at the top of the house, but quite comfortable. She looked at Renée.

"Perhaps madame would prefer to see them?" Renée shot a wicked glance at me and burst out laughing. We all laughed. Madame appeared hurt, until the joke was explained to her, and then she joined in too. She shuffled back to the main body and explained the joke to them. More laughter followed, and the consultation began all over again. Once more the emissary approached, this time with amended terms. We clinched at two separate rooms for the girls and a sort of dormitory for the men. Either the house was amazingly elastic or, as I shrewdly suspected, the family was turning out for us. The little girl produced a can of hot water and the three of us trooped off to exchange our soiled garments for something clean. Monsieur, still displaying an expanse of nightshirt magnificent with red embroidery, escorted us up an uncarpeted flight to a long, narrow room distempered in pale blue and decorated with the ghastly photographic enlargement of himself in *poilu's* uniform and tin hat. He left us with a candle that had guttered badly and went on guttering while we washed.

We had brought up our own cases. Karolin, awaiting his turn with the only wash-basin turned down the coverlets and examined the beds.

"They're clean," he announced, "but I can't say much for the springs!"

"We're lucky to get in anywhere," I retorted. Burnett was making the best of a towel that would have been better employed as a table-napkin. An array of reeking garments littered the floor. We smoked and washed and exchanged fatuous remarks, while the portrait of mine host on the wall watched us with a fatherly interest.

Renée and Margharita were consuming coffee when we descended. I thought they made a charming picture without their hats. The daughter of the house brought in plates and things and an enormous omelette, assisted by a sleepy-looking youth in a baize apron and carpet slippers. Karolin and the youth embarked upon an exploration of the cellars and returned with a bottle of excellent wine. On the whole, it was very pleasant, a happy sequel to a breakneck drive from Paris and an adventure in a marsh. Karolin was quite at home. He addressed the girl as "Simone" and the youth as "Louis"; the rumomelette, it transpired, had been his own idea. There were rumors, too, of cold chicken.

"I'll he up with the lark in the morning," he announced. "I think we'll manage to get the car out all right. Louis has given me the address of a man with a lorry."

Renée glanced up from her plate.

"Do tell them to be careful. Fancy, Dick, we only had her this morning!—Are you feeling better?"

"Fine, thanks."

She surveyed me anxiously.

"You wouldn't like my hotwater bottle? I've asked Simone to fill it."

I shook my head.

"Baines ought to be here," she continued, "to be looking after you."

"I think I'm being very well looked after," I assured her. "Frankly, I'm rather glad to be rid of Baines for a bit. He annoys me. He sucks his teeth!"

Renée smiled.

"I suppose we shouldn't have left him and Marie together like that. It isn't respectable. Mrs. Baines would never forgive me, if she knew. I've a very soft spot in my heart for her, you know, Dick. How long have you had her?"

"Heaven knows!" I said.

The cold chicken materialized, escorted by a regiment of fried potatoes. It amazed me to reflect how these people worked. It would all go down in the bill, of course, but you couldn't have secured a similar repast at that hour in England for a king's ransom. Karolin informed me that the village was called Le Broc, and that Limoges was roughly fifty kilometers south of us. The meal came to an end. Margharita excused herself and retired. Burnett went up too, working, he assured us, on the principle that if one went to bed immediately after a meal one's slumbers were not interfered with. Karolin and Louis, now bosom friends, conversed across the bar. Simone had disappeared. Renée crept to the door and tried it; it was open. She beckoned me outside. Looking back as I went, I saw a family of mice feeding on the crumbs under our table.

The night was clear now. We stood together on a cobbled road, looking at the fountain. Her arm slipped through mine. "I feel a beast," she said. "I don't know what came over me tonight."

"It was my fault," I answered. "I was a fool."

"You weren't; you were simply wonderful. You know, you're an awful babe in some respects, Dick. It was a shame to take advantage of you. I don't know why I did it. It was the utter loneliness of the swamp, I suppose, and you carrying me like that. I felt like the siren of the pool! Stupid, wasn't it?"

Gray buildings frowned at us across the pave road, a butcher's with the shutters up, an *épicerie, a* draper's—crazy jalousies above that wanted a coat of paint . . . jagged, uneven roofs of clumsy tiles. The water at the fountain dribbled out in an unceasing stream. Ghosts lurked there—the ghosts of women who had washed their clothes there on well-worn boards for centuries. Beyond it another phantom lurked—Juan Mitzakis, my friend, the friend who had been betrothed to the woman who was by my side.

"I'm thinking of Juan," I answered. "It wasn't cricket, was it?"

She eyed me a little curiously, shuddered and withdrew her arm.

"You're tremendously loyal, Dick."

I didn't answer.

"Some people would say he had had his innings."

"Yes, I suppose some would."

She waited, but there was nothing to say or do. A car, with a single headlight, cluttered out of the night and was gone. An inner voice reminded me that Juan had tried to kill us all; another recalled me to a sense of duty.

"It's cold out here," I said. "We'd better go in."

"Good night, Dick," she whispered, and passed through the doorway out of sight.

Chapter 26

TRUE TO HIS PROMISE, Karolin rose early. The sound of water being poured into a basin aroused me from my slumbers, and I hastened to join him. Burnett's dental plates reposed in a tooth-glass
on the wash-stand. Burnett himself, minus these aids to perennial
youth, lay on his back beneath a tremendous eiderdown affair that
I had christened *the corpse,* snoring lustily. His clothes were
neatly folded on a chair, his bowler hat ornamented a bedpost. The
resemblance to a ferret was not so marked.

We stripped to the waist and washed in turn, shivering in the
icy blast from the open window. It was twenty past six by my
watch when we gained the passage and stole down the wooden
stairs, trying not to wake the girls. Early as it was, the family was
up and busy. Madame, a duster tied around her head, was plying a
bass-broom, toiling in a dust-cloud that all but eclipsed the small
tables with their burden of chairs. Simone smiled at us from behind the bar. Louis was outside, washing wine bottles at the fountain. He whistled Monsieur from the yard at the back. Between
them, they directed us to the house of Monsieur Charvoz, the gentleman with the lorry.

Monsieur Charvoz, a stout, thickset brigand, was oiling his ve-
hicle a good half mile down the road. Karolin explained our pre-
dicament, the exact position of the Morbizon, the necessity for
haste. Monsieur Charvoz dug out a grimy list of the tasks the lorry
was already committed to undertake that day, waved his arms violently and trudged into the house. Karolin, nothing daunted, followed on his heels, myself at a more discreet distance. Fair words,
argument that seemed interminable, bribery and corruption, eventually secured us first place on that list. We made the acquaintance
of Charvoz's two sons, climbed with them into the back of the
lorry, and Charvoz *père* started the engine.

We had put on our soiled clothes, anticipating something re-
sembling a repetition of the night before. Before many minutes
had elapsed, we were grateful for the precaution. The methods of
the Charvoz firm were inclined to be rough and ready; they would
have rescued the Morbizon, in some sort of condition and any side

up, in half-an-hour. Directed by Karolin and myself, helped by ropes, chains and a good deal of swearing, she came to the road-side on even keel, with nothing bent or damaged and the paint-work hardly scratched. Lifting her to the road itself was another matter. After several abortive attempts and a lot of discussion, one of the younger Frenchmen hurried off on foot and returned after a lengthy interval with the breakdown gang from a local garage. Shortly before nine the Morbizon left her bed of ooze and shambled somewhat ungracefully on to terra firma.

She was as filthy as I have ever seen a car and a good deal of water had slopped inside. There was water in the carburetor and the engine declined to answer either to self-starter or cranking-handle. The Charvoz family towed her to the village, the break-down gang gathered up their tools and Karolin and I went in to breakfast.

Burnett was strolling about outside, his hard hat just visible above a pale green newspaper.

"Hullo!" he greeted us. "You've been busy, I see. I suppose that was our car that passed just now. Why didn't you wake me?"

"We hadn't the heart," I told him.

He thrust the paper into my hand.

"It's all in here now," he declared; "that business at the Cartha-gena, the scene in the Rue Solferino . . . the whole bag of tricks, in fact. It's on the front page, whole columns of it . . . *'Mystery of a White Car'* . . . *'Desperate Drive through Paris'* . . . *'Two Detec-tives Killed in Collision'* . . . *'Private Car Gives Chase'* . . . He did another spectacular drive, apparently, through Limoges."

"They haven't got him?" I asked. Burnett shook his head.

"Not up to the moment that 'rag' was published. But it's only a question of time. The whole country's out to get him. The police'll be on the look-out everywhere."

I carried the paper inside and sat down, wondering how far Juan had gone, where we should go next. The whole thing seemed hopeless. How could one help a man, argue with him, bring him to his senses, when he was blazing a trail of diabolical crime across a continent? Glancing through last night's casualty-list, I almost hoped that the police would take him. Renée had been queer last night, overwrought I thought. She had said Juan had "had his in-nings." A remark which appeared to imply that even she had lost interest in the man she had persuaded me to seek. A temptation seized me to turn back and throw in my hand—until I remembered that the affair had started when I had fired at the White Owl in Mexico.

Karolin reminded me I was wet. We went up and changed. The girls were still absent when we commenced breakfast. I told Simone to give them *petit déjeuner* in their rooms. Karolin gulped down his second cup of coffee and went out to see what sort of a job the mechanics were making of the Morbizon. He paused in the doorway on his way out.

"Fill her right up, I suppose?" he queried.

"Oh, yes."

"Any idea where we're bound?"

"Not the remotest."

He rubbed his chin reflectively.

"What about running through Valdao's papers? I gave you them in that packet, just before we pushed off. They might be helpful."

I went up and fetched them.

When I got down again I found a couple of bronzed-faced, blue-clad gendarmes at our table talking to Burnett. They had heard from the proprietor that there were strangers in the village. Possibly, too, Charvoz had told them about the car. Decent, clean-limbed young fellows they were, keen on their job and pleasant enough to converse with. I noted that Burnett had had the good sense to offer them *vin blanc*.

"I've just been explaining to these gentlemen," he called to me, "that it was your car that followed the white saloon from Paris."

"Quite so," I stammered; "that's right." I joined the group and shook hands all round, not a little anxious to discover to what extent Mr. Burnett had compromised us. But I need not have worried. Burnett had not been a police officer for nothing! It transpired that he had related his half of the story and omitted ours. He had recognized that the Paris police had the number of our car as well as Juan's, and that nothing we could say, or omit to say, could alter that. His testimony, reduced to simple terms, ran as follows: He had been summoned by a member of the Spanish Embassy in London to inquire into the supposed recognition of the murderer of the late Luiz Manzanarez in Paris. The Señorita Margharita had directed him to the flat where Juan was living. We, friends of Margharita's, had turned up with a car. Believing the man who called himself Julian Murray to be on the point of departing for Spain, we had driven with our luggage to the Gare d'Orleans, witnessed the encounter with the police in the Solferino, and done our best to overtake him. Then followed a brief history of the journey south and the final climax in the swamp.

I corroborated this, brought down Renée and Margharita, who corroborated it too. Karolin turned up with the Morbizon. The officers examined it inside and out and jotted down full particulars. We settled our bill, disposed our baggage in the container and on the grid, indulged in more hand-shaking, squeezed in the gendarmes somehow and drove off to repeat the story at the nearest police-office. A bearded gentleman cross-examined us and appeared satisfied. Burnett's credentials were eminently satisfactory. As for the rest of us, our faces corresponded more or less with the ghastly portraits stuck on our passports. Renée, Karolin, and I, had, in effect, become back-numbers. They were only interested in Margharita, because she had seen Juan both in London and Paris —and in Burnett, because he was acting for her. The bearded gentleman parted from us in the main street, having obtained Burnett's promise that he would proceed to Paris as soon as possible and get in touch with the authorities there. Renée was thanked for the public-spiritedness that had prompted her to lend her car.

We lunched there and drove on afterward to Limoges. We saw Margharita and Burnett off by the afternoon train. Margharita, I fancy, was sorry to go. Her companion seemed less sorry— possibly because he knew there were less smells in Paris than outside! The train started, there was the usual waving of handkerchiefs. Renée and I were alone. I took her arm.

"Now, young woman," I said, "you've got to behave."

She grimaced at me.

"Have you promised to write to Margharita?" she asked.

I felt like shaking her.

"I'm not infatuated, if that's what you mean. I've hardly said a dozen words to her since we met."

For a wonder, she didn't comment on this. We went back to the car and drove to an hotel. It was a place of comfort and running water. Taking things easy between tea and dinner, I dug out Valdao's papers and placed them in a smelly heap on the dressing-table. There was roughly two thousand francs in notes and some odd coins. I examined a perfectly good passport issued in Tampico: "Valdao . . . Anton . . . 54 . . ." and the usual descriptive details. The rest comprised a couple of hotel-bills, a London tram-ticket, an ear-marked map of Paris, published by some tourist agency, a black leather wallet that was empty, and the torn half of a foreign envelope with an address scrawled on it in purple ink:

"Helvetia, Rue Tarbes, Bordeaux."
Underneath was the single word "Amazon."
I recognized the writing as Juan's.

Chapter 27

"HELVETIA, RUE TARBES, BORDEAUX!"—"AMAZON!"

I sat in my shirt-sleeves staring at it, wondering what its significance might be. In the absence of other written matter, it built itself up in my estimation as a clue of paramount importance. Another important factor was that Valdao had insisted to Karolin that he was Juan's servant, and not the evil influence we had previously thought him. Since the beginning of time it has always been the outlook of fond parents, of staunch friends, to adhere to the belief that the prodigal was more sinned against than sinning—that "bad company" was at the back of his misdeeds. That, I fancied, was where I had tripped up, and Renée. And yet, the deeper we had probed into the mystery, the more apparent it had become that Juan Mitzakis was the driving force of that mysterious trio, although on two distinct occasions he had seemed to display fear of the White Owl. Somehow I jerked back to the possible supernatural aspect. Supposing, purely for the sake of argument, that Juan Mitzakis has dabbled in the "black art" in which none of us seriously believed; supposing he had succeeded in securing the cooperation of an evil spirit in the guise of a bird. Dabbling in mysteries, like an unskilled mechanic let loose in a power station, he might still be afraid of the spirit that was serving him. Something might fuse and destroy everything, the formula might fail, the White Owl might turn on its master! Utter madness, of course! but every bit as feasible as a bird of such extraordinary intelligence that it could be trained to baffle the police in a crisis or force the driver of a high-powered car into a swamp! And then, of course, there was the mystery of the bullet-wounds Valdao himself had shown me . . .

I pulled on my jacket and went down to the hall. The sleek young man at the desk came to my assistance. Between us, we discovered that the Helvetia was, as I had imagined, an hotel; it was marked "first-class" in all the books. *Amazon* of course, might have meant anything, but it was interesting to learn that the Compagnie Generale Bordelaise owned a vessel of that name, that made spasmodic sailings from Bordeaux to the West Indies and

Vera Cruz. The young man promised to ascertain when next she was due out.

I sauntered into the street and bought some tobacco. A late edition, purchased at the same time, satisfied me that Juan was still at large. The same extraordinary luck that had helped him in London and through Paris seemed to be persisting. It was surprising the number of people all over France who had seen a mysterious white saloon moving at a high speed! The paper published an account of Burnett's interview with the police that morning. Margharita, I noticed, obtained "honorable mention"; Renée and I, fortunately, were not mentioned at all.

By the drive-in to the lock-ups I ran into Karolin. He had bought a new overcoat—a blue rainproof with a belt. From the state of his hands I judged he had been tinkering with the Morbizon.

He murmured something about one of the tappets. I gave him the paper to read. He did so, leaning against the wall. It seemed that the habits of taxi-drivers had become ingrained in him.

"He's having a good run for his money!" he remarked at length. "But they're bound to get him."

"You'd think so," I agreed.

"Will you be wanting the car tonight?" was his next question.

I shook my head.

"Unless something unusual occurs to alter our plans, we shall be stopping here. Miss de Salis is tired."

We entered the hotel together. In the elevator he recollected something.

"What about that packet? Did you find anything there?"

I nodded.

"Come to my room, as soon as you've washed," I suggested. "There are one or two matters about which I would rather like your opinion."

For an hour or more we smoked and talked, while traffic rumbled its way through the street below and the wind that had come up with the darkness sent great pockets of rain lashing against the panes. Karolin, that creature of many tongues and many callings, propounded theory after theory, sometimes sitting astride a chair, his arms folded on the back, sometimes pacing the room, distributing little heaps of cigarette-ash over the carpet. The writing on the envelope, he asserted, might be a ruse, a trick invented by Juan to induce his pursuers to concentrate on Bordeaux while he and Naia crossed into Spain. In any case, one could always put in a long-

distance call to the Helvetia and find out if he were there or expected to arrive. I objected that he might have changed his name
and that, not having seen him, they could scarcely be expected to
recognize him by his description. His comment on this was that
they would know if they had reserved rooms for three passengers
for the *Amazon.* His main argument was always that the address
that Juan had written could be of little use to Valdao, because he
doubted if he could read. And the more he talked, the more I became convinced that the clue was genuine. Possibly, if Valdao on
his trip to Europe had learned to read only a little, the address had
been given to him to memorize and destroy; possibly, supposing
that his education had not advanced that far, it was given him to
show to people when he was asking the way. Juan must have recognized the risk of their being separated, and provided for that
eventuality. Bordeaux and the *Amazon,* I contended, formed his
last card when everything else had failed.

Gradually we found ourselves caught in a vicious circle, that
always brought us back to the same question: Who or what was
Valdao? That he was a *solid* human being was proved beyond
doubt. We had seen him run from the police in Paris, Karolin had
fastened him in a box . . . both of us had seen and handled him
when dead . . . And Valdao was not the White Owl, nor the White
Owl Valdao. That, too, was firmly established. Glimmerings came
to us as we talked, glimmerings of something outside the accepted
order of things. Wide-eyed, half-ashamed, we had stumbled on to
the threshold of a strange world. Which of us voiced it I forget.
Juan Mitzakis, driven half-insane by the fall down the shaft had
come under the influence of the White Owl—a spirit, if you like—
disembodied, yet still haunting the earth in a shape that was visible
or invisible, at will . . . the emblem of a strange creed. Acting in
the guise of a medium, a half-human link between these two, came
Valdao, the man with the green eyes. And thirdly, comprehensible
in a way to ourselves, yet utterly incomprehensible to Renée, figured Naia, priestess at the shrine, another "influence" perhaps,
given to Juan, not as his mistress, but rather as his soul-mate.

It was seven by the church clock outside when Karolin's voice
broke the silence that had fallen.

"The police know him as 'Julian Murray.' We don't know what
name appears on his passport. He may have renewed the old one,
the one he had when you knew him. The British Consulate might
never have heard that he was supposed to be dead."

I looked up.

"Well?" I demanded, "what then?"

"In that case, if there's anything in this *Amazon* clue, he'll appear on their passenger-list as 'Mitzakis.' Why not telephone the shipping-company instead of the Helvetia?"

I nodded.

"Yes," I agreed, "we'll do that. If their reply is satisfactory, we'll push on to Bordeaux."

"You see," he pursued, "Mitzakis may not want to return to Mexico. According to the yarn he pitched to you, he believes himself invulnerable, impervious to arrest. The others may not have been quite so confident. The hornet's nest they've raised about their ears may have scared them badly. Naia, too, may have been homesick."

"You think he's succumbed to a majority of two to one?"

"It's just possible. But then, of course, he's mad as they make 'em, so what's the use of bothering with his motives! Even if he's booked rooms at the Helvetia and berths on the *Amazon*—there's no saying we shall find him. He may change his mind."

"If he suspects we're in possession of that paper," I said, "most probably he will . . ."

He added another link to the endless chain of cigarettes he had smoked since he came into the room. It was as catching as a yawn or an epidemic. I found myself following suit. Bordeaux loomed up big on my mental horizon; it seemed certain we must go there, at all costs. Better, I argued, to be on a false scent than on none at all! And yet, for Juan to enter Bordeaux at such a moment appeared to be the height of all folly. It would be madness to go there with Naia, suicide to take with him the White Owl . . . As for the *Amazon,* a boat in these days to a man escaping from justice was little better than a prison. There was the imminent risk of recognition *en route* . . . irons . . . wireless communication with the shore.

On the stroke of the half-hour we joined Renée in the dining-room.

"Feel better?" I asked as we sat down.

She laughed.

"Tons, thanks. I've been asleep, and I'm not the least bit ashamed to admit it. You look as if you could do with a course of the same medicine!" She caught the waiter's eye. "Let's have a cocktail; it'll do us all the good in the world!"

She had come down in excellent fettle. Throughout the meal she chattered almost incessantly, remarking on the sprinkling of people at the other tables, entertaining us with stories she had heard in Nice, Bordighera, Monaco. Listening to her, one would have imagined she hadn't a care in the world. But there were moments, too, when the smile vanished completely and a hard expression took its place, moments when her dark eyes searched my face as if anxious to discover what my private thoughts were. I felt that, but for Karolin, she would have whispered: "You don't really think me an abandoned woman, do you, Dick?" And I knew she wouldn't have believed me if I had told her.

We moved presently to a small, rather shabby *salon,* where ponderous chairs offered a minimum of comfort. Poised on a corner-cabinet, a cone loudspeaker was playing gramophone records from Toulouse. It was harsh and unpleasant; the sepulchral voice of the announcer, sandwiched between the items, hardly bore comparison with our soft-voiced careful-speaking gentlemen at home.

Renée pointed to it.

"Can't we turn it off or something?"

I looked around helplessly; Karolin, the man with the practical turn of mind, advanced towards the instrument intending, in the absence from the room of the set itself, to disconnect it altogether. Suddenly a strident band selection petered out midway . . .

A fresh voice began speaking, a woman's this time . . . distinctly preferable.

Renée caught my arm.

"Listen!"

In the tense silence an important item of news came over: *"The White Owl Mystery: A white saloon-car corresponding to the one being sought by the police, has been found in the Gave near Luz-St-Sauveur, Hautes Pyrenees . . . Apparently, it had crashed through a parapet and fallen over a precipice some fifty metres deep . . . The machine has been completely wrecked. Little hope is entertained that its occupants have survived. The Gave has been flooded by recent torrential rains, and a heavy fall of snow is rendering the search for the bodies more difficult . . ."*

The music started again, and Karolin disconnected the loudspeaker. Renée looked at me.

"Poor Juan!" she whispered.

Chapter 28

POOR JUAN!

I wondered, and I could see that Karolin wondered too. It was tragic but, however one chose to look at it, the best way out. The name of Juan Mitzakis, that was still dear to me, need never be besmirched; it would go down in the annals of French criminology that Julian Murray had murdered and fled and died . . . and nobody, outside our charmed circle, would be any the wiser. The White Owl would survive longer than Juan. When his memory had faded men would still be recording the exploits of that mysterious bird, speculating as to its origin, its significance. Visitors to Paris would be shown the spot in the Rue Treille where it had first appeared, and the spot in the Rue Solferino where it had launched its second attack on the gendarmes. The Carthagena, however, would not make Valdao's room an exhibit: rather, they would endeavor to live it down. The Carthagena was a respectable hotel!

And, because it was the best way out for everybody concerned, Karolin and I doubted if it had ever happened. In other words, it was too good to be true. Renée, on the other hand, had taken it for granted.

"Of course it's true," she insisted. "They would never be allowed to broadcast a thing like that if it wasn't. It sounds so sensible to me—the heavy snowstorm and Juan driving like that . . . I suppose he missed the road and couldn't stop. I'm told things like that often happen in the winter."

I declined to argue.

"We'll run down there tomorrow," I decided, "and try to find out something. It's over two hundred miles. We ought to start early."

Karolin bent forward in his chair.

"Wait a bit," he said, his eyes gleaming with excitement. "One of us had better go to Bordeaux."

Renée frowned.

"Why Bordeaux?"

I explained that we had found an address and what appeared to be the name of a vessel on an envelope among Valdao's belongings. I had barely finished when Karolin burst in again.

"This last piece of news has altered the entire aspect of the case," he insisted. "Up to now I'd thought that Spain was the destination and Bordeaux the false scent. Although even that was open to doubt, because he was by no means certain of either the police or ourselves hitting on that envelope. To have served any useful purpose, it should have been left behind in Valdao's room."

"That's rather what I thought," I interposed.

"Now," continued Karolin, emphasizing the point with his clenched fist, "you've a situation that might have been calculated to set us all doubting—a magnificent false scent that'll satisfy the gendarmerie for a bit, because they don't know about Bordeaux—and that should unsettle us, knowing even what we do, because when we last sighted Mitzakis he was driving pretty madly. You see, I know that district; I've driven there from Pau. A charabanc-party of twenty-two went over there once, roughly I imagine in the same spot where Mitzakis is reported to have fallen. Everybody knows about it; there's an inscription built into the wall. Some of the bodies were picked up miles away, and that was in the season. In winter the Gave will be far worse. It may be weeks before they're satisfied whether Juan and the girl were in that car or not—and by that time Mitzakis could be in Mexico."

Renée gasped.

"Then you don't think he's dead?"

"Not a bit of it! He had to get rid of the white saloon somewhere. Mr. Burnett foresaw that. The make of his car and his number was in every local paper. He couldn't hope to get a second fill-up except at the pistol-point. I contend that he kept the engine running, pushed in a gear and jumped off, letting the saloon crash her own way through the stone wall and go down. It had to drop clear; there was nothing to stop it. It would pitch into the middle of the torrent and have the water washing right through it in no time."

"How would they get away?" asked Renée.

Karolin bit his lip.

"That I can't tell you. On foot for a spell, I suppose. I doubt if they would have risked the train. It's quiet there and strangers would be noticed. They might have hailed a chance car, driven from the district and bribed the driver to keep his mouth shut—or knocked him on the head and left him somewhere. Anyhow, the snow would have covered up any tracks they might have made near the scene of the accident."

The youth from the hall came in, stared at the loud-speaker and at us, then connected it up again and went out. He must have visited the machine, too, and put on more reaction, for we were treated to a frenzied crescendo of American dance music.

Renée stuffed her fingers in her ears.

"Supposing," she shouted above the din, "Juan left Naia behind somewhere—to rejoin him somewhere else? He might have, you know. He could have got away easier alone."

We trooped from the room to the elevator and, by means of the elevator, to my own particular apartment. Karolin had been pondering her statement all the way up.

"Sapristi!" he ejaculated as I closed the door, "I believe that's right. Tarbes would have been a handy spot, handy for Bordeaux too. Nobody was likely to suspect her while she was by herself. She could have had the Owl . . . in a box . . . That's what I should have done—Who's going to Bordeaux tomorrow?"

"I will, if you like," I said.

Renée objected to this arrangement.

"No, Dick, let Mr. Karolin go. He knows his way about better than you do. And you can drive the Morbizon. You did it quite nicely in Paris." She rose and I opened the door for her. "Good night, Mr. Karolin," she said from the corridor, "I don't know what we should do without you! I'm writing a note to Marie, Dick, before I go to bed. Do you want me to include a message for Baines?"

"No," I returned, "I don't think so."

"Very well, I'll just send him your love."

She fluttered off with a wave of the hand. I closed the door again and looked at Karolin.

"Go carefully in Bordeaux when you get there," I warned him. "Remember we killed Valdao! . . . *and the White Owl never forgets . . . !*"

"Whatever that may mean!" he laughed. He went out shortly afterwards, whether to bed or to have another look at those tappets I never knew. I dug out a book and began reading. Around ten I rang for whisky and a siphon of soda. The waiter, a grinning, dark-haired boy in an absurdly long tail-coat, brought me a brand I had never heard of, informing me it was all they had. Half-an-hour later he was back with a message from Renée:

"The English mademoiselle would be glad if you could oblige her with a stamp."

I sent her all I had and settled down to my book again. I heard eleven strike somewhere . . . half-past . . . midnight . . . No traffic rattled over the roadway below. There were no voices, nothing . . . A mouse popped up by the radiator, saw me and promptly disappeared . . . We seemed to have dropped into the realm of mice . . . There had been some at Le Broc. I caught myself dozing over my book, drank some more whisky and endeavored to concentrate, knowing full well that I ought to undress and turn in. But the novel and the intense stillness of Limoges after Paris held me. I nodded again, rose and stretched my arms, looked for my pipe and filled it resolutely, giving myself another half-hour.

I was standing by the round table in the center of the room, feeling for matches, when the door opened quite suddenly. I looked up and started. Instead of the youth with the flapping tails, Juan Mitzakis stood in the entry, surveying me with a face like thunder.

"*So!*" he whispered in a tone I had never heard him use before. He lurched in like a man who had been drinking, yet when he closed the door there was hardly a sound. He looked like an Apache, with the shabby check cap pulled over his eyes, the muffler at his throat, the wide-legged trousers falling over cloth-sided boots. His lip and chin showed two days' growth of dark beard, and his eyes were the eyes of a hunted creature.

"It's you!" I retorted, getting command of myself. "Come in and sit down. I'm glad you've come. Now we can see about getting you out of this mess."

Scorning my invitation apparently, he lolled against the wall, mouthing at me in a disgusting, uncanny way. It didn't occur to me then to inquire how he had found us out, or how he had succeeded in passing the night-porter. The thought that was uppermost in my mind was that he was here, a fugitive from justice. I believed, now that he was driven into a corner, that there were chances of reasoning with him and getting him away.

"I warned you to keep out of this," he jerked out suddenly. "Why didn't you?"

I shrugged my shoulders.

"You know very well why I didn't. I wanted to help you; that's why—separate you from companions that are no earthly use to you—stop you continuing this mad business of yours—get you back to myself—and Renée."

At the mention of her name he raised both arms aloft and grimaced at the ceiling.

"She—? Oh, yes! Very nice too! We'll talk to her presently." He advanced a couple of paces towards me. "Where's Valdao?" he rapped out. "What have you done with him?"

"I—?" I stammered, taken off my guard.

"Valdao—?"

A thought crossed my mind. So that was why he had come? The Owl perhaps had directed him, but Valdao was dead—and the "contact" was weakening!

"Valdao—yes—" he rapped at me again.

"Where is he? You know; you must know. God! what a fool you are, Dick! I told you to keep away. You're no use at handling—*devils!*"

I lit my pipe.

"And you," I retorted, detecting what I believed to be signs of weakening in his manner, "are a mighty poor sort of devil! They've got you on the run, my friend—not devil doctors either, but the police. And you've had to rig yourself out like that to get away!"

He had lurched against the wall again and the mouthing had ceased. I saw him bury his head in his hands and a shudder pass through his frame.

"What about sitting in that chair," I suggested, "and talking sense for a change? You don't suppose I left England for my health, do you? I wanted to do you the best turn I could. If you doubt that, tell me why I haven't exposed you. It would have been a simple matter, you know."

The room seemed to stifle him. He staggered to the window, fumbled with the catch and threw it open to its fullest extent. The night air came in, damp and chill; great gusts shook the casements. I could see water dropping past the opening from a faulty gutter, see it trickling inside. He was upon me almost before I knew it.

"Come on," he hissed. "Where is he? Where's Valdao?"

"If it comes to that," I hedged, putting the table between us, "where's Naia?" I was maneuvering towards the trestle and my suitcase; my automatic was there. I fancied the sight of a gun might shake him into a more reasonable frame of mind.

My shaft pulled him up short.

"Naia—" he muttered, a vein on his forehead twitching, "Naia—" He clutched the edge of the table with both hands and his laugh was horrible to hear. "You liked her, didn't you, Dick?

Met her in your tent—in Mexico. You like Renée too. Well, I killed her, if you want to know. She stood me out, you see—wouldn't confess why she spoke to you in Paris." The laugh resounded again. "I pushed her over the cliff in the car—and jumped as it fell! I had the luck of the devil there, Dick! But then, you see, I am a devil, aren't I?" His expression changed to one of diabolical fury. "Give me Valdao! I must have him—I'm lost, don't you understand?" With a sudden movement he pitched the table behind him—book, siphon, everything. "My God! you can't trifle with me, Dick! I want Valdao—and I mean to have him. You know who had him last, what they did with him—I tell you I don't often give people so long to make up their minds. I kill!" He folded his arms and laughed once more—the same unearthly paroxysm that Karolin and I had heard through the shutters. "Oh, I can kill, Dick! You've seen how I kill. People we hate—people who annoy us—people who don't do what we want!"

His hand slipped to his coat. He came at me, brandishing a knife.

"Where is he?"

Hands in pockets, I waited for him. "You'll be a fool if you bother any more about him," I retorted. "Valdao murdered a detective in Paris. They want him as much as they do you."

A sight of papers on the dressing-table checked him. He shot off at a tangent, pawing over them. I scented real trouble now, flicked open the lid of my case and found the automatic. Valdao's papers were among that heap; he was bound to see them there. I had half withdrawn the pistol when a blow like a sledge-hammer sent me flying across the bed. Fingers like so many steel bars clutched at my throat. Struggling, I saw Juan's leering face above me—the broken peak of that preposterous cap—six inches of gleaming steel poised in midair.

Something fluttered at the window and, with it, poisonous and nauseating, came the familiar odor. The whole room was full of it. The White Owl flew in, hovered between Juan and the window, until there seemed nothing back there but green eyes and wings that stretched from wall to wall . . . Juan glanced back at it and muttered something that sounded like a question. The fingers all but strangled me, but my own that held the pistol still had power. I raised the barrel furtively, directed it, hooked a forefinger over the trigger. I felt I could kill too, but I didn't want to. It was a question of self-preservation.

His eyes were on me again. The knife was descending—moving with slow deliberation towards my heart. I swung to one side, blinking to avoid those green eyes that hovered by the ceiling. The fingers at my throat twisted me back. I stuck the barrel into his coat.

The door-handle rattled and I heard a scream. The grip at my throat relaxed, faded away and was gone. The smell still hung in the room. I saw the White Owl shrink and flash through the window, as if panic-stricken, saw Juan backing in horror across the carpet, stride the low sill and vanish. The room was empty again; there was only Renée at the door—Renée in a blue silk wrap, staring with scared eyes. She ran to the window and closed it, fastening it with shaking hands. Presently she was bending over me, sobbing hysterically.

"I felt something was wrong, Dick," she whispered, "and had to come. You didn't mind, did you?" Something cold touched my cheek, something that dangled from the chain at her throat. It was the silver crucifix Juan had dropped on the hillside in Mexico!

Chapter 29

"A SUDDEN HUSH fell on the temple and every man present cov-
ered his face. There came the sound of a gong and a fluttering of
giant wings, as the grim bird of sacrifice was released. Only one
of all that vast multitude felt the creature pause, the touch of its
talons on his flesh. Not daring to look, he called his own name
aloud and the High Priest by the stone altar repeated it. Again the
fluttering, fading off into the distance, an eerie shriek perhaps—
and then the gong... In the tense silence that followed, a
woman's voice, clear and penetrating, chanted the single sentence
of a simple creed: 'He who sees the White Owl dies...!' "

This, the only connected portion of Juan's book that I had
heard, came to me word for word almost as Renée had quoted to
me at the New Venice, while I lay there gasping for breath. And,
close on its heels as it were, came a jumble of something Juan
himself had told me:

"... came to the earth in fantastic shape in 1527 ... was driven
into a cavern by the presence of mind of a Spanish priest *and a*
crucifix..."

It was strange that! Mitzakis had dropped the chain with the
crucifix while we were pulling up that door. I had picked it up,
intending to give it to him, but had forgotten. Could it be that that
was the reason that the White Owl had turned its attentions to Juan
rather than myself? It certainly looked like it. But for that trifling
incident, it might have been I who was roaming the world, mur-
dering at random, while Juan and Renée were drifting around, trying to stop me. I stared at the ceiling, wondering if they would.
They would have been married by then, with possibly a baby in
the offing. In any case, to imagine a complete reversal of things
was difficult.

It dawned on me quite suddenly that I was undressed and in
bed. My head throbbed ... there was a bandage of sorts, that felt
cold and damp, wrapped around my neck. Somebody had shaded
the light. Figures pottered around in the gloom—Karolin, with
pyjama-legs jutting from his new rainproof, messing about by the
wash-basin: Renée measuring out some fluid into a tumbler. The

stupidity of the whole business annoyed me. I wasn't ill! I was on the point of protesting when a ghastly fear swept over me, a kind of vague suspicion that I had gone mad and been imagining things. The sight of an unsheathed knife on the round table reassured me. It was the weapon Juan had flourished over me when I had been screwing up my nerve to shoot him.

I sat bolt upright.

"Hullo!" I said; "what's the time?"

They both jumped. Renée hurried across to me with the glass.

"You must lie down," she said in a hushed voice; "you must really."

"Why?" I demanded.

"Because you're not well."

"But I am," I lied. "I'm as fit as a fiddle. Why on earth shouldn't I be? You haven't told me what the time is yet."

"Half-past four," interposed Karolin from the basin. "We've been over three hours bringing you round."

I stared at Renée.

"Bringing me round from what?"

She burst into tears.

"Oh, Dick," she wailed, "they nearly killed you. You were at your last gasp when I came in. It—it frightened me to death! That horrible dream I told you about had begun all over again. I awoke with a ghastly premonition of disaster. Then I heard voices along the corridor . . . yours . . . then Juan's, chanting some terrible dirge . . ."

"Dirge!" I repeated. "I don't remember that."

"I slipped on a wrap and hurried to your door. There was a noise inside like somebody choking . . . and a beastly indescribable smell . . . I tapped, but nobody heard me. Then I threw it open and screamed at the top of my voice. I don't think there can be anybody else sleeping on this floor, because nobody came . . . You were lying half across the bed. Juan was bending over you, muttering gibberish, with the point of a knife held against your chest . . . The White Owl was there too, bigger, worse than I had ever imagined . . . It saw me and made for me. I screamed again—and it went—out of the window . . . Juan saw me and started up, snarling like a savage beast. There was blood already on the point of his knife—your blood, Dick! He stared hard at me and went too, swiftly, silently . . . I expected to hear him fall on the pavement, but he didn't—and there was nothing outside when I looked. I closed the window and came to you. Then I fetched Mr. Karolin."

"It was the crucifix," I muttered, and pointed to her throat.

Karolin moved to the table and picked up the knife.

" 'Laroche, Boulevard des Italiens, Paris,' " he read aloud, looking at the printing on the blade. "Curious that, don't you think? The Señorita Manzanarez saw him outside that shop."

I sank back on the pillow, feeling stupidly weak and exhausted. Renée held me up and forced some liquid between my lips. The room was going round and round. It stopped and I could think quite clearly. Her story of the incident varied from my own recollection and yet, oddly enough, I knew that she was right and I was wrong. For the first time I became conscious of a pain over my heart. There was a pad of something under my pyjama-jacket, fixed there with adhesive plaster.

I suppose I fell asleep.

It was light when I awoke again, but the curtains were still drawn across the windows. Renée was seated at the table writing letters. Karolin was not in the room.

She looked up presently and saw that I was awake.

"How are you?" she asked, coming over.

"Fine!" I said, and I spoke without exaggeration. The throbbing at the temples had gone, a chest-wound that could merely have been superficial gave me no pain. I sat up and stretched. "The trouble with all you young women is," I smiled, "that you want to make a hospital case out of a cold in the head!"

She tried to prop me up with a pillow.

"There's gratitude for you!" she retorted. "D'you realize I haven't slept a wink since two this morning?"

"Sorry!" I murmured contritely, "but you should have. What's happened to Karolin?"

"I sent him to Bordeaux by an early train. I thought you would be annoyed if I didn't. I wanted to send for a doctor, but he advised me not to do so, unless I could possibly help it. He thought it would make a lot of talk and we should have the police here, asking awkward questions.—What do you feel like?"

"I feel like dressing."

"Don't be difficult, Dick. I'm sure you oughtn't to be getting up yet. I meant what would you like to eat?"

"Anything you can lay your hands on."

"Honestly?"

She examined my throat externally with a critical eye; she threatened to make an internal observation with the aid of a dessert-spoon, but I firmly refused to allow it. Indisputably, she made

a very charming amateur nurse, but I was certain she hadn't the remotest idea what to look for. I had to show her how to take my
pulse! Her watch told me it was ten minutes to twelve.

"I tell you what," I said, "order lunch for both of us up here,
and tell 'em to put in a bottle of the Pommard we had last night. I
feel I could tackle some of that."

She gave me a thermometer to suck. "I wish I knew more about
this sort of thing, Dick," she sighed. "I feel certain you shouldn't
attempt 'solids.' Wouldn't you prefer bread and milk?"

"There is nothing in this world that I detest more!"

"But if it's good for you—?"

"I don't believe bread and milk was ever good for anybody," I
returned.

"Very well," she replied; "I'll run down and see what's on the
menu."

As soon as she had gone, I got up and locked the door. I was a
bit unsteady on my pins, but a cold sluice at the basin pulled me
together. Fearing she might return at any moment, I half dressed
before shaving. I had just lathered when she tried the handle, then
knocked. Razor in hand, I went over and let her in. At sight of me,
she recoiled.

"Well!—If you aren't the limit!"

I stropped my razor cheerfully.

"You see," I remarked, "I decline to be a stretcher case. I always have and I always shall. I disliked that means of transport in
the war!"

She hesitated.

"What do I do now? Go away until you've finished?"

"No," I insisted, "It's your job to stand by—in case I swoon or
something. Not, of course, that I have any intention of swooning,
but you never know!'

She watched me passing an old-fashioned "cutthroat" over my
cheek—a job that required concentration, for my hands, I discovered, were none too steady. As a general rule, I hated people
watching me shave, but somehow Renée was different. It didn't
annoy me even when she talked.

"How funny! Do you have to go through that performance
every morning?"

"Every morning."

"And don't you ever cut yourself?"

"Damn! I have now! You needn't get excited; it was just a
'snick.' There! that's finished . . . Shaving, my dear Renée, is one

of those irritating modern necessities. It began to come in when soup was invented."

"Don't be disgusting!"

"I'm not. I'm merely trying to educate you."

She perched herself on the bed, feet dangling.

"Do you really think I want educating, Uncle Richard?" I paused in my ablutions and stared at her. She hadn't called me that since that vampire business by the swamp. It had amused me at first; now I was feeling that I didn't like it a bit. It accentuated the difference in our ages, made one feel damnably old!

"There are times," I retorted, "when I think you want *smacking!*"

She burst out laughing.

"Such as—?"

A devil danced in her eyes, the swamp-devil I thought. It sent the blood to my head, prompted thoughts that were hardly in keeping with convalescence. It was a mercy perhaps that the youth with the over-large tail-coat selected that moment for blundering in with the tray.

I got through that meal somehow, although it hurt me considerably to swallow. Renée went out and bought some cards and we played various games, culminating with poker-patience. Tea came up, a tactful concession to Anglo-Saxon habits, and somewhere round that time Renée made an announcement which frankly astonished me:

"Do you know what I'm going to do with Juan's money?" she said. "I'm going to establish a fund to help all those people who've suffered through the White Owl. Not Margharita, of course; she has plenty of her own. But the relatives of that detective Valdao murdered, all those who were injured in accidents during that drive and the relatives they had to support. Don't you think it a good idea?"

"Excellent," I agreed. "Can you spare it?"

"I shall have to. I couldn't possibly keep it after all this . . . I'm telling you this because I feel frightfully virtuous today, and tomorrow I may feel quite different—and I want you to keep me up to it. You know, there is such a thing as having too much money, Dick. I've never believed it before, but I do now. I've never known what it's like to be really poor. Ever since Juan disappeared and left me all that I've been like a lonely statue, stuck up on a golden pinnacle.—It makes one awfully selfish being stuck up like that!" She sighed and looked down at her hands. "The only people

who bother about you are shop-keepers and fortune-hunters . . .
The really decent men keep away. It frightens them."

I stumbled to my feet and stood over her. My hands dropped to
her shoulders and hers came up and met them, holding them
tightly.

"You're a brick, Renée," I whispered. "I only wish I were a
really decent man."

She pulled me down to her, to a contrite, plaintive little being
all quivering with emotion. There had been no lipstick that morning, no powder, nothing that was artificial. The Circe of the pools
was gone, the golden pyramid. I gazed into the dark eyes of the
real woman, tear-filmed, tilting back at me.

"You're the best man I have ever known, Dick," she answered.
"Won't you kiss me?"

The phone call from Karolin came at six. Renée ran down to
the hall to answer it. For ten minutes I waited in a room of varied
memories, memories crushed into the space of a few short hours.
Mechanically my fingers passed from my throat to the wad of lint
at my chest. I felt I had nothing to be ashamed of. The question of
disloyalty no longer arose. Juan Mitzakis had had his innings! She
came in very quietly, closing the door. "Dick dear, what do you
think? Juan had booked berths on the *Amazon,* but he didn't em-
bark; nobody did . . . Karolin's just seen the people and made sure.
He's coming back tonight."

"Ah!" I remarked. "That's a pity. I only expected Juan to go . . .
The others are both dead. Valdao died in the trunk on the way
from Paris, but I didn't tell you. Naia went over the cliff in Juan's
car."

She nodded gravely. Suddenly she drew a newspaper from behind her and thrust it into my hands.

"Juan's dead too," she whispered. "It's all in there. It was the
fall from this window after all. They found him in a doorway. He
must have crawled there."

She buried her head on my shoulder.

Epilogue

HEAT!—HEAT THAT HUNG HEAVY in primeval forest and descended scorching on the plains . . . that blistered one's arms and neck until it was agony to move . . . Unguents, salves, native remedies that failed to achieve their purpose, but merely attracted flies! And then, presently, just when one's sense of humor appeared to have deserted one forever, when life was a curse and the faults of one's friends had become a thousand times more obvious than their virtues, there came a morning when one's epidermis reappeared in tougher guise, a night when the roving mosquito seemed less interested!

I remember following a rough track through tumbled boulders, over a vast plateau with a blue mountain panorama behind. It was an hour after dawn. There, high up, the air was like a spring day in England, fresher perhaps and more exhilarating. I had been that way before, but at a different time of the year and under different circumstances. A quarter of a mile ahead, his broad straw hat bobbing among the rocks, our Indian guide sat astride his pony. A hundred yards to our rear there began a straggling line of peons, stumbling along under a load of supplies and kits . . .

Renée, brown as a berry, reined in her mount and waited for me.

"Isn't it just too wonderful, Dick!" she cried, and her sweeping arm took in the landscape. "I'm glad we came."

I was glad too, if only for the pleasure of watching her develop in so surprising a manner that none of her friends on the Riviera would have believed it possible. Her adventures had begun almost before mine had started. A storm at sea, the first view of Tampico, persuading a sturdy, hard-mouthed white pony that people who had acquired the rudiments of riding in the neighborhood of Hyde Park were not to be trifled with . . . sleeping in tents, putting up with the vagaries of native cooks, forgetting to be startled when large and nauseous insects invaded one's sleeping-quarters . . . Mere incidents to one who has voyaged before, eye-openers to a girl who had only traveled *de luxe* by the *Golden Arrow* or the

Blue Train, and to whom a lipstick was as indispensable as a pocket handkerchief!

Shirt and riding-breeches; brown top-boots, whose erstwhile shiny surfaces showed a multitude of scratches! A colored handkerchief knotted at the throat! A bewitching, gipsy face smiling from under the picturesque sombrero! Sunburn, fever, those thousand and one other minor ingredients that combine to form the baptismal fire awaiting all venturers into tropical hinterlands, had taken promising material and wrought wonders. The change was subtle at first; it had grown almost without one's realizing it.

I unslung my camera and took a snap of her. The track broadened. We rode side by side, through a wilderness of rocks and scrub and giant Mexican cactus. The sun climbed up its vault of blue and presently two little streams of perspiration began at my temples under my hat and ran down, making dark marks on the khaki shirt below. But it was very wonderful, all the same . . . Looking backwards, I saw Karolin waving to me, jogging along in the rear with the sturdy brigand who had supplied the bearers for both the first expedition and this. Karolin was in his element; he was picking up a new dialect! I gathered that he wanted me to admire the view.

"Marvelous, isn't it?" I bellowed, but I doubt if my voice reached him. I gazed ahead and my thoughts traveled back to France seven weeks ago, to Paris, Le Broc, Limoges, Bordeaux . . . It seemed a far cry; it might have been seven years! And we, for some strange reason that none of us properly understood, were forging ahead with a single object in view—to put back the stone Juan and I had shifted, to cement it firmly in place and come away! Knowing what we did, it seemed to us the most sensible thing we could do—a sort of shutting down the lid on a chamber of horrors that nothing this side of the grave could satisfactorily explain. Somehow we were convinced it would make a difference. There was nothing else left to be done. We were not archaeologists, and the supposed treasure in the caves left us without a thrill. Ghosts walked the streets with me in Tampico—the ghosts of Juan and of Lindsay, the captain of the *Felicidad.* I began picking up old friends, vice-consuls, traders, guides . . . Things moved a little quicker than they had the last time. I could grapple with the philosophy of *mañana.* I had been through all that before . . . There were fewer mistakes; I found I knew what to take and what to leave behind. Bearers came to me for employment that I knew were no good at all.

Our setting out was an event; people got up with the sun to see it. A number of children and dogs accompanied us and gradually dropped off. The seaboard town thinned out to *adobe* dwellings; the *adobe* dwellings became scarcer. The wilds loomed up and enveloped us ... and still there were ghosts along the route, friendly ghosts; Juan again with his boyish smile and endless endurance, queer stunted *leperos* who had walked that way with me and never would walk again ... One thought of Cortes and his legions and the great Aztec civilization that had flourished before the Spaniard came ...

The train of thought stopped. I was back on the plateau once more, riding beside Renée. Her thoughts, it transpired, had been quite different.

"I suppose we shall keep Baines?" she said. I nodded, "I suppose so."

"We shall have to," she decided. "Mrs. Baines is such a dear. And, of course, she's a wonderful cook. I can't cook for toffee, Dick; I shall have to learn." She edged her mount closer and reached for my hand.

"You don't mind my coming here, do you? I mean, you don't imagine that if Juan could suddenly come to life now it would make any difference? It wouldn't you know. I'd realized long before he disappeared that we were making a mistake. Two extremely pampered children wanting to try a new experience! That was all, Dick. I should hate you to think you were playing second fiddle."

I pressed her fingers and laughed.

"I don't think I should mind very much. However you may have felt, I still feel rather a poor substitute for Juan."

She frowned at me.

"That's not true. He was a dear thing and I liked him tremendously, but our marriage would have been an utter fiasco. My dear, if there were another pretty girl in the room he couldn't keep his eyes off her! You know that's so. We should have been virtually divorced inside a month! He would have wanted his own room, his own car, his own weekends ... We should have been extraordinarily polite to one another when we met—and in the end I should have run off and eloped with you! So, you see, it would have come to roughly the same in the end."

"Fatalism!" I suggested. Renée sighed.

"I believe in happy endings," she said. Conversation lapsed there and we rode on in silence, pitching a temporary camp at noon in the shelter of the first belt of trees we had encountered all day. We ate, took our *siesta* and pressed forward again until just before sundown. Since lunch we had been climbing steadily, following the course of a torrent. In the brief twilight the temperature dropped appreciably; after dinner it became bitterly cold. Renée, Karolin and I sat huddled in our blankets, glad of the cheerful blaze of our own private camp-fire. Karolin had bought a ukulele-banjo in Tampico; he played it most nights when the portable gramophone wasn't in operation. Tonight he assured us he had hit on some new chords. Sitting cross-legged in the natural amphitheater where the camp lay, he twanged the strings and gave us a selection of Russian peasant melodies, with vocal accompaniment; switched off to "Swanee River,"

"Camptown Races" and "Polly-wolly-doodle," in which we all joined. From the cluster of peons round the bigger fire a hundred yards or more away there drifted the strains of an opposition concert. Big stars looked down on us from a velvet pall. The moon came up, a benign lady not quite at the full, casting strange shadows from the rocks, the tents, the ragged group of backs in the horse-lines.

Karolin broke off in the middle of a song and yawned.

"It's probably raining in Paris," he said somewhat inconsequently. "Who would think we celebrated Christmas last week."

Renée laughed.

"And we hadn't any plum-pudding! That was a serious omission, Dick."

"Yes," I admitted; "wasn't it?—And next week, with any sort of luck, we should be on our way back."

Karolin was making doleful noises, trying to tune his instrument by ear.

"How long before we get there?" he demanded.

"We should make it by the day after tomorrow. Charro thinks tomorrow night, but I fancy he's erring on the optimistic side. It's not far, but the going's hard for the ponies." I lit my pipe. "What about another tune, Ivan?"

"Whistle something," he returned, "and I'll try it. What was that thing they were all playing when we left?"

"Honolulu Moon," suggested Renée, snuggling closer to me for warmth. "Play that, Karolin; it would be almost appropriate. It's cold, Dick. I ought to have brought my furs." Suddenly she clung to me and pointed. *"Look, Dick . . . look there."*

A string broke and Karolin swore softly.

Looking along her outstretched arm, I saw a figure standing on a great wedge of rock that formed part of the giant circle that hemmed us in. The next moment we were all on our feet, staring at what might have been the statue of a woman in barbaric attire, with a white bird perched on her shoulder.

As if somebody had shouted a word of command, we dropped our blankets and began running towards it. Fifty paces from the phenomenon Renée stopped, holding her side. I stopped with her, but Karolin raced on, bent on solving the mystery. The figure was very clear now, the moonlight glittering in an array of gleaming ornaments. I saw Ivan at the foot of the rock, staring upwards. The White Owl launched itself into midair and bore down on him, shrieking mournfully. He picked up something and hit at it, but it had wheeled away by this time, flying rapidly. It dipped below the barrier of rock and, simultaneously almost the figure vanished from the summit.

We explored farther, looking for them both, but found nothing. Coming back towards the fire and our discarded blankets, Karolin glanced up at me.

"Naia!" he exclaimed; "I saw her face. That sets one thinking, doesn't it?"

"By heaven, Dick. It's here. We've found it!" Ivan Karolin's voice broke the silence, a strange echo of practically the words that Juan Mitzakis had used nearly two years before. It had become "Dick" and "Ivan" now, convenient, familiar terms that one accepted as a general part of a common adventure; although he always called Renée "Miss de Salis," and was just "Karolin" to her.

One spot in a wilderness is like another; things grow and storms destroy landmarks. It had taken us two whole days to locate the spot. During that period, on each occasion at twilight, we had sighted the White Owl twice. Karolin was convinced that it had deliberately misled us . . . Once more in the light of a tremendous moon, I stood amid the crumbling ruins of a civilization that had flourished before Cortes, gazing down at an iron door, rusted and pitted with age. It was just as the Indians and I had left it— slightly askew, partly overlapping the hole.

Renée hung on my arm. Looking down at her, I saw that she was white and trembling and that her free hand held a large ivory crucifix she had bought in Bordeaux.

"Not frightened?" I whispered.

She shook her head.

"Emotion, Dick! Stupid feminine emotion! I'm never afraid with you.—Is—is that where it happened?"

"Yes; that's it."

She drew me to the edge where Karolin, immersed in some scheme of his own, was busily uncoiling rope.

"It's deep, isn't it?"

"Very," I said. As we had done on that far-off eventful night, I found a stone and dropped it in. Neither of us heard it fall. The incident struck a chord in iny memory. There had been fumes then— like a fog, and later pallid tongues of fire! There was none of that now. Whatever had caused it must have burnt itself out.

We both watched Karolin, hitching one end of his rope to a tree, testing it, fastening the other end around himself. The truth dawned on me.

"You're not going down?" I said.

He surveyed me with a broad grin.

"I am," he returned. "I want you to take the strain and pay out as I tell you. I was born curious, Dick. I can never see an open door without wanting to know what the house inside is like. The rope's first-class; I bought it myself. It's made for this sort of job. If I meet any horrors on the way down—I'll yell to you to haul me in . . . Ready?"

I dropped my hand on his shoulder.

"Don't be a fool," I said sternly. "If any one goes down that shaft tonight it's going to be me. Juan was my friend, not yours—"

Renée broke in with: "Don't either of you go, please. Let's just fasten it up and get away."

Karolin laughed. He shot a glance at Charro, the guide, standing at a distance with arms folded, under the trees. "Hey!" he called. "Come over here and lend a hand. We want you." He turned to Renée. "I'm a rebel tonight, Miss de Salis—and I think you will admit it is for the first time since you engaged me. But tonight I want my way. When all this is over, you will only be employing me out of gratitude, charity, or whatever else you choose to call it. I shan't be any real use—unless to play to you on the ukulele! I've been thinking this out all the way up. I've formed a theory, you see, and I want to prove it." He produced an electric torch from his pocket and tested its light on Charro's unlovely countenance. "If I go from here without trying out my theory—I shall be desolate!"

Renée wavered.

"How much rope have you?"

"Sixty feet. You can only lower me about forty-five; there'll be a lot of waste up here."

"And supposing the White Owl attacks you?" He shrugged his shoulders and showed her the little cross she had given him.

"I have my talisman—and my gun. I shall be harnessed so that I have both my hands free. If it's a bird, I shall shoot it at closer quarters than Dick did; if it's a devil, I'm adequately protected."

We argued with him for another half-hour, but he had his way in the end. Charro and I looped the rope around a stump and paid out that way. He clambered over, held on to the edge of the hole with his hands, let them slip—and we took the strain. I had an angular view and saw his light descending slowly. Renée was stretched at full length on the ground, peering over. Minutes passed. The rope was still going out. A hollow voice came up to us:

"Stop! Stop a bit! I've found something."

Charro and I put the brake on and waited.

And then, screeching, venomous, like a white phantom from the trees, the White Owl came at us. It flew in a halo of eerie light, a queer phosphorescent aura that made it appear twice its size. Charro uttered a wild yell and let go the rope. Renée was on her knees, both hands clasping the crucifix.

I yelled to both of them.

"Hang on to that rope, you fool!—Renée! pull out my revolver and blaze at it. If it gets in there, he's done!"

The first round, that startled Renée more than it did the bird, brought Charro back to his senses. He understood birds and guns, although he understood knives better. I remember a story now of a man whose throat he had slit in Yucatan. I heard this prince of ruffians muttering prayers to the Madonna, but he hung on to the rope again, and that was all that mattered. The crucifix theory was exploded— or perhaps it partly worked. Possibly, too, the forces of evil were stronger here on the threshold of its temple. It would be difficult to say. But this I do know: The thing came at us like a flash of summer lightning, two balls of vivid green in an ocean of white, dazzling us, tempting us to side-step towards that hole and fall. And the smell that hung on the hillside was as if the tombs of all the Toltecs that had departed this life had been suddenly opened and their gases spread abroad. I could hear it, see it, feel and know that it was there, but it never touched me, nor I it. And yet those repeated intangible attacks were sapping my vitality minute by minute. Somehow we gave the rope a second twist around the stump. I dragged Renée over to take my place, snatched the automatic from her fingers and fired the remaining rounds into that mass of reeking light . . . As the last report stopped echoing amid the hills, I saw the big crucifix lying at my feet. Desperate, furious at my impotence, I groped for it—and flung it, aiming at the green eyes . . .

A wild cry, like a mingling of a thousand voices, came from the bowels of the earth—millions of wings seemed to be flapping everywhere. Not a cloud flecked the heavens—and yet I'll swear a peal of thunder rolled from horizon to horizon, echoed and died down again.

There was no bird above us now, no aura—only the memory of a smell. Something like a dark human body, with waving arms, hurtled past me and pitched, head first, into the hole. A pallid flame licked my boot. Endowed with renewed vigor, I pushed past Renée and began pulling in, hand over hand again, toiling like a madman. Charro had dropped to his knees. From the length of his fervid address to the star-strewn firmament I guessed that he was confessing his sins. I found time to kick him to his senses. The coils of rope grew at my feet. A head and shoulders showed above the edge and I grabbed at them and held on. The flames were everywhere; they scorched me as I drew him over—Karolin, bleeding at the mouth, his fair hair singed and smoldering. Laying him clear, I left him to Renée. Charro and I edged the door into place and stood back, staring at one another, exhausted.

Ivan Karolin stirred in his sleep and saw us bending over him.

"I found a watch," he said simply. "It had fallen on a ledge. There was nothing else there." He smiled at us faintly and dropped off again. Renée glanced up at me.

"Poor Karolin," she murmured. "We must look after him, Dick. He's been awfully good."

I found the watch in one of his pockets and carried it to the lamp. We both recognized it; it was the one Juan had always worn. Renée had given it him when they became engaged. The glass was broken and the hands twisted, but there was extraordinarily little rust. Shreds of a leather wrist-strap still clung to it. Renée carried it to her tent and that was the last I saw of her that night.

In the gray of a Mexican dawn Charro and I cemented the door. One had "nerves" up there . . . it was both the beginning and the ending-point of an inexplicable thing. When Charro was putting the last touches to his work, I could have sworn I saw Naia gazing at me reproachfully from the trees. Imagination perhaps? Mirage? One could never be sure.

Halfway back to Tampico, with the camp-fire lighting up our faces, Ivan Karolin interrupted a wild Russian folk-song to a banjo-ukulele accompaniment to tell me his thoughts:

"I believe in deities and devils," he declared, "just as I believe in good motives and bad ones. Some things are better left alone . . . but you can't always fight against blood and heredity. Mitzakis had it in his veins; you couldn't blame him. Possibly there are other people where he met Valdao; we shall never know that either. Valdao lived, of course, but Naia and the White Owl came from what some people call 'The Other Side.' Valdao had bridged the gulf; others have done that too. He taught Juan something, but not enough. After he died, this 'contact' began to peter out. The devil's last kick was when he tried to kill you. That wasn't Juan, you know; he liked you tremendously . . . It was just the devil . . . the White Owl. That hit on the head was the beginning of it all."

He broke off and began strumming softly "Honolulu Moon." I thought Renée was crying. Away down by the bigger camp-fire the peons were laughing and chattering over some game of chance.

THE END

RAMBLE HOUSE's

HARRY STEPHEN KEELER WEBWORK MYSTERIES

(RH) indicates the title is available ONLY in the RAMBLE HOUSE edition

The Ace of Spades Murder
The Affair of the Bottled Deuce (RH)
The Amazing Web
The Barking Clock
Behind That Mask
The Book with the Orange Leaves
The Bottle with the Green Wax Seal
The Box from Japan
The Case of the Canny Killer
The Case of the Crazy Corpse (RH)
The Case of the Flying Hands (RH)
The Case of the Ivory Arrow
The Case of the Jeweled Ragpicker
The Case of the Lavender Gripsack
The Case of the Mysterious Moll
The Case of the 16 Beans
The Case of the Transparent Nude (RH)
The Case of the Transposed Legs
The Case of the Two-Headed Idiot (RH)
The Case of the Two Strange Ladies
The Circus Stealers (RH)
Cleopatra's Tears
A Copy of Beowulf (RH)
The Crimson Cube (RH)
The Face of the Man From Saturn
Find the Clock
The Five Silver Buddhas
The 4th King
The Gallows Waits, My Lord! (RH)
The Green Jade Hand
Finger! Finger!
Hangman's Nights (RH)
I, Chameleon (RH)
I Killed Lincoln at 10:13! (RH)
The Iron Ring
The Man Who Changed His Skin (RH)
The Man with the Crimson Box
The Man with the Magic Eardrums
The Man with the Wooden Spectacles
The Marceau Case
The Matilda Hunter Murder
The Monocled Monster

The Murder of London Lew
The Murdered Mathematician
The Mysterious Card (RH)
The Mysterious Ivory Ball of Wong Shing Li (RH)
The Mystery of the Fiddling Cracksman
The Peacock Fan
The Photo of Lady X (RH)
The Portrait of Jirjohn Cobb
Report on Vanessa Hewstone (RH)
Riddle of the Travelling Skull
Riddle of the Wooden Parrakeet (RH)
The Scarlet Mummy (RH)
The Search for X-Y-Z
The Sharkskin Book
Sing Sing Nights
The Six From Nowhere (RH)
The Skull of the Waltzing Clown
The Spectacles of Mr. Cagliostro
Stand By—London Calling!
The Steeltown Strangler
The Stolen Gravestone (RH)
Strange Journey (RH)
The Strange Will
The Straw Hat Murders (RH)
The Street of 1000 Eyes (RH)
Thieves' Nights
Three Novellos (RH)
The Tiger Snake
The Trap (RH)
Vagabond Nights (Defrauded Yeggman)
Vagabond Nights 2 (10 Hours)
The Vanishing Gold Truck
The Voice of the Seven Sparrows
The Washington Square Enigma
When Thief Meets Thief
The White Circle (RH)
The Wonderful Scheme of Mr. Christopher Thorne
X. Jones—of Scotland Yard
Y. Cheung, Business Detective

Keeler Related Works

A To Izzard: A Harry Stephen Keeler Companion by Fender Tucker — Articles and stories about Harry, by Harry, and in his style. Included is a compleat bibliography.

Wild About Harry: Reviews of Keeler Novels — Edited by Richard Polt & Fender Tucker — 22 reviews of works by Harry Stephen Keeler from *Keeler News*. A perfect introduction to the author.

The Keeler Keyhole Collection: Annotated newsletter rants from Harry Stephen Keeler, edited by Francis M. Nevins. Over 400 pages of incredibly personal Keeleriana.

Fakealoo — Pastiches of the style of Harry Stephen Keeler by selected demented members of the HSK Society. Updated every year with the new winner.

Strands of the Web: Short Stories of Harry Stephen Keeler — 29 stories, just about all that Keeler wrote, are edited and introduced by Fred Cleaver.

RAMBLE HOUSE's Loon Sanctuary

A Clear Path to Cross — Sharon Knowles short mystery stories by Ed Lynskey.

A Jimmy Starr Omnibus — Three 40s novels by Jimmy Starr.

A Roland Daniel Double: The Signal and The Return of Wu Fang — Classic thrillers from the 30s.

A Shot Rang Out — Three decades of reviews and articles by today's Anthony Boucher, Jon Breen. An essential book for any mystery lover's library.

A Smell of Smoke — A 1951 English countryside thriller by Miles Burton.

A Snark Selection — Lewis Carroll's *The Hunting of the Snark* with two Snarkian chapters by Harry Stephen Keeler — Illustrated by Gavin L. O'Keefe.

A Young Man's Heart — A forgotten early classic by Cornell Woolrich.

Alexander Laing Novels — *The Motives of Nicholas Holtz* and *Dr. Scarlett*, stories of medical mayhem and intrigue from the 30s.

An Angel in the Street — Modern hardboiled noir by Peter Genovese.

Automaton — Brilliant treatise on robotics: 1928-style! By H. Stafford Hatfield.

Beast or Man? — A 1930 novel of racism and horror by Sean M'Guire. Introduced by John Pelan.

Black Hogan Strikes Again — Australia's Peter Renwick pens a tale of the 30s outback.

Black River Falls — Suspense from the master, Ed Gorman.

Blondy's Boy Friend — A snappy 1930 story by Philip Wylie, writing as Leatrice Homesley.

Blood in a Snap — The *Finnegan's Wake* of the 21st century, by Jim Weiler.

Blood Moon — The first of the Robert Payne series by Ed Gorman.

Chelsea Quinn Yarbro Novels featuring Charlie Moon — *Ogilvie, Tallant and Moon, Music When the Sweet Voice Dies, Poisonous Fruit* and *Dead Mice*. An Ojibwa detective in SF.

Cornucopia of Crime — Francis M. Nevins assembled this huge collection of his writings about crime literature and the people who write it. Essential for any serious mystery library.

Crimson Clown Novels — By Johnston McCulley, author of the Zorro novels, *The Crimson Clown* and *The Crimson Clown Again.*

Dago Red — 22 tales of dark suspense by Bill Pronzini.

David Hume Novels — *Corpses Never Argue, Cemetery First Stop, Make Way for the Mourners, Eternity Here I Come.* 1930s British hardboiled fiction with an attitude.

Dead Man Talks Too Much — Hollywood boozer by Weed Dickenson.

Death Leaves No Card — One of the most unusual murdered-in-the-tub mysteries you'll ever read. By Miles Burton.

Death March of the Dancing Dolls and Other Stories — Volume Three in the Day Keene in the Detective Pulps series. Introduced by Bill Crider.

Deep Space and other Stories — A collection of SF gems by Richard A. Lupoff.

Detective Duff Unravels It — Episodic mysteries by Harvey O'Higgins.

Dime Novels: Ramble House's 10-Cent Books — *Knife in the Dark* by Robert Leslie Bellem, *Hot Lead* and *Song of Death* by Ed Earl Repp, *A Hashish House in New York* by H.H. Kane, and five more.

Don Diablo: Book of a Lost Film — Two-volume treatment of a western by Paul Landres, with diagrams. Intro by Francis M. Nevins.

Dope and Swastikas — Two strange novels from 1922 by Edmund Snell

Dope Tales #1 — Two dope-riddled classics; *Dope Runners* by Gerald Grantham and *Death Takes the Joystick* by Phillip Condé.

Dope Tales #2 — Two more narco-classics; *The Invisible Hand* by Rex Dark and *The Smokers of Hashish* by Norman Berrow.

Dope Tales #3 — Two enchanting novels of opium by the master, Sax Rohmer. *Dope* and *The Yellow Claw.*

Double Hot — Two 60s softcore sex novels by Morris Hershman.

Dr. Odin — Douglas Newton's 1933 racial potboiler comes back to life.

Evidence in Blue — 1938 mystery by E. Charles Vivian.

Fatal Accident — Murder by automobile, a 1936 mystery by Cecil M. Wills.

Finger-prints Never Lie — A 1939 classic detective novel by John G. Brandon.

Freaks and Fantasies — Eerie tales by Tod Robbins, collaborator of Tod Browning on the film FREAKS.

Gadsby — A lipogram (a novel without the letter E). Ernest Vincent Wright's last work, published in 1939 right before his death.

Gelett Burgess Novels — *The Master of Mysteries, The White Cat, Two O'Clock Courage, Ladies in Boxes, Find the Woman, The Heart Line, The Picaroons* and *Lady Mechante*. All are introduced by Richard A. Lupoff who is singlehandedly bringing Burgess back to life.

Geronimo — S. M. Barrett's 1905 autobiography of a noble American.

Hake Talbot Novels — *Rim of the Pit, The Hangman's Handyman.* Classic locked room mysteries, with mapback covers by Gavin O'Keefe.

Hollywood Dreams — A novel of Tinsel Town and the Depression by Richard O'Brien.

I Stole $16,000,000 — A true story by cracksman Herbert E. Wilson.

Inclination to Murder — 1966 thriller by New Zealand's Harriet Hunter.

Invaders from the Dark — Classic werewolf tale from Greye La Spina.

J. Poindexter, Colored — Classic satirical black novel by Irvin S. Cobb.

Jack Mann Novels — Strange murder in the English countryside. *Gees' First Case, Nightmare Farm, Grey Shapes, The Ninth Life, The Glass Too Many.*

Jake Hardy — A lusty western tale from Wesley Tallant.

Jim Harmon Double Novels — *Vixen Hollow/Celluloid Scandal, The Man Who Made Maniacs/Silent Siren, Ape Rape/Wanton Witch, Sex Burns Like Fire/Twist Session, Sudden Lust/Passion Strip, Sin Unlimited/Harlot Master, Twilight Girls/Sex Institution.* Written in the early 60s and never reprinted until now.

Joel Townsley Rogers Novels and Short Stories — By the author of *The Red Right Hand: Once In a Red Moon, Lady With the Dice, The Stopped Clock, Never Leave My Bed.* Also two short story collections: *Night of Horror* and *Killing Time.*

Joseph Shallit Novels — *The Case of the Billion Dollar Body, Lady Don't Die on My Doorstep, Kiss the Killer, Yell Bloody Murder, Take Your Last Look.* One of America's best 50's authors and a favorite of author Bill Pronzini.

Keller Memento — 45 short stories of the amazing and weird by Dr. David Keller.

Killer's Caress — Cary Moran's 1936 hardboiled thriller.

League of the Grateful Dead and Other Stories — Volume One in the Day Keene in the Detective Pulps series. In the introduction John Pelan outlines his plans for re-publishing all of Day Keene's short stories from the pulps.

Man Out of Hell and Other Stories — Volume II of the John H. Knox weird pulps collection.

Marblehead: A Novel of H.P. Lovecraft — A long-lost masterpiece from Richard A. Lupoff. This is the "director's cut", the long version that has never been published before.

Master of Souls — Mark Hansom's 1937 shocker is introduced by weirdologist John Pelan.

Max Afford Novels — *Owl of Darkness, Death's Mannikins, Blood on His Hands, The Dead Are Blind, The Sheep and the Wolves, Sinners in Paradise* and *Two Locked Room Mysteries and a Ripping Yarn* by one of Australia's finest mystery novelists.

More Secret Adventures of Sherlock Holmes — Gary Lovisi's second collection of tales about the unknown sides of the great detective.

Muddled Mind: Complete Works of Ed Wood, Jr. — David Hayes and Hayden Davis deconstruct the life and works of the mad, but canny, genius.

Murder among the Nudists — A mystery from 1934 by Peter Hunt, featuring a naked Detective-Inspector going undercover in a nudist colony.

Murder in Black and White — 1931 classic tennis whodunit by Evelyn Elder.

Murder in Shawnee — Two novels of the Alleghenies by John Douglas: *Shawnee Alley Fire* and *Haunts.*

Murder in Silk — A 1937 Yellow Peril novel of the silk trade by Ralph Trevor.

My Deadly Angel — 1955 Cold War drama by John Chelton.

My First Time: The One Experience You Never Forget — Michael Birchwood — 64 true first-person narratives of how they lost it.

Mysterious Martin, the Master of Murder — Two versions of a strange 1912 novel by Tod Robbins about a man who writes books that can kill.

Norman Berrow Novels — *The Bishop's Sword, Ghost House, Don't Go Out After Dark, Claws of the Cougar, The Smokers of Hashish, The Secret Dancer, Don't Jump Mr. Boland!, The Footprints of Satan, Fingers for Ransom, The Three Tiers of Fantasy, The Spaniard's Thumb, The Eleventh Plague, Words Have Wings, One Thrilling Night, The Lady's in Danger, It Howls at Night, The Terror in the Fog, Oil Under the Window, Murder in the Melody, The Singing Room.* This is the complete Norman Berrow library of classic locked-room mysteries, several of which are masterpieces.

Old Times' Sake — Short stories by James Reasoner from Mike Shayne Magazine.

Perfect .38 — Two early Timothy Dane novels by William Ard. More to come.

Prose Bowl — Futuristic satire of a world where hack writing has replaced football as our national obsession, by Bill Pronzini and Barry N. Malzberg.

Red Light — The history of legal prostitution in Shreveport Louisiana by Eric Brock. Includes wonderful photos of the houses and the ladies.

Researching American-Made Toy Soldiers — A 276-page collection of a lifetime of articles by toy soldier expert Richard O'Brien.

Reunion in Hell — Volume One of the John H. Knox series of weird stories from the pulps. Introduced by horror expert John Pelan.

Ripped from the Headlines! — The Jack the Ripper story as told in the newspaper articles in the *New York* and *London Times.*

Robert Randisi Novels — *No Exit to Brooklyn* and *The Dead of Brooklyn.* The first two Nick Delvecchio novels.

Rough Cut & New, Improved Murder — Ed Gorman's first two novels.

Ruled By Radio — 1925 futuristic novel by Robert L. Hadfield & Frank E. Farncombe.

Rupert Penny Novels — *Policeman's Holiday, Policeman's Evidence, Lucky Policeman, Policeman in Armour, Sealed Room Murder, Sweet Poison, The Talkative Policeman, She had to Have Gas* and *Cut and Run* (by Martin Tanner.) Rupert Penny is the pseudonym of Australian Charles Thornett, a master of the locked room, impossible crime plot.

Sand's Game — Spectacular hard-boiled noir from Ennis Willie, edited by Lynn Myers and Stephen Mertz, with contributions from Max Allan Collins, Bill Crider, Wayne Dundee, Bill Pronzini, Gary Lovisi and James Reasoner.

Satan's Den Exposed — True crime in Truth or Consequences New Mexico — Award-winning journalism by the *Desert Journal.*

Gelett Burgess Novels — *The Master of Mysteries, The White Cat, Two O'Clock Courage, Ladies in Boxes, Find the Woman, The Heart Line, The Picaroons* and *Lady Mechante.* All are edited and introduced by Richard A. Lupoff.

Sam McCain Novels — Ed Gorman's terrific series includes *The Day the Music Died, Wake Up Little Susie* and *Will You Still Love Me Tomorrow?*

Sex Slave — Potboiler of lust in the days of Cleopatra by Dion Leclerq, 1966.

Shadows' Edge — Two early novels by Wade Wright: *Shadows Don't Bleed* and *The Sharp Edge.*

Sideslip — 1968 SF masterpiece by Ted White and Dave Van Arnam.

Slammer Days — Two full-length prison memoirs: *Men into Beasts* (1952) by George Sylvester Viereck and *Home Away From Home* (1962) by Jack Woodford.

Sorcerer's Chessmen — John Pelan introduces this 1939 classic by Mark Hansom.

Star Griffin — Michael Kurland's 1987 masterpiece of SF drollery is back.

Stakeout on Millennium Drive — Award-winning Indianapolis Noir by Ian Woollen.

Strands of the Web: Short Stories of Harry Stephen Keeler — Edited and Introduced by Fred Cleaver.

Suzy — A collection of comic strips by Richard O'Brien and Bob Vojtko from 1970.

Tales of the Macabre and Ordinary — Modern twisted horror by Chris Mikul, author of the *Bizarrism* series.

Tenebrae — Ernest G. Henham's 1898 horror tale brought back.

The Amorous Intrigues & Adventures of Aaron Burr — by Anonymous. Hot historical action about the man who almost became Emperor of Mexico.

The Anthony Boucher Chronicles — edited by Francis M. Nevins. Book reviews by Anthony Boucher written for the *San Francisco Chronicle*, 1942 – 1947. Essential and fascinating reading by the best book reviewer there ever was.

The Best of 10-Story Book — edited by Chris Mikul, over 35 stories from the literary magazine Harry Stephen Keeler edited.

The Black Dark Murders — Vintage 50s college murder yarn by Milt Ozaki, writing as Robert O. Saber.

The Book of Time — The classic novel by H.G. Wells is joined by sequels by Wells himself and three timely stories by Richard A. Lupoff. Lavishly illustrated by Gavin L. O'Keefe.

The Case of the Little Green Men — Mack Reynolds wrote this love song to sci-fi fans back in 1951 and it's now back in print.

The Case of the Withered Hand — 1936 potboiler by John G. Brandon.

The Charlie Chaplin Murder Mystery — A 2004 tribute by film scholar, Wes D. Gehring.

The Chinese Jar Mystery — Murder in the manor by John Stephen Strange, 1934.

The Compleat Calhoun — All of Fender Tucker's works: Includes *Totah Six-Pack, Weed, Women and Song* and *Tales from the Tower*, plus a CD of all of his songs.

The Compleat Ova Hamlet — Parodies of SF authors by Richard A. Lupoff. This is a brand new edition with more stories and more illustrations by Trina Robbins.

The Contested Earth and Other SF Stories — A never-before published space opera and seven short stories by Jim Harmon.

The Crimson Query — A 1929 thriller from Arlton Eadie. A perfect way to get introduced.

The Curse of Cantire — A classic 1939 novel of a family curse by Walter S. Masterman.

The Devil Drives — An odd prison and lost treasure novel from 1932 by Virgil Markham.

The Devil's Mistress — A 1915 Scottish gothic tale by J. W. Brodie-Innes, a member of Aleister Crowley's Golden Dawn.

The Dumpling — Political murder from 1907 by Coulson Kernahan.

The End of It All and Other Stories — Ed Gorman selected his favorite short stories for this huge collection.

The Fangs of Suet Pudding — A 1944 novel of the German invasion by Adams Farr

The Ghost of Gaston Revere — From 1935, a novel of life and beyond by Mark Hansom, introduced by John Pelan.

The Gold Star Line — Seaboard adventure from L.T. Reade and Robert Eustace.

The Golden Dagger — 1951 Scotland Yard yarn by E. R. Punshon.

The Hairbreadth Escapes of Major Mendax — Francis Blake Crofton's 1889 boys' book.

The House of the Vampire — 1907 poetic thriller by George S. Viereck.

The Incredible Adventures of Rowland Hern — Intriguing 1928 impossible crimes by Nicholas Olde.

The Julius Caesar Murder Case — A classic 1935 re-telling of the assassination by Wallace Irwin that's much more fun than the Shakespeare version.

The Koky Comics — A collection of all of the 1978-1981 Sunday and daily comic strips by Richard O'Brien and Mort Gerberg, in two volumes.

The Lady of the Terraces — 1925 missing race adventure by E. Charles Vivian.

The Lord of Terror — 1925 mystery with master-criminal, Fantômas.

The N. R. De Mexico Novels — Robert Bragg, the real N.R. de Mexico, presents *Marijuana Girl, Madman on a Drum, Private Chauffeur* in one volume.

The Night Remembers — A 1991 Jack Walsh mystery from Ed Gorman.

The One After Snelling — Kickass modern noir from Richard O'Brien.

The Organ Reader — A huge compilation of just about everything published in the 1971-1972 radical bay-area newspaper, *THE ORGAN*. A coffee table book that points out the shallowness of the coffee table mindset.

The Poker Club — Three in one! Ed Gorman's ground-breaking novel, the short story it was based upon, and the screenplay of the film made from it.

The Private Journal & Diary of John H. Surratt — The memoirs of the man who conspired to assassinate President Lincoln.

The Secret Adventures of Sherlock Holmes — Three Sherlockian pastiches by the Brooklyn author/publisher, Gary Lovisi.

The Shadow on the House — Mark Hansom's 1934 masterpiece of horror is introduced by John Pelan.

The Sign of the Scorpion — A 1935 Edmund Snell tale of oriental evil.

The Singular Problem of the Stygian House-Boat — Two classic tales by John Kendrick Bangs about the denizens of Hades.

The Smiling Corpse — Philip Wylie and Bernard Bergman's odd 1935 novel.

The Stench of Death: An Odoriferous Omnibus by Jack Moskovitz — Two complete novels and two novellas from 60's sleaze author, Jack Moskovitz.

The Time Armada — Fox B. Holden's 1953 SF gem.

The Tongueless Horror and Other Stories — Volume One of the series of short stories from the weird pulps by Wyatt Blassingame.

The Tracer of Lost Persons — From 1906, an episodic novel that became a hit radio series in the 30s. Introduced by Richard A. Lupoff.

The Trail of the Cloven Hoof — Diabolical horror from 1935 by Arlton Eadie. Introduced by John Pelan.

The Triune Man — Mindscrambling science fiction from Richard A. Lupoff.

The Universal Holmes — Richard A. Lupoff's 2007 collection of five Holmesian pastiches and a recipe for giant rat stew.

The Werewolf vs the Vampire Woman — Hard to believe ultraviolence by either Arthur M. Scarm or Arthur M. Scram.

The Whistling Ancestors — A 1936 classic of weirdness by Richard E. Goddard and introduced by John Pelan.

The White Peril in the Far East — Sidney Lewis Gulick's 1905 indictment of the West and assurance that Japan would never attack the U.S.

The Wizard of Berner's Abbey — A 1935 horror gem written by Mark Hansom and introduced by John Pelan.

Wade Wright Novels — *Echo of Fear, Death At Nostalgia Street, It Leads to Murder* and *Shadows' Edge*, a double book featuring *Shadows Don't Bleed* and *The Sharp Edge*.

Welsh Rarebit Tales — Charming stories from 1902 by Harle Oren Cummins.

Through the Looking Glass — Lewis Carroll wrote it; Gavin L. O'Keefe illustrated it.

Time Line — Ramble House artist Gavin O'Keefe selects his most evocative art inspired by the twisted literature he reads and designs.

Tiresias — Psychotic modern horror novel by Jonathan M. Sweet.

Totah Six-Pack — Just Fender Tucker's six tales about Farmington in one sleek volume.

Trail of the Spirit Warrior — Roger Haley's historical saga of life in the Indian Territories.

Ultra-Boiled — 23 gut-wrenching tales by our Man in Brooklyn, Gary Lovisi.

Up Front From Behind — A 2011 satire of Wall Street by James B. Kobak.

Victims & Villains — Intriguing Sherlockiana from Derham Groves.

Walter S. Masterman Novels — *The Green Toad, The Flying Beast, The Yellow Mistletoe, The Wrong Verdict, The Perjured Alibi, The Border Line* and *The Curse of Cantire*. Masterman wrote horror and mystery, some introduced by John Pelan.

We Are the Dead and Other Stories — Volume Two in the Day Keene in the Detective Pulps series, introduced by Ed Gorman. When done, there may be as many as 11 in the series.

West Texas War and Other Western Stories — by Gary Lovisi.

Whip Dodge: Man Hunter — Wesley Tallant's saga of a bounty hunter of the old West.

You'll Die Laughing — Bruce Elliott's 1945 novel of murder at a practical joker's English countryside manor.

RAMBLE HOUSE

Fender Tucker, Prop.   Gavin L. O'Keefe, Graphics
www.ramblehouse.com   fender@ramblehouse.com
228-826-1783   10329 Sheephead Drive, Vancleave MS 39565